HOMELAND
CONSPIRACY

HOMELAND
CONSPIRACY

Gary Fuller

Virtual Bookworm Publishing
College Station, TX

HOMELAND CONSPIRACY

ISBN 978-1-62137-664-4 (softcover)

ISBN 978-1-62137-665-1 (hardcover)

ISBN 978-1-62137-666-8 (ebook)

Library of Congress Control Number: 2015901851

Virtual Bookworm Publishing
PO Box 9949
College Station, TX 77849

To my wife, Johanna Gabriel
Dessert is the sweetest part of the meal
and it is usually served as the last dish.
YOU are the dessert of my life.
Let's enjoy our lives together,
— Forever !

Also written by Gary Fuller:

LETHAL CONSPIRACY

Dr. Stephen Grant, Columbia University professor of political science and special assistant to the UN Secretary General, is recruited by the CIA to identify a terrorist cell formed inside the United Nations. Still recovering from the death of his wife a year ago, Grant hopes this new adventure will spring him from the deep depression he's suffered.

When an undercover Mossad agent posing as an Arabic aide at the UN discovers the terrorists' plan, Grant knows he's got to put everything he has into this mission. The terrorists want to explode bombs at an Iranian facility storing three fully developed nuclear warheads and blame Israel, forcing Iran to retaliate using their secret nuclear weapons.

Grant becomes entangled with an alluring female psychologist while tracking down the terrorists. Unfortunately, the terrorist organization wants to eliminate them both. In his frantic efforts to survive and stop the radicals before they launch their planned attack and start a nuclear war, Grant faces Iraqi insurgents, Hamas militants, and Egyptian Secret Police from New York to the Middle East.

Just as alarming to him, though, is that he must also face the very real possibility that he's falling in love.

ACKNOWLEDGEMENTS

There are always many people to thank with such a project as this. I am eternally grateful to all who helped, directly or indirectly, in any way whatsoever. My apologies to those not specifically mentioned here—your contributions are reflected within these pages.

My wife, Johanna Gabriel, proved to be an invaluable asset as always, both through the strength and encouragement she imparted, and through extensive input from a psychologist's point of view examining the various characters and their personality traits. Her extensive efforts at proof reading, rereading and checking final changes caught many errors I missed, and her suggestions aided my struggles attempting to discover the right words.

Win Fiandaca helped review the first few chapters. Her editing skills were well-honed, and she provided excellent insight in establishing the story beginnings.

Many people contributed ideas and information helping understand various methods, processes and procedures. These sources need to remain anonymous, either at their own request or to protect them as a source. Included were consultants and advisors to various government agencies, security contractors, and members of the FBI, CIA, and NSA. You know who you are, and I am grateful to each of you.

CHAPTER 1

June 1, 2013
West Bank Territory

There it was again.

Panic grabbed him, squeezing so hard he couldn't breathe. *What was it? Who might be out there?* Heart pounding, his mind raced over possible causes of the sound outside the house at this hour of the night.

Sitting closest to the window, he would be the first to notice if something did happen in the darkness outside. Cocking his head, he listened for the noise again. Nothing. No sound of any kind. He began feeling a bit paranoid.

The curtains had been closed on the window near where Kamran Khan sat, preventing him from seeing outside the house. More importantly, it kept anyone outside from looking in. And no one sat in front of the window to avoid casting a shadow which might become a sniper's target.

Khan checked his watch. Three A.M. He knew in this section of the West Bank it was not wise for anyone to be roaming about during the early morning hours.

Ramallah is considered the most affluent and cultural, as well as the most liberal, of Palestinian cities. It features a lively nightlife with a good number of shops, restaurants and bars open late. A common habit of the citizens of the city is going out for a late night drink, dinner, or some Rukab Ice Cream, which is based on the resin of chewing gum and thus has a distinctive taste. Still, many older residents prefer an Argila, a flavored tobacco waterpipe sometimes called a hubble bubble.

Both locals and countless tourists flocked to the nicer coffee shops, bars and restaurants seeking an enjoyable evening near the old city, not far from where a few select people attended this

1

secret meeting. Once the businesses closed around midnight, everyone would go straight home or return to their hotels.

That was the reason the meeting had been planned for this time of night.

But Khan had heard a sound. Sweat began soaking his faded yellow shirt.

He turned from the window back to the large room, to look at the guests gathered there. The conversation indicated no one else had heard the noise. Maybe it was just his imagination. Khan shook his head and tried to focus on the meeting.

Khalid Khan stood a few feet to the right, next to the empty fireplace, his blue sport jacket open to reveal the gray polo shirt underneath as he leaned his back against the wall. He raised his left hand under his chin and brushed his short beard. "So the arms deal is done?"

Although Kamran Khan dearly loved his brother, he did not reveal any visible display of such emotion. He could not. This was all business, serious business. But whenever Kamran looked at, or thought of, his older brother Khalid, he felt huge respect and deep love swell up inside him. There was no one like his big brother.

Kamran remembered growing up in Sukkur, in the Sindh province of Pakistan. A trying time for Kamran, he struggled as young boy in a small family, living in one of the poorest neighborhoods in a city of 400,000 people. His father would disappear after breakfast and not return until evening, sometimes very late. Kamran never knew what his father did; only that he was never around the home, never really with the family. As a boy growing up, he would have been alone had it not been for his older brother.

Kamran looked up to Khalid as the mature man and depended on him for guidance and advice. He also depended on him for love. Khalid took time to assure Kamran that he mattered, he was indeed someone, and someday he would grow up and become a man to be respected.

Often Kamran would wander off to spend time down by the Indus River. He enjoyed walking along the yellow stone and steel Sukkur Barrage, formally called Lloyd Barrage. Over 5,000 feet long, the barrage has 66 gates and controls one of the largest irrigation systems in the world. Kamran liked watching the water sweep into the seven various canals that would provide water for nearly 10 million acres. A few of the canals are actually larger than the Suez Canal.

Khalid would find his brother there and they would walk together, talking about their future, the meaning of life, and the many Islamic teachings they learned in the Government Al-falah High School.

Once schooling was complete, Kamran was recruited into the Pakistani Inter-Services Intelligence or ISI, somewhat similar to the United States' CIA. Enthralled with his job, Kamran persuaded Khalid to join also. They met often, always sharing their separate experiences together over the past four years. Now on this one assignment, they were finally working together. Kamran loved it.

Thirteen people from three different countries met here in this secret meeting, discussing how to conduct major attacks against Israel. Thirteen—a lucky or unlucky number?

Malik Ahmad, the third member of Khan's team representing the ISI, purposely sat across the room to observe members of the other two groups. His face reflected interest in the discussion, but revealed no emotion. He appeared relaxed and casual in his blue shirt, jeans and sandals.

To his left were two men from Lebanon, both high-ranking Hezbollah officials. The dark face and penetrating eyes of the first man revealed nothing of his thoughts, but gave everyone the feeling that he knew theirs.

The second and much heavier Lebanese was also in his mid 30s and appeared to be the spokesman. "Negotiations and payment arrangements have been completed."

Still trying to identify what caused the sound outside the house, Kamran Khan's thoughts drifted. He knew the Israeli military occasionally entered Ramallah in the dead of night to arrest someone they considered a Palestinian terrorist, and then disappeared before anyone realized they were there. But ever since the hanging, this rarely happened.

Enraged by incidents in Gaza, Palestinians in the West Bank had demonstrated against the Israeli army. Shortly after a large demonstration, two Israeli army reservists had taken a wrong turn and were set upon by a mob. The frenzied crowd killed the two IDF (Israeli Defense Force) reservists, mutilated their bodies, and dragged them through the streets before hanging what was left of them. Israel retaliated with an air strike on Ramallah.

Since that time, it had been quite a while since any member of the IDF had been seen in Ramallah, and most Palestinians wanted to keep it that way. But if Israel somehow learned of this meeting, the entire Israeli army would invade the city.

Across the room, a young Palestinian bobbing in his chair seized Khan's attention. "Yes, we did. That's why we —"

The man seated next to him on his left reached over and slapped his hand down on the man's leg. "Silence, my young friend. Be quiet and learn."

Jabr Butrus looked slowly around the group of men sitting and standing in the large room. "You must forgive my friend for his outburst. He is young and still learning. But he is a dedicated soldier to the Palestinian cause and can be trusted completely."

He paused.

"To show how much you can trust him, I tell you my story." He took a deep breath. "I lived in Jerusalem, where I have a wife and two beautiful daughters. I was forced to flee my home and leave my family. As you are aware, Sayeret Matkal is the Special Forces unit of the Israeli Defense Forces and reports to the intelligence directorate Aman. They connected me to some street café bombings. I came here to the West Bank to take refuge and hide from them. Here, I am also dedicated to the Palestinian cause." He nodded his head. "Now you all know."

He motioned to a man on the other side the room. "Ali, would you like to continue?"

To the right of the Pakistani ISI observer sat an older Palestinian dressed in a white shirt, brown vest and darker brown baggy pants. His beard and eyebrows had turned gray a long time ago, although his shoulder-length hair remained almost black.

Leaning forward, Ali Abbas spoke in a soft, gentle voice. "We want to conduct several major attacks on Israel so they will finally agree to an independent Palestine—at least for the West Bank." He paused, took a deep breath and looked at Khalid, still leaning against the wall. "We have agreed upon the weapons, and we have made a substantial payment up front ... to assure we can receive them."

He continued in his soft voice. "Hezbollah will transport the weapons. But that is where we need your assistance." He leaned back and elbowed the thin man seated next to him. "Right, Abdul?"

The man on his right nodded. Everyone knew Abdul Hakim was a trusted member of the organization to liberate Palestine, but only the other three Palestinians knew he had lived in the Gaza Strip for thirty years. He held a work permit for daily passage to his job in Tel Aviv. He learned that Israel planned to cancel all work permits from Gaza, so he finished work one day and made his way to the West Bank Territory, and had lived there ever since.

Kamran's brother Khalid spoke up. "What kind of help can we provide to this process?"

Kamran looked down at the floor and closed his eyes, listening. Still nervous, he realized he had not heard another sound outside the house. It had been quiet this whole time. Relieved, he thought to himself, *Relax. It must have been the wind, or perhaps a stray cat*, and dismissed his fear.

The nervous young Palestinian watched him. Kamran could tell he was curious and wanted to ask if Kamran was all right, but he glanced at the man next to him and remained silent.

A third member of Hezbollah also stood, leaning against the wall next to Kamran's brother. He too had been quiet, observing the others. He shifted his weight and looked over at Khalid. "We plan on going through Syria. Their civil war will provide excellent cover for transporting the weapons and explosives."

Ali Abbas, the older Palestinian with the soft voice, spoke again. "Pakistan has trained many of the rebels fighting in Syria. Your country has helped arm several groups of the soldiers. You have even sent food to some of them." He paused only a moment as he looked from one Pakistani to another. "We need you to negotiate safe passage with the rebels, so we can bring these weapons here to use against Israel."

———————

Daniel Shavit shivered. A light breeze from the south taunted him with its chilling breath. The temperature, below 0 degrees C and mixed with 63% humidity, made it more than uncomfortable.

Cold, Shavit remained motionless, waiting. They had to avoid making more noise. Glad it would be over in a few minutes, he turned to his left and stared into the darkness. Other members of his team, wearing black face paint and commando black tactical uniforms, could not be easily identified unless they moved. They, too, stood frozen in place. Gradually, his eyes began to penetrate the darkness, and people's outlines became visible.

This was not the first time Colonel Shavit had trespassed into the Palestinian West Bank Territory seeking to destroy enemies of Israel. The first time, the Iraqis provided several bombs and tried to bribe a group of Palestinians with counterfeit money to use them against Israel's Defense Force soldiers. The second incursion into this territory was to raid a meeting between Iranians, Syrians and some Palestinians. They wanted to plant bombs in elementary schools, blackmail the Israeli government, then explode the bombs anyway. Fortunately, Shavit's team succeeded in stopping both plots before they could be implemented.

Combat experience gained in the South Lebanon Conflict tempered Shavit's skills in assessing a bad environment and refined his abilities to lead a successful strike in enemy territory, escape and survive to fight another day. This made him the perfect leader for Mossad pinpoint strikes in Palestinian territory.

Shavit gestured for two men to join him. Slowly and quietly, the three men moved to within 30 feet of the house. Shavit then signaled the rest of the Mossad team to position themselves behind cover, but with a clear view of the large picture window on the side of the house. One man moved to cover the front door. They could not afford to let even one person escape.

Putting a hand on the two men's shoulders, Shavit nodded. Dropping to their knees, the two men raised their weapons.

———————

Once again, Kamran thought he heard a sound coming from outside the house. His mind, still seeking possible reasons, finally settled on one that could not be denied. He leaped forward out of his chair, landed on his stomach and clutched at the floor, trying to make himself part of it while shouting at the others the last word some of them would hear. "DOWN!"

By the time they heard the WHOOSH, the window glass had already shattered and the rocket had entered the room. A fireball of orange-yellow flame erupted, filling the room before the sound of the explosion could be heard.

The flash of flame evaporated as another WHOOSH sounded, followed immediately by another. But the men in the room did not hear it, nor the two subsequent explosions as those missiles smashed into the house.

Flames danced through what had been a pleasant, middle class home with a large kitchen-living room combination and three bedrooms. Piles of rubble converged with the few partial walls still standing to give evidence the home ever existed. A creaking, groaning noise called attention to one of those partial walls toward the back of the house as it lost hold of an adjoining wall and crumbled to the ground. The huge flame quickly muted into several small fires scattered around the structure.

Three of the team members started toward the house. "Wait!" Daniel Shavit held a pencil flashlight and waved his hand for the rest of the team to see. "No one could have survived that." He glanced around to ensure everyone was present. "Let's get the hell out of here before others come. We're in enemy territory, and we don't want to start another damn war here tonight." He signaled with his hand, "Let's go."

Rapidly moving away from the scene, the Mossad team did not detect the small movement in the wreckage. Everyone in that house should have died. No one could have survived.

———————

Kamran Khan struggled to move his arms away from his face. Wincing, he almost screamed from the searing pain in his left shoulder. Blinking several times, he tried to clear his mind and comprehend what had happened.

The pain helped him understand that he should not be alive. His first thought was that he had to move — to get out of there, away from that house. Death had looked him in the face. It lasted for only one fleeting second, but felt like a very long, incredibly terrifying moment. Then it was over and somehow, he was still alive. Blinding orange flames from the rocket explosions repeatedly lashed out at him, but couldn't quite touch him. The intense heat had tried to scorch him, but the two dead bodies on top of him became a shield that saved his life.

Summoning what seemed like his last bit of strength, he forced himself up between the bodies. The awesome devastation caused by the Israeli rockets overwhelmed him. Tears filled his eyes and, in his pain, he praised Allah. It was a miracle. Through Allah's grace, he remained alive.

Khan knew the attack had to be the Mossad. Somehow they had learned about the secret meeting. There could be no other explanation. With immense difficulty, he pushed and pulled until the charred bodies moved aside and he managed to stand. Stumbling, he managed only a few steps. Slowly turning his head, he checked everywhere for any sign of movement.

"Khalid." He tried to shout, but his burning throat constricted. Gasping for air, the after-smoke from the explosions filled his lungs, making him cough. He bent over and rested his hands against sore legs just above the knees. He finally succeeded in getting a breath. Then another.

He managed to stand up straight and attempted once more to look around. Tears still present, he had difficulty discerning the wreckage. He took a deep breath and tried again.

"Khalid? Khalid, my brother," he cried out. "Khalid, where are you?" There was no answer. "Khalid, are you alive?" He scanned the wreckage a second time, specifically searching for his brother.

Nothing moved except the smoke rising from the small fires scattered about.

"Allah!" he shouted. A different, deeper pain filled his heart. He dropped his head and sobbed. It became a full cry. "Allah, why?" He shook his head no. "Why Khalid?" He wiped tears from his face. "Why not me?"

A strange sensation came over him. A wild look appeared on his face. With enlarged eyes, he lifted his face to the sky. Shaking his head yes, he said aloud, "Okay. I understand. You let me live so I could take your revenge."

Clenching his teeth, fighting the pain, he struggled to raise his right hand high into the air. "Allah is good. Allah is great." The smoke cleared and he sucked the cold night air into his lungs. Stumbling, he regained his balance and again pushed his clenched right fist above his head. "Yes, I will do your will. Your revenge will sting Israel."

He paused. His eyes glazed over as a smile crept across his lips. "With your help, I will wreak your vengeance upon Israel — and upon everyone who has helped her."

He thought of America. *They help Israel financially, politically, militarily, in every way. They are also responsible.*

Again he gasped for breath and pushed his fist as high into the sky as he could reach. "Yes, Allah, yes! America, too. They have propped Israel up long enough. The day will come when they can no longer pay to support Israel. They will not be able to protect her." With his throat aching from the smoke and his hoarse voice almost gone, he summoned enough strength to shout, "They shall pay — Little Satan and the Great Satan — Israel and her friend America shall pay!"

CHAPTER 2

April 10, 2014
New York City

She waited.

Sensing it was hard for her, he thought how it must challenge her spirit to compel herself to just stand there. He saw her lift her head a bit, seeking his eyes, trying to send him the message.

The night grew still and the moment of truth confronted him. Stepping closer to her, Stephen Grant hesitated again. Still afraid that she would reject him, even though all the signals had been sent, all the subtle encouragement given. With all the wonderful time they had spent together over the last few months, it remained difficult for him.

He gazed into her soft, sensual eyes that sent the message. He understood her message. At least, he hoped he did. And he realized he had to make the move. She couldn't do it.

Images from the fantastic evening they had just shared flashed through his mind, filling him with warm, pleasant sensations. He pictured the two of them laughing and smiling at each other during the musical comedy at that cozy little theater off Broadway. He recalled how pretty she looked in the candlelight at dinner as he peered over the edge of his wine glass at her, and that look of tenderness. And yes, it was there. Love! In her eyes! Then, once more, he felt her in his arms as they danced, moving with the rhythm, her alluring body pressed against his.

This presented a dilemma for Stephen. This woman was truly enticing. She sparked intense feelings of desire within him. He wanted to kiss her, to hold her all night. In fact, he had wanted that for several dates now. He even fantasized about them making love. But whenever he was with her and these feelings were at their strongest, another woman interfered.

Every time he felt like taking this new woman in his arms, the face of Samantha Sorkin would appear. Whenever he wanted to kiss her, Samantha would move in between them. Samantha would be there with that mischievous sparkle in her eyes, her teasing smile taunting him. Though never present physically, she became a barrier keeping him from his longings.

Feeling the urgency of making a commitment to this woman was tearing him apart. He couldn't continue like this, for his own sake as well as hers. She had been patient, but he knew she wouldn't wait forever. She was charming, educated, intelligent, and beautiful. All of which made her exquisitely hot and foxy.

He was sure other men would find her desirable and try to capture her heart. "*But*," he thought, "*she's with me. We've spent considerable time together — without physical intimacy — just holding hands, a little nudge here and there, and an occasional warm hug. Still she has accepted all of my invitations and seems happy when she's with me.*"

She was so easy to talk to, about anything, about everything. He became alive when he was with her. They were relaxed and comfortable together, whether at a formal benefit or wearing blue jeans for a picnic in the park. He thoroughly enjoyed just being with her.

She tilted her head and gazed into his eyes. Her lips parted just a little, waiting.

He took a small half step toward her, put his arms around her and pulled her to him. Slowly, he brought his head down, his face close to hers, and stopped.

She didn't move. Her dark, sexy eyes said it all — go ahead.

Barely touching, he brushed her lips with his. He felt her shudder. He felt her arms go around him. She pulled him tight against her. He already knew she wanted him. Now, he knew he wanted her too, more than anything.

As they kissed, her soft, moist lips moved against his. He responded, moving his hands across and around her back, giving and taking pleasure.

The chains surrounding his heart snapped and fell away. Repressed emotions rushed through his body, igniting the fire of desire. Their embrace locked them together, pushing the rest of the world away as fantasies transported him to another universe.

Stephen didn't want the kiss to end. He floated in ecstasy and would have happily stayed there, but a distant siren coming closer brought his feet back to the ground.

Stephen pulled his head back a little without loosening his embrace. He smiled. She did too. He followed her eyes as they moved down his face and then back up to his. She spoke. "Once more."

The second kiss again filled him with emotion and desire. He pulled her even tighter against him as they once again soared toward the height of ecstasy. Soon the delicious moment faded when the car with the screaming siren turned the corner and sped down the street past them, dragging the rest of the world with it.

Their lips parted. Slowly letting out his breath, he opened his eyes and stared into her dark, beautiful, passion-filled eyes. Suddenly feeling warm all over, he smiled. This evening was one he would remember.

Almost breathlessly she said, "I've waited a long time for that, Stephen."

He lowered his head and smiled. "I know, Sheryl." He looked away, raised his left hand, and began tracing an elliptical scar running horizontally from near his left eyebrow to just inside his hairline. He often did this when deep in thought, or when anxious.

He looked back at her. "I told you it would be difficult for me to become involved with anyone. That I could enjoy your company and doing things together, but not to expect much more."

"Yes, you said that." Her eyes sparkled and her lips spread in a small smile. "And you've said a lot more. We've gotten to know each other pretty well over these past few months."

Pausing, looking deep into his eyes, Sheryl's eyes narrowed and her soft voice became much stronger and more forceful. "Now I have something to say."

Dr. Stephen Grant, Columbia University professor of political science, Middle East expert, and special assistant to the UN Secretary General, presented a handsome image. At just over six feet and one hundred ninety pounds, he maintained a trim figure and moved with an athletic grace that reflected continual physical conditioning.

A full head of light brown hair, just beginning to thin and gray around the edges, betrayed his maturity of nearly 50 years. Sensitive blue eyes revealed his normally compassionate nature, but could change instantly to convey sheer anger when appropriate.

He loosened his grip, but kept his right arm around her. "Yes, my dear." He realized he had never called her anything other than her name. He smiled. "Yes."

Without looking away from his eyes, she said, "I know you'll always love Becky. And you should. She was your wife."

Stephen knew he would love her forever. Rebecca, or Becky, a pretty, petite blonde, had been the joy of his life for 21 years of marriage, constantly filling his life with sunlight.

"Cherish her memory and the love you shared." Sheryl began slowly shaking her head no. "But she died, Stephen. She can't share this life with you anymore — other than in your heart."

A terrible traffic accident had taken her away and robbed him of his happiness. For a moment, he again felt that excruciating emptiness in the pit of his stomach. The pain of her death had crushed his heart, and the joy in his life had been sucked out. He forced a deep breath.

He pictured Becky's smile, the wind gently blowing her hair, and the warmth in her eyes when she mouthed the words, "I love you." Their time together was incredible, filled with love and laughter.

He recalled the shock he had after her death when he walked into the next room of his apartment and saw her standing there. Surprise yielded to warmth as his heart leapt into his throat. He couldn't speak. He couldn't say anything. He wanted to run to her and put his arms around her. But before he could do anything, her motionless figure disappeared. She was gone. Emotions hammered him as he realized she was never there. She was dead, and he would never feel her in his arms again.

Stephen had lived in severe depression for over a year, almost losing himself. His best friend Peter had helped him climb out of that dark hole.

Peter Standish, also a professor at Columbia, had become a friend when he and Stephen first started their teaching careers at Harvard. Peter had introduced Becky to Stephen. It was Peter who helped him finally get through the grief and restart his life again.

Stephen stood still, listening. Sheryl continued. "And there was Samantha." She continued to stare deeply into Stephen's blue eyes. "I know you loved her, Stephen." She paused. "I understand you still do, and that's okay. But now she's gone too. The women you loved — neither of them are here for you anymore."

He felt a longing in his heart, and tears formed in his eyes as he recalled how deeply he'd come to love Samantha Sorkin. Sam, as she liked to be called. She was a psychologist with a special clearance granted for treating members of the UN. And she was gorgeous. She set his heart on fire.

Stephen admired Samantha's intellect also. She was quick, bright, always thinking. Yet in spite of her knowledge and experience, she often acted childlike in many ways. She seemed to live in fear of being swallowed up in a relationship and losing control of her individuality.

Stephen had learned from losing Becky that one could not live life successfully being fearful. You must force yourself to move forward, beyond that fear. In fact, his only real fear was not being able to love again. But Sam helped relieve that.

Thanks to his best friend Peter's recommendation, Stephen had been drafted by the CIA to help identify and stop some terrorists who had formed a cell within the United Nations. The terrorists planned to start a nuclear war that would annihilate Israel and end world domination by the United States. Stephen became much more involved in that situation than anyone would have imagined, with repeated life-threatening events while traveling to Iraq, Egypt, and the Gaza Strip.

Samantha had also become involved and was eventually kidnapped. They both almost lost their lives before it was over. They came very close to death and ended up in the hospital afterward.

He pictured the last time he saw Samantha. She told him she had to go on a spiritual journey to find herself, and that she had to go alone, without him. She said goodbye and walked out of his life without looking back.

Knowing he had been lucky enough to have two loves in his lifetime, it took quite some time to get over them—first Becky, and then Sam. He had been alone now for what seemed like an eternity.

Then he met Sheryl Hauser. Five feet seven inches of dynamite, captivating looks, enticing smile, long dark brown hair, darker eyes, and curves in all the right places.

Having a cup of coffee while waiting for a friend at the Columbia campus New York Presbyterian hospital, his small table had the only vacant seat left in the cafeteria. He recalled hearing her soft, pleasant voice over his shoulder asking if she could join him until another seat became available. He remembered asking himself, as she sat down, how a woman could look and act that sexy without trying. Smiles led to pleasant conversation, which led to another meeting, and then the casual dating started. That was five months ago.

Stephen shared his feelings about his two loves and how it might be difficult for him to overcome that. However, he would welcome having someone to share some time with, do a few special things and just have some fun.

Sheryl explained she had experienced love in her life too, becoming engaged to a man while in medical school. They were to be married after she completed her residency. However, a tall redhead with big boobs and rich parents convinced Sheryl's fiancé to accompany her to Rio, and Sheryl had not heard from him since.

Sheryl had joined a small group of doctors in her specialty at Manhattan Pediatrics on East 72nd Street and enjoyed a comfortable practice for the last seven years. Now in her late thirties, she had learned patience, wondering if she would find love again someday. In the meantime, she was open to sharing adventures and camaraderie with Stephen.

Now with both arms around her, Stephen felt her heart racing as she struggled to control her emotions. He saw the seriousness with which she spoke. He noticed her expression soften as she continued. "It's okay to still love them — and it's all right to love me, too."

She rose up on her tiptoes, bringing her face closer to his. "I love you, Stephen. Do you hear me? I love you. And it's okay. Our love is different. It doesn't have to take away from your other loves. This is just ours, and it's separate from the others."

Her arms went back around him, and she put her head against his chest. She pleaded, "Let yourself go," the urgency in her voice clear. After a moment, she pulled back and looked up at him. He saw tears flowing down her cheeks. "It's okay to love me. It will grow. Just give it a chance."

She snuggled against him. He enjoyed her movements and the sensations various parts of her body gave him — gifted him. But he also knew that what he felt was more than just the physical sensations. She satisfied his longing, his loneliness, without consuming him. He didn't want to lose this. He had lost enough in his life already. He was not willing to give up more.

Stephen blinked as tears formed in his own eyes and he, too, tightened his arms around her. She felt so good against him, like she belonged there.

For a moment he didn't have the strength to say anything, but a fire kindled within him. He felt it spread, rising up inside his very being. His voice finally returned with renewed strength. "I love you, too, Sheryl."

CHAPTER 3

Electrifying pain flashed through his body.

Opening his mouth wide in a desperate attempt to gasp for air, his muscles constricted, immediately stopping his ability to breathe. He wanted to scream, but the intense pain and the shock of surprise delivered the instant knowledge that he had just drawn his last breath. His strength evaporated rapidly as wide eyes rolled upward to see white clouds fade into a darkening blue sky.

Excruciating pain shot through him again, even in the darkness, as the four and a half inch steel blade thrust into his back moved. The sharp, acute point on the recurved blade of the folding Kopis knife tilted upward, tearing into the man's heart. Death enveloped him, and his body crumpled to the deck.

Pulling the knife free as the boat captain fell, Rana Saleem laughed. "These new style lifejackets are so thin, they offer no resistance." He kicked the lifeless body. "My blade pierced the jacket like it was made of tea." He bent over and wiped the blood from the knife blade on the captain's expensive, white European life vest.

"Here, Rana, I will help you." Kamran Khan had been in the first mate's chair to the right of the captain when Saleem, standing beside the boat's driver, thrust the knife into the captain's back. "Remove the lifejacket. We want no chance of anyone identifying him."

Freeing the dead captain's arms from the vest, Khan instructed, "Lift his shoulders. I'll get his feet. There is not much strength in my left arm. It hurts when I use it, but I will help. Let's get him over the side. If there are any sharks within two miles, they will smell the blood and devour the evidence of our crime."

Originally slowed by the captain to obtain an accurate GPS reading, the forty-five foot motor yacht from Cuba, chartered with the captain, glided smoothly across the calm water. The body made only a small splash as it dropped into the water six miles from the southeastern coastline of the United States.

"You do know how to run this boat, do you not?"

"Yes, Rana. I do." Khan smiled as he slipped into the driver's chair. "The captain was extremely proud of this boat, and of his own skills. He showed me many things and demonstrated how to use the controls. I am ready."

"Good. There is still a long way to go."

"Do not worry, my friend. I know what to do."

"I hope you have many more good ideas, Kamran, like the one for the Coast Guard."

"Yes, I know the American Coast Guard watches their shoreline and checks incoming vessels. We looked like tourists having fun, with Leena sunbathing in her bikini and the rest of us in shorts with fishing poles. Waving at the helicopter told them we didn't have anything to hide."

"They waved back and took off. We won't see them again, will we?"

"I hope not, Rana."

Scanning the horizon, the only other boats visible were those in the distance toward the shore. Khan checked his watch. "I wonder what's keeping Saboor. He and Leena went to their cabins to change some time ago."

"Saboor's probably having a drink," Saleem answered. "He wants to be more like the Americans."

Khan replied wearily, "I wanted to review our plans in more detail, now that the captain is no longer with us."

"Kamran." Saleem appeared hopeful, smiling, "With our plan, we will get a real chance, won't we? It will be truly something to kill the President of the United States. We will be famous."

"Yes, Rana. We will have our chance." Khan thought for a moment before answering. "It will be more than an opportunity, it will work!"

Excited, Saleem smiled broadly as he danced around the yacht's bridge, humming his favorite tune.

Exhaling a deep breath, Khan stood. "Rana, take the wheel. Steer toward those boats straight ahead of us there in the distance." He pointed toward the horizon. "All those boats gathered over there. Head for them. I'm going below for a minute."

Cruisers Yachts made the 4550 Express Motoryacht impressive by any standard. Unlike most yachts this size, the cockpit and bridge deck features a crossover design, with fluid integration of the bridge and plush seating areas that merge into one large entertainment area. To the rear of this area is the helm station, with seating for the captain and first mate. Two ultra-plush sofa seats are aft, with a plush recliner on each side. The entertainment area features a standard wet bar, ice maker, refrigerator, 20 inch LCD television, DVD player and a top quality sound system as well.

While the 4550 is well laid out above decks, she's just as attractively arranged below. The space here, which is accented throughout with standard cherrywood, is, unlike many express boats, voluminous, with headroom averaging six foot five. The Master Stateroom features a catty-corner queen-size berth, spacious cabinets and vanity, and a full size bathtub. There is also a queen-size bed in the VIP Stateroom. The Third Stateroom features two standard beds. Each stateroom has a private head and its own private shower.

Nearing the bottom of the steps below deck, Khan heard scuffling and a muted scream coming from the Master Stateroom where Leena stayed. Quickly opening the door, Khan saw Leena Wateeb, minus her bikini, on the bed with a scared look of terror on her face. She struggled with Saboor Rajput on top of her. He had forced her legs apart and showed a big grin as he thrust in and out.

Khan ran to the bed, grabbed Rajput by the shoulders from behind and twisted, spinning Rajput off Wateeb and flipping him to the floor. "Saboor, what do you think you are doing?"

Surprised and somewhat dazed, Rajput made no attempt to stand. "It is all her fault, Kamran. She was teasing all of us." He stopped to get his breath. "She wore that ..." he pointed, "bathing suit. No good Muslim woman would wear a bikini like that in front of other men who are not her husband."

Leena Wateeb turned on her side, away from the two men, and began crying. Straight black hair drifted down over her shoulders and spread onto the bed. If she had been standing, the long hair would have provided a sexy, peek-a-boo curtain, partially covering her breasts. Deeply tanned, flawless skin displayed the backside of a high-priced swimsuit model from Sports Illustrated.

Wiping tears from her face, she hollered, "We are supposed to be like American tourists. I tried."

"She asked for it," Rajput said, "showing her body that way." He put his head down.

She turned her head around to look at Rajput. "You leave me and my family with no honor."

He became angry. "Nothing will happen." He looked at Khan. "She cannot prove anything. Sharia requires three male witnesses." He sucked air in short, quick breaths. "Come on, Kamran. We can both enjoy a good time with her."

"*Enough!*" Khan said forcefully. "We are supposed to be a team here, working together. We have to ... to make this thing work." Pausing for a breath, he continued. "Saboor, take your clothes, go to your room and get dressed. I will see you on deck."

As Rajput left the room, Khan's voice softened. "Leena, this should not have happened this way. I apologize for Saboor. For the rest of our team, too. We all enjoyed looking at you too much. You will not have to do this again. Get dressed. Give yourself a few minutes, then come up on deck with the rest of us." After pausing, he spoke very tenderly. "It will be all right, Leena."

Back on deck, Khan took over the captain's chair, confirmed his heading, and pushed the single lever electronic speed control all the way forward. The twin 480-hp Volvo Penta 75P diesel inboards reacted, increasing the forty-five foot yacht's speed to its maximum of 32 mph.

After some time they neared the U.S. mainland. Khan checked the GPS and killed the engines. The yacht bounced in the water a few hundred yards off the coast of South Carolina as the entire crew waited and watched. They got the signal just before sunset.

As the yacht moved slowly toward the spot of the signal, just south of Sand Island, a hidden inlet revealed itself. Khan maneuvered the boat through narrow twists and turns as they travelled up the inlet for over a quarter mile. Rounding a corner, they entered a huge opening over a hundred yards wide. Surrounded by trees, large bushes and thick underbrush, it appeared like it was in the middle of a jungle.

Khan slowed the boat even more. At the middle of the opening, he turned the wheel toward the only manmade item there, a small wooden dock on the northwest side of the water. He killed the engines and let the yacht drift silently.

As they reached the dock, a dark-haired young woman wearing a khaki shirt, blue jeans and sandals emerged from the bushes. She had the appearance of a Playboy Girl of the Month. As she bounced toward them on the dock, she smiled broadly at the boat crew and announced, "I am Umara."

While the woman grabbed the boat's railing to stop it, Khan took the lead and jumped off the boat to the dock. "Umara, it is good to see you." He moved to the woman for a quick embrace, then turned to the others. "Umara is one of our advance team. She is here to meet us and take us to Baltimore."

As the others began disembarking, Khan put their fears to rest. "Umara and Tariq were sent here early to help prepare for us. They flew from Havana to Mexico City more than three months ago. Once in Mexico, it was easy for them to obtain false papers stating they were Mr. and Mrs. Tariq Gorshani. They obtained a fake tourist visa to the U.S., travelled to Baltimore and found a house to serve as home base for our team during the operation."

"Hurry," she said. "I have a car near here, and we don't want to be seen."

"Follow Umara to the car," Khan instructed. "Saboor, help me with boat, then we can join the others."

"Khan, the car is about 100 meters straight back and to the left," Umara said. "It's an old, gray Chevy. It's getting dark, so you might have to look a bit to find it."

"An old Chevrolet?" An alarm went off in Khan's mind. "How old?"

"Tariq thought it was a 1958 or '59 model. Why?"

"Umara, when did you get the car?"

"Two days ago. It was parked overnight at a gas station. No one was there when we took it. Everything should be all right."

"Umara, an older car will stand out and people will notice it. That's not good. We don't want people's attention. Here in the U.S., people drive newer automobiles."

"Okay." Umara shrugged. "It's night time. We'll head down the road and steal another. One that won't be so noticeable."

Khan shook his head. "Umara, I think you fit into the American way of life too well." He changed his voice to mimic hers. "Okay, we'll just head down the road and steal another one." He exhaled loudly, then smiled. "Well, I guess we'd better get a different one. We don't need trouble with the police so soon."

Saboor Rajput and Kamran Khan climbed back onto the boat as the others moved off through the brush and out of sight. Rajput asked, "What are we going to do?"

"Sink the boat," replied Khan. "Follow me."

Below deck in the galley, they found and opened the water cocks. "Let's check the Master Suite first, then the others."

As Rajput entered the larger suite, Khan followed and closed the door behind him. "There are no water cocks in this room, Saboor."

Rajput turned to Khan. "What do you mean? Then why are we here?"

"Saboor, this is where you raped Leena." He glared at Rajput. "I needed you to be part of the team, but you couldn't do it." He reached under his shirt and pulled out a Kahr PM45.

Easy to conceal, the black polymer frame .45 caliber semi-automatic pistol weighs just over a pound, at 17.3 ounces, with a barrel length of 3.24 inches and an overall length of 5.79 inches. The textured black polymer grips provide an easy hold around the five-round magazine. The matte blackened stainless slide has an ultra hard, super thin coating, which has been used successfully in the knife industry to protect blades from corrosion and scratches.

The pistol uses a striker pin and is double-action only. Khan carried a sixth round in the chamber, making it easy to shoot. He didn't have to work the slide or even cock a hammer. All he had to do was point the gun at Rajput and pull the trigger.

"No! *Kamran!*"

Khan raised the pistol, and the Kahr PM45 spit its messengers of death three times.

Catapulted backward, Rajput's body slammed against the wall, twisted sideways, and slid to the floor, painting the polished wood paneling with blood.

After making certain Rajput was dead, Khan left the boat and hurried through the brush to where the others waited with the car.

"Kamran, over here." Umara spoke in a low, soft voice, not wanting to be overheard if strangers were anywhere near. She blinked her flashlight.

Khan saw the flashing light through the thick brush and moved to her. "I am here, Umara."

"Good. I saved you a place in the front seat. You can see where we are going."

Turning her head and glancing around, she asked, "Where's Saboor?"

Khan motioned with his hand. "Let's go to the car. Have you seen anyone else around here?"

"No. No one," she replied. "Fishermen will come, but I am not sure how soon. We will be gone. It should be safe for us. No one will find the boat very soon."

Reaching the car, Umara got into the driver's seat and Khan entered from the other side and sat on the front seat beside her. "Let's go."

The two people in the back seat, Saleem and Wateeb, glanced questioningly at each other. Saleem asked, "What about Saboor?"

"He's not coming." Khan turned around and stared back at Leena, into her dark eyes. "He could not work as part of a team."

CHAPTER 4

"It's been stolen?"

"Yep. Along with most of our stuff. We pulled into the Best Western here in Fayetteville late last night and were so tired, we just went to our room and crashed, all four of us." Charlie Grant, Stephen's older brother, sounded excited and out of breath.

"Have you called the police?"

"Yeah, they bin here." Charlie took a breath. "They said they cain't do much, but they put word out to the rest of the highway patrol 'bout the car."

"Wow." Stephen could only imagine how his brother felt after this happening. He didn't sound angry, only frustrated. "At least no one was hurt in the process. That was fortunate. And your family completed your visit to Disney World before it happened. How was that?"

"Oh, the kids loved it. They must have gone on every ride at least twice. And it's crazy. That place is so expensive, and way, way too crowded. It's sure not like Kansas."

Stephen couldn't help but smile. "No, it's not like Kansas. I'm glad all of you are all right."

"Stephen." He took a breath. "You know I believe things happen for a reason, but this one sure sets me back. I cain't figure it out."

"What do you mean, Charlie?"

"I parked the car down at the far end of the parking lot. It's new and I didn't want to get it all scratched up. When I went out this morning, the car was gone. A beat-up old gray Chevy with no license plates was parked in its spot. Can ya beat that?"

"That's a great trade."

"Yeah, but not for me. My car only had a couple thousand miles on it. The leather still smelled new."

"What did the police say?"

"Ah, they said they'd try to find out who owns the Chevy. Maybe it was reported stolen or something, and maybe not. They said it would take a couple days, at least."

"No, I mean what did they say about your car?"

"You know, they didn't seem all that excited about that. You'd think they'd 'a wanted to do something to try and find my car. They did put out a notice over the radio. I guess they were goin' to send some sort of notification to other police agencies in the state." He let out a deep breath. "But it seemed more like, 'Ho-hum. Let your insurance company know. Then it's between them and me.'"

"Yeah. They probably get their share of auto theft, Charlie. So they don't get too excited."

"Well, you must be right. They said they have no idea when they may get it back, if at all. They said a newer car like mine will probably be over the state line in just a couple hours."

"What are you going to do now?"

"The insurance company said what they call 'trip interruption' is part of our policy. They'll pay expenses for us to get home. You know, rental car, food, motels, that sort of thing. I am sorry, brother, but we won't be able to come visit like we planned. I was looking forward to it."

"Yes, so was I, Charlie." He sighed. "It's been awhile." Pausing a moment, he took a deep breath. "There's a new change in my life. I have someone I wanted you to meet."

"Oh, yeah? And just who might that be?"

"Someone new." Stephen paused. "Her name is Sheryl Hauser." He pictured her standing with him, grinning. He smiled back at her. "She's lovely, big brother. She's a pediatrician here in New York." He shook his head, acknowledging what he was saying. "She's so sweet." He felt warm all over just talking about her. "I think I'm in love, Charlie."

"She must be somethin' special."

"She is. You guys would like her. She's very charming."

"And beautiful, I bet. Knowing you, she's got to be a seriously hot, foxy thing."

"Of course," Stephen laughed.

"Well, you'll have to bring her to Kansas to meet the family. If you wanted us to meet her, she must be special to you. Come on out to our place, and Mom and Dad can meet her too."

"We'll plan for that."

"Yeah. That'll be nice." He paused a moment, then added, "Please do come out. We'd all really like to see you, but you understand how this thing is, don't you?"

"Yes, I understand. You can't help it. We'll come see you."

Charlie waited a moment. "Say, Stephen, how 'bout keeping your eyes open for my car up there in the big city. All right? Who knows where it'll turn up. The car is a new, maroon Tahoe with custom Kansas plates that say PRECHR."

Both Charlie and Stephen's father were country preachers in Kansas. They loved it there, both the country and the people. Their father had hoped Stephen would follow the family tradition and do the same, but Stephen was called to do something else. He loved the glamour and excitement of the big city, and he loved being involved in international affairs with people from various cultures.

He had been an exchange student and lived with a family in Egypt for two of his high school years. After college, he completed an internship with the State Department that included helping draft two treaties between the U.S. and several Middle Eastern countries. When he finally settled at Columbia University, he had been asked to split his time and serve as a special assistant on Middle Eastern affairs to the Secretary-General of the United Nations.

"Yeah, Charlie." Stephen shook his head and laughed. "Like I'm really going to see that car here in New York City. But don't worry, brother, I'll keep an eye out for it."

CHAPTER 5

Nervous, Khan held his breath as he stepped out of the car and glanced around. A light breeze stirred the branches of only a few pine trees. Small white clouds drifted slowly across the pale blue sky, forcing the sun to play hide and seek. Khan noticed no automobiles were visible and he could not hear any traffic sounds anywhere. He nodded, speaking barely above a whisper. "Very peaceful." He turned to Umara. "It appears you and Tariq did well, finding this place." Umara enjoyed seeing him smile.

The others tried to be quiet exiting the car, eager to see the house.

"It's okay. You don't have to be totally silent." Umara spoke with a smile. Waving her arm, she said, "You can see the house has a very large yard all around, what the Americans call four acres. Tall, thick evergreen trees are close together, lining the property and completely shielding us." Her smile grew even wider, proud of the place she and Tariq found. "Can you smell them, the trees? Everything is so fresh here—the flowers, the trees. I love it."

Umara continued, "We are in Baltimore County, not the city. All the homes here along Cedar Garden Road have very large yards. Plus," she motioned with both hands, "the houses on both sides are empty. None of the neighbors are close enough to overhear us. We can talk freely."

Khan shook his head. "We still must be cautious. It may be all right for others listening to us as we come and go, to know we are here. But be careful what you say when you are outside. We cannot take unnecessary risks."

Umara's smile would not be deterred. She pointed at the three-story brick colonial that seemed like a mansion to her.

"Let's go inside." Obvious excitement showed on her face. "It is a huge house. There is room for everyone here."

Tariq greeted them as they entered, giving Khan the first embrace. "My brother, it is good to see you." After greeting Rana, then Leena, he peered questioningly at Khan. "Where is Saboor?"

"He could not work with us as a team," Khan answered, shaking his head. "He will not be coming."

Tariq's expression said he understood—something went wrong and Saboor had to be eliminated. Tariq nodded. "Too bad. I liked Saboor." Shrugging, he continued. "Oh, well. I hope you had a good trip."

Donning a smile, he said, "Let me show you the house. You can see it's very big. Afterward we can talk about what we must do."

Inside, Tariq led them across the spacious living room toward the back of the house. "This next space is the dining room. This beautiful table and all the chairs came with the home. We rented the house with all the elaborate furniture you will see. We did not need to buy anything."

"Across over here," he remarked, pointing, "is the kitchen."

They continued moving through the kitchen and back into the entryway. "I'm sure you noticed the circular staircase when you came in. The open ceiling goes all the way to the third floor." He smiled.

"Impressive," replied Khan. "Let's go ahead upstairs."

A crystal chandelier hung at the top of the stairs, its light spreading over the staircase and well down the hall to another, smaller chandelier. "There are two bedrooms and one bathroom on this top level," Tariq informed them. "Leena, you and Umara will stay here."

Umara walked to an open doorway to one of the rooms. "This is my bedroom. Leena, you can have the other room." She smiled. "I know you will like it." She spread her arms and spun in a circle. "Everything here is so elegant."

Beaming, she said, "Tariq, why don't you take the men downstairs? I'll show Leena the rooms here."

"It's so big," Leena exclaimed as they entered her bedroom. "All this just for me?"

"Yes. Isn't it magnificent?"

Leena turned in a complete circle, taking it all in.

Umara walked over to her. "Leena, all of the men have gone downstairs. Please, tell me what happened to Saboor."

Leena quickly dropped her head and stared at the floor. A tear formed in the corner of her eye. In a hesitant voice barely above a whisper, she told Umara, "I am so ashamed, Umara." Leena looked up at Umara, her face full of emotion, seeking understanding. The words came slowly. "He ... he raped me."

"Oh, Leena!" She reached out and took hold of Leena's hand. "I'm so sorry."

Still hesitant, Leena continued. "We acted like Americans to fool their Coast Guard. I was in a bikini. The men all had shorts and fishing poles. After the Coast Guard helicopter flew away, Saboor and I went to our cabins to change clothes." She coughed and peeked at Umara, blushing. "I had just removed the bikini when Saboor came into my cabin. He rushed over and threw me down on the bed."

She wiped her eyes and swallowed hard. "He took his shorts off and got on the bed before I could do anything. He didn't say a word. He just looked at me and grinned." She started to cry. "I tried to stop him, but he was too strong."

Umara saw a flash of anger in Leena's eyes, but it quickly returned to overwhelming shame. She continued, still speaking slowly. "After a couple minutes, he forced my legs apart and began raping me."

As Leena cried, Umara could hear that shame in her voice. "That's when Kamran came into the room. He stopped it."

Umara took hold of Leena's other hand and held them both. "It's okay, Leena. He didn't hurt you badly, did he?"

Dropping her head again, Leena closed her eyes. After a moment, she shook her head. "No. It hurt bad right at that time, but I'm okay."

Umara stared into Lena's eyes and continued to hold both her hands. "Leena, listen to me. You're strong. You'll get beyond it."

"But I am so ashamed."

"You don't have to be." She nodded yes with her head and smiled at Leena. "Let me tell you about me and Tariq."

Umara kept smiling as she spoke. "After we got here, in Baltimore, Tariq told me we both were uneasy when we talked about our pretend marriage. We were uncomfortable talking about it to others. He said we needed to practice being married so it would appear better to others. If we practiced, it would be more natural for us to act like a couple. Others would see that and believe it."

Umara shook her head yes. "He said Allah would understand. We were doing His will to fight against the infidel Americans, so it was not wrong. Now we practice every day, sometimes twice."

"At first I was afraid when he wanted to touch me. I was always nervous when we would practice, but I got over it. He enjoys playing with my body. Now I enjoy it too. We are like a married couple. No one can tell the difference."

"It will be okay, Leena." She gave her a compassionate hug. "Remember that. And if you need to talk about it, you can come to me anytime." Smiling, she added, "Now let's go downstairs and join the men."

Descending to the second floor, Khan noticed that the soft gray carpet covering the stairs only covered the middle of each step. About four inches of space left on each side of the carpeting revealed the polished dark oak wood of the staircase. The color matched the paneling covering the lower half of the walls in the halls of both floors. An off-white color adorned the walls above the paneling to prevent the hallways from appearing too dark. The same light gray carpeting brightened the floor in each hallway.

On the second level, Tariq said, "There are three bedrooms and two bathrooms here." He looked at Khan. "Kamran, please take the large bedroom with private bath. Rana and I will each have a bedroom here and will share the second bathroom." Khan and Saleem both nodded.

Returning to the main floor, Tariq said, "There is a small bathroom on this floor, and one in the basement. We have plenty of room to work our plans here."

"It's perfect," Khan replied. "Great job, Tariq. Tell me, how did you find this place?"

"I studied available rentals on the Internet. Then I expanded the search to include those for sale. This house had been for sale for over six months. The price had been reduced twice during that time. The owners moved to a new home in Georgia and left it empty. I offered to rent it if they included the furniture, and they accepted."

"Again, you did a good job."

Tariq nodded. "Thank you." He motioned with his hand. "We are close to the Interstate 95 highway, and it is only a twenty-minute drive to the convention center."

"Twenty minutes? Excellent. This will be perfect." Khan rubbed his hands together. Turning to Leena and Umara, he asked, "Umara, do you have any tea?"

"Yes, of course."

In Pakistan, tea is popular all over the country and holds an integral significance in local culture. One of the most consumed beverages in Pakistani cuisine, the local name for tea in Urdu is 'chai'.

"However," she added, "all the closest grocery store had was tea bags. They will have to do."

Throughout Pakistan, tea is made from loose tea leaves, steeped for a few minutes and then poured into cups through a strainer. It is always served with milk. Sugar is served separately so each individual can sweeten their drink according to their own taste. Teabags are reserved for when time constraints do not allow one to prepare tea from the loose leaves.

"We are in America," offered Tariq. "It is the land of instant gratification."

Khan nodded. "Umara, if you have some biscuits, it would also be nice, like the custom back at home."

A few minutes later, all five people sat around the dining room table enjoying the biscuits and tea. Khan reminisced, "This is great, but it's too bad there isn't some paan to share."

The consumption of paan has long been a popular cultural tradition throughout Pakistan. Paan is a stimulating and psychoactive preparation of betel leaf combined with areca nut, mixed with a lime paste. It is chewed for a time, then spat out or swallowed. A delicacy enjoyed by many, it is almost exclusively bought from street vendors instead of being prepared at home.

"You know, it is too bad," offered Tariq. "America is such a rich country," he motioned, swinging his arm around, "with beautiful places like this, but yet it is still so uncivilized."

Khan agreed. "Yes, and they don't even know they are missing anything. They have become so self-centered, seeking only their own immediate pleasure." He nodded. "It is too bad."

Khan motioned to Tariq with his tea cup. "Tell me, were you able to get all the items on the list I gave you?"

"Yes. I had a little difficulty obtaining the specific rifle you requested, but I finally got the right one."

"You had specific models you requested?"

"Yes, Rana. I researched these items carefully. I want to be sure I have exactly what I need."

"Which is … ?" inquired Rana.

"The rifle is a Savage Law Enforcement Series 110 BA in 338 Lapua magnum with bipod. It is extremely accurate and an excellent long range weapon. Unlike most sniper rifles, this one has a five-round magazine. It is much easier to get off successive shots if needed."

"The scope is a Vortex Viper PST. Passive Shooting Tactical riflescope. It is a 6-24 power, 50mm scope with constant illuminated MOA ranging reticles. The scope is made from aircraft grade aluminum and provides waterproof, fog proof, dust proof performance."

"It is an expensive combination, but it will do exactly what I need," Khan concluded.

"Yes," said Tariq. "The total cost was a little over four thousand U.S. dollars." He looked at Khan. "I had the telescopic sight mounted on the sniper rifle and flip cap covers added. I even purchased a carrying case for it." Tariq waited a second. "But please tell me, Kamran, what is this for? It was not part of our plan for killing the President of the United States during the conference here at the convention center."

"It is, in a way. Rana, Leena and I will go to New York City. We will create a distraction so federal forces cannot focus everything on the conference here. That will help us."

Tariq glanced at Rana, and then looked back at Khan. "Can you tell us what you plan?"

Taking a bite of his biscuit, Khan sipped his tea and sat back. While focusing on Tariq, he glanced at each of the others also. "You know my brother and I were agents for the ISI. The Mossad somehow learned about a secret meeting we were attending in the West Bank, in Ramallah. They raided the place, killing everyone else, including my brother. My left shoulder and arm were severely injured. I will never regain strength in that arm."

He took another sip of tea. "The ISI learned that Colonel Daniel Shavit led that raid for the Mossad. They would not allow me to seek revenge, so I resigned. Since then, I discovered that Israel rewarded Colonel Shavit for his success." He paused. "He is in New York City. He is now UN Ambassador Shavit."

Tariq nodded. "So you are going there to kill him."

"Yes." Again Khan sipped his tea. "The rifle is for backup if I need it. I do not think I will. I have arranged a business lunch meeting at a particular restaurant with several members of the Israeli delegation—including, and especially, the Israeli Ambassador." Khan smiled and a strange look swept across his face. "I brought semtex to plant in the restaurant ahead of time," he paused, "lots of it ... to ensure the Ambassador's luncheon will be a blast." He laughed.

CHAPTER 6

The silver knife blade flashed, slashing through the air aimed right at him. A quick parry and dodge to the side altered the weapon's path, narrowly missing Stephen's throat. The follow-through utilized his new skills to grab the wrist holding the knife and pull in the same direction as the thrust. With a twisting motion, Stephen wrestled the man's arm down and around, coming up behind the man's back, and held it with his left hand. Bringing his own right arm up and around, Stephen brought his forearm against the man's throat and applied pressure.

"Good move." Pleased, the instructor added, "Great job, Stephen. Your training is paying off."

Stephen relaxed his hold, and the other trainee gasped for air. He turned to face Stephen, tried to smile, and with a slight bow, offered his hand in congratulations.

"That will end our lesson for today. Good job, both of you. Time to hit the showers."

The refreshing shower relaxed him and brought a multitude of thoughts, including how well he was doing with these hand-to-hand combat lessons for self defense. Then she appeared. Samantha Sorkin. He recalled her warning that he should seriously learn how to fight, to defend himself. And her words concerning the CIA. "Since they came to you for help once, they'll come back to you again." So far that had not happened, but he acknowledged that it was a possibility.

Dressed and exiting the locker room, Stephen heard his name called, along with, "Phone call." Walking into the gym's office, he picked up the phone. "Dr. Grant."

"Stephen, how's the self defense training going?"

"Peter," he replied. "Pretty well. I think I'm finally learning enough to not get myself killed, at least in the first few minutes. So how are you doing? What's up?"

"I thought if you're up to it, we might have lunch. You still taking the afternoon off?"

"Yes, I am. And if you're going to enjoy an afternoon off, I know just the place to go. I've wanted to go back to a special restaurant, and I'd be delighted if you would be my guest."

———————

Khan placed the black attaché case on the floor next to him. With his foot, he pushed it against the wall at the back of the booth.

He snickered as he visualized the Israeli Ambassador and his aides sitting around one of the small tables, placing their food order with a waiter. His thoughts were like a knife stabbing at them. *They are so smug, so proud, so falsely secure. Just wait. Your reward is coming soon.* He laughed out loud.

Sitting across the table, Leena and Saleem peered at him. "What is it, Kamran?"

"Just thinking about what is going to happen." He nodded. "So richly deserved."

Glancing over at Leena, Khan smiled. "Try not to kick the case, Leena, That's the Ambassador's present."

Saleem offered, "You don't even know where he will sit, Kamran."

"There is enough plastic to not make any difference. It will be sufficient if he is inside the restaurant."

Khan pictured the Ambassador's face. He'd obtained photographs from the ISI and found several more on the Internet. His eyes narrowed as he thought about the surprise Daniel Shavit would experience and how his expression would morph into a look of sheer horror. Khan's mouth formed a sinister grin as he felt the mounting satisfaction that would be his. Not just revenge—retaliation! Shavit would pay with his life today. He would not be a hero any longer. He would be dead.

Picking up a menu, Khan said, "Since there is lots of time, what would you like to eat?"

Leena whispered, "The food here in this restaurant is so expensive."

Khan countered, "This is New York City. Everything is expensive."

———————

"Ready to go, gentlemen?" he asked the three men waiting. Daniel Shavit did not think the meeting with these businessmen would generate anything positive, but he could not afford to take that chance, so he agreed to go. If these businessmen were correct and proved to be successful, it would mean a great deal to Israel and them. However, he had heard so many wishful ideas from American dreamers that he became doubtful about the reality of most of those ideas. It would most likely be a waste of time. He would be glad when it was over.

"Mr. Ambassador?" The clerk held the phone with his hand over the mouthpiece. "The U.S. Secretary of State is here. She is downstairs."

With a questioning look, Shavit said, "Her appointment is not until three o'clock. Sure she is downstairs now?"

"She offers her apologies. Said she had to rearrange her schedule at the President's request. She will be meeting with him this afternoon."

Exhaling a deep breath, Shavit answered, "All right. Ask if she could come up to this office."

Turning to the other men, he spoke to his assistant. "Gil, you're going to have to take this one for me. I'm sorry. The meeting is at the Midtown Steakhouse on 53rd, right across from the New York Sheridan. Find out what their business is, see if you can determine anything about their financial stability, and if this is a business that would benefit the Haifa area. See if they have any new ideas that might make this work for them and us. Remember, don't agree to anything. Tell them we're interested, but we need to discuss it. And thank them for the meeting."

The Ambassador started to turn away, but stopped. "And guys, no one talks to the press about this. Understand?"

———————

"So what do you think, Peter? Pretty nice place, right?"

""Yes, it is. I love the ambience. Busy, but very nice." Best friends, Dr. Stephen Grant and Dr. Peter Standish relished their lunch break away from everything. "I've never been to the Midtown Steakhouse before."

"It's convenient, but far enough away to provide a pleasant respite. No classes, no students, and no UN." He looked at Peter, and the look on his face revealed the deep respect and warm friendship they held for each other. Stephen motioned, "Enjoy finishing your steak."

"I will. This is a great steak, and it's seasoned just right. It's delicious." He raised his eyebrows. "And it's cooked to perfection. Done, but still pink in the center. Just the way I like it."

Smiling, Peter lifted his cocktail glass in a toast. "I'm glad we took the rest of the day off. Here's to a pleasant, lazy afternoon."

Stephen picked up his glass and reached over to clink it against Peter's. "Hear, hear."

Sitting back in his chair, Stephen luxuriated in the cool liquid slowly flowing down his throat. "I have an idea." He motioned for the waiter, and requested the bartender come to the table.

"We'd like you to try to make our favorite drink. Here, I've written down the recipe."

The bartender took the napkin. "Hmm. Three parts vanilla vodka, one part white chocolate liqueur, shaken over ice, and garnished with a cherry." The bartender smiled. "Okay. I have all that. Let's try it."

Peter raised a finger. "And what we really need is a bowl of mixed nuts. If you don't have that, peanuts will do."

Still smiling, the bartender strode back to the bar.

Pleased, Peter added, "Now we're talking," and again lifted his glass in mock salute.

After the new cocktails were delivered along with a bowl of peanuts, Stephen inquired, "How is your new wife doing, Peter?"

"Great. Married life is wonderful. I think Olivia likes being Mrs. Standish." Grabbing a handful of peanuts, he put several of them in his mouth and took pleasure with each bite. He grinned and said, "I enjoy her delight and happiness. I like being married."

Stephen nodded. "That's a good thing."

Peter asked, "How are things going with you and Sheryl?"

Olivia Newman, now Olivia Standish, was best friends with Sheryl Hauser. She had asked Sheryl to be the maid of honor at her wedding. The four of them shared an occasional late-night dinner at a north side restaurant.

"I think we've turned a corner. We said we love each other."

"Wow."

"Yes, but ..." Stephen put his head down. "I don't know, Peter. She keeps doing things that remind me of Becky, then she says something just the way Sam would." He shook his head no. "It makes it hard."

"I'm sure it does." Peter sat back in his chair and smiled. "But you have to get beyond that. You're going to have to do that no matter what." He paused, took a deep breath and reached for more peanuts. "Does Sheryl know?"

"I think so ... I don't know."

"In order to get on with the rest of your life, you must get over this. You have to move on. Stephen, there will always be someone doing something that reminds you of Becky or Sam." Peter shook his head. "Neither of them are physically in your life anymore. They can't be. They're only part of your past. Put it behind you. Let it go, Stephen."

"Yeah. Well, I'm trying."

———————

Three people were waiting in the maroon SUV parked a few cars down the street when a dark limo stopped in front of the restaurant, and the Israeli delegates exited the car. "Wait until they get inside," Tariq cautioned.

The Israelis walked to the front door of the Midtown Steakhouse without speaking. As Gil reached for the handle, the door swung open. Two men leaving the restaurant stopped and stepped back to allow the Israelis to enter. As they did, the door closed. Gil smiled, "Stephen, it is nice to see you." He offered his hand.

Stephen accepted and shook his hand. He introduced Peter to the others and wished them a pleasant lunch. Smiling, he pushed the door open for he and Peter to leave. As they emerged from the restaurant, thinking it was a wonderful afternoon, Stephen remembered the papers.

"I have to go back, Peter. I left the folder with my papers on the table. I'll just be a minute."

"Okay. I'll wait here."

Stephen turned and walked back toward the door to the restaurant.

Several feet away in the opposite direction, holding the remote in his hand, Khan said, "Now," and pushed the button.

CHAPTER 7

She couldn't move.

Knowing she was right where he wanted her, she felt his body pressing against her.

She realized whatever happened next, she would never forget this night: the feel of his warm breath on her cheek, the smell of his aftershave. It would be a part of her life forever.

His hands moved. She felt his body push against her even more as his grip tightened. She could feel his desire growing.

She closed her eyes, waiting. A fearful anticipation swept over her, then a strange excitement sprouted from within.

Forcing herself to move her head, she looked up at him. He brought his face down close to hers. Gazing into his eyes, all fear left as their lips met.

Her cell phone interrupted the memories. "Hello, this is Sheryl."

"Hi, girl. This is Olivia. How's my BFF?"

"Oh, great, Olivia. Great."

Girl talk took several minutes, catching up and sharing life's pleasures along with a little laughter. They enjoyed being best friends. Then came the question. "How are you doing with Stephen?"

"Oh, Olivia, we had a spectacular evening last night, truly. Fabulous dinner, wonderful music, great dancing." She felt lighter than air. "It was beautiful."

"Sounds good."

"Oh, it was. It really was." She paused, inhaling deeply. Alone, sitting at the desk in her office, she pushed the file folder in front of her over to the side. With her left hand she reached out and picked up a small framed picture. She looked longingly at Stephen and smiled.

She raised her right shoulder to hold the phone against her ear. The fingers of her right hand touched his face. She ran her fingers down his soft cheek. He smiled back at her.

"We had a special moment last night." She sighed. "Olivia, he kissed me."

"Ah-ha. Finally."

"Yes, and it was even better than I imagined. It felt so good with his arms around me, pulling me against him. Ohh," she shuddered, "I wanted to stay there. His lips were so soft ... to start ... but his kiss became so passionate, I couldn't let him stop with just one."

"Oh, girlfriend, you did have a good night."

"Oh, yes." Pausing, she put the picture back on her desk, but continued staring at him. Her gaze dropped to the floor. "It took a long time coming, but we hit a turning point last night. I'm glad. I'm not sure how much longer I could have waited. Sometimes, it seems Stephen has a hard time deciding what he wants ... or at least doing something about it."

"True. That's our man, Stephen. But once he does, he really goes after it. And it sounds like he made a decision about you, my dear friend."

"I sure hope so. I do want him, and I told him so last night. I told him I love him."

"You go, girl."

"We had quite a talk, too."

"Good for you, girlfriend. What'd you say? Tell me all about it."

"We talked about his past, or rather I did: Rebecca ... and, of course, Sam." She took another deep breath. "I was rather firm. I hope just enough. I felt I had to be. I told him they were gone and he needed to get over them."

"How did he respond?"

"Quiet. Very quiet. He was listening ... and, I hope, thinking about what I was saying."

She paused as a young couple passed outside the window, on their way to the front door of the office. She smiled again. "I'm glad we're not the age of the young couple that's now entering the office." She shook her head. "It's enough to worry about our own tangled lives. I'm happy neither Stephen nor I wanted children. It's complicated enough with only us."

"Oh, that's good. You don't want kids, but you're a pediatrician?"

"Yeah, well ... as long as they're somebody else's."

Still sitting behind her desk, she swung her chair around to face the wall displaying her degrees and other certifications. She leaned back and continued. "The look on his face told me what I said was right on the mark." Her voice became determined. "It's time for him to get some balls and man up. He needs to come to grips with this whole thing: me, the past, the future. Olivia, he has to face reality sooner or later. I'd rather it be sooner. I want it to be now."

"Maybe he likes it the way it is."

"No." She shook her head. "I don't believe that. Not the way he kissed me. He pulled me so tight against him. It felt good. I could tell he thought so too. I know he wants more ... and I'm sure he wants the same thing I do. Olivia ...," she could hear her friend breathing, waiting. "Olivia, he said he loves me too."

"Wow. That *is* a big step for Stephen. I'm so happy for you, both of you." From the sound of her voice, Sheryl could picture the huge grin on Olivia's face.

"So what happens now?"

Sheryl shook her head. "I'm not sure, my friend. When I was in his arms, I showed him the kind of love he can have. Now it's up to him. He said he loves me. I hope and pray that he has the courage to reach for it."

"Oh, me too. Me too. You guys are meant for each other. Would you like me to ask Peter to talk to him?"

"They're spending the afternoon together. I hope Peter has an opportunity to say something, and that Stephen listens."

"If there's an opening, dear friend, I have no doubt Peter will use it."

"I know, Olivia. You guys are so great. You're the best friends a person could have." She hesitated. "Oh, Olivia, I love Stephen, and I know he wants this, too, I just don't know how much."

"I sense some hesitation there, Sheryl."

"It's not hesitation, Olivia, it's fear. I'm not sure Stephen is motivated enough to follow through with his decision. I'm here for him. He just has to reach for me."

CHAPTER 8

Stopping before reaching the door to the restaurant, Stephen turned to Peter and started to say something when they both sensed the roar of the explosion rather than hearing it.

A gigantic force smashed against their backs, raised them into the air and threw them across the sidewalk as a brilliant flash of white light surrounded them, blinding them to their surroundings. Invisible pavement grabbed at their skin as they belly-flopped onto the street and slid across the concrete, finally rolling the last few feet. A tidal wave of hot air rushed over them and stunning pain cut into their bodies, burning deeply everywhere.

Air was pulled from Stephen's lungs and he struggled, unable to get a breath. He felt like he was on fire.

Forcing his eyes open, Stephen's mind raced over incomplete thoughts as he tried to look around and comprehend what had happened. He started shaking from within, unable to focus on anything more than a few feet away. Unconnected images flashed before his face, out of order.

He and Peter were enjoying their lunch. Stephen poured the wine and handed a glass to Sheryl, who was standing beside the table at last night's restaurant. Smiling, she tasted the wine, set the glass down, and offered her hand to Stephen. Taking her hand, Stephen led her to the dance floor, turned, and took Samantha into his arms.

Colorful birds sang their melodious delight, fluttering in soft sunlight above while the pale blue sky yielded to exploding cannons thundering in distant fields as they sped closer and closer to UN Headquarters.

The mental fog began dissipating and he felt the concrete beneath him. *I'm lying in the street.* As his vision began clearing, he discerned debris scattered all around him, while objects in the distance remained blurry.

Using his hands and arms, he checked himself, but there was no flame, no fire. Just pain. He remembered Peter and shouted his name. No answer.

He forced himself to roll over and attempted to stand, but didn't have enough strength and fell back to the concrete. He looked around again, calling Peter's name. Still no reply.

Wet and sticky all over, every part of him hurt. Raising his hand to his face, Stephen discovered he had blood spread all over him. Lifting his head, he called, "Peter! Peter, where are you? Are you okay?" Still no response.

He thought he heard a car start up nearby. The blurry shape of a huge maroon SUV pulled away from the curb and accelerated down the street, moving away quickly.

He closed his eyes and thought, *That can't be Peter. He wouldn't leave in a hurry like that. He wouldn't leave me here.* He tried to make a face, but everything hurt too much. "Peter," he screamed. "Where are you?"

Finally managing to stand, he felt a bit woozy, not sure of his balance. A hand grabbed his arm. "Here, let me help you."

Squinting, he could see someone standing there looking at him. The younger man asked, "Are you all right, sir? Are you hurt badly?"

Stephen attempted to shake his head. "No. I ... I think ... I'm okay ... nothing serious."

"Okay. I'm going to let go, now. Can you stand? I need to help your friend over there on the ground."

Stephen's vision began clearing more and he saw the young man bend over a man's body, also covered in blood, lying a few feet away on the sidewalk. He was not moving. Stephen took a couple shaky steps toward the reclining figure and stopped.

"Oh no! Peter!"

Stephen felt another man's hands take hold of his arms from behind. "It's okay. We called 911. An ambulance and the police are on the way."

Stephen thought he nodded his head, but couldn't be sure. He closed his eyes. The air smelled like a big fireworks show had just ended. He felt his strength slipping away from his body.

Slowly slumping to the ground, Stephen realized he was crying. The young man turned back to him. "He's alive. For now. Sir ... " Stephen looked up. "He's hurt, but alive." Stephen managed a half-smile. He was still sitting on the sidewalk crying when the ambulance arrived.

"Some friend you are." Smirking, Stephen stood at the end of the hospital bed and winked at Peter. "You scared the shit out of me. I thought you were dead."

Lying in the hospital bed, Peter had both arms partially wrapped in bandages, only exposing the skin on his lower left arm where the IV was connected. "Yeah, well that's what you get for taking me to that place for lunch."

Blinking a couple of times, Peter acted as if his eyes lost focus for a minute. "My head hurts like hell. Did they give me something for this killer headache?"

"I don't know," Stephen replied. "But they've got you wrapped up like you're wearing some kind of turban or something."

"Well, you don't look so good yourself, my friend." He tried to point, but the bandages stopped him. Wincing, he moaned and said, "All those bandages on your arm. And you're wearing a head dress, too. What do you say about that?"

"Hmph. You're right, we both look like a mess."

"Yes. You may have had a few stitches, but I'm confined to this wonderful bed for a little while."

"Yes, but you have all the good-looking women on staff waiting on you. What a guy."

"Well, that may be true, but if this headache doesn't let up soon, I'm going to ask for some more of whatever they have." He looked at Stephen. "And I'm telling them to put it on your bill." He tried to smile. "You and your Israeli friends," Peter said playfully. "And I don't want to spend lunch with any of your Palestinian friends, either."

"Don't worry. That's not until next week." They both laughed, and Stephen sat down beside the bed to visit with his friend.

"You have to admit it was a good lunch."

"Yes, that's true." Peter replied. "That was a great steak." He sighed. "Too bad there's not enough left of the place to go there again." He managed to point at Stephen. "It's a damned good thing we walked out of there when we did."

"Yes, and I'm glad we didn't talk longer with the Israelis." Stephen raised his left hand and used his finger to trace along the scar extending from his eyebrow to his hairline. "But then if we did, we wouldn't get to wear these fancy hospital gowns."

"You mean if we did, we wouldn't be wearing anything." Peter paused and nodded, "Did you get a chance to call Olivia and Sheryl?"

"Yes. I told them we were both okay, but knowing them, they'll both be here shortly." Stephen tried to cross his legs, but winced from the pain and decided against it. "I suppose they're going to want to keep us here overnight for observation."

Peter nodded. "Probably. It's a wonder we weren't hurt any worse. The explosion demolished that whole building. The TV news said they're still searching for survivors."

"Yes, I heard that, too. It appears everyone inside the restaurant was killed in the explosion. They don't even know how many people were there yet, only that the place was packed. The casualty numbers are going to be pretty high. The explosion was so large it knocked down the wall to the store next door and injured several people there."

Peter concurred. "Those poor people didn't even know what hit them. We were lucky, just far enough out the door to survive." He waved his finger at Stephen. "There are better ways to enjoy an afternoon off. This is not what I had in mind."

"Don't I know it." Glancing over at Peter, he added, "I bet we can't even get room service to bring us our favorite drink."

"Yeah, or peanuts either." Peter shook his head, rather slowly. "What kind of rinky-dink place is this?"

"You're sure you're all right?"

"Doc said 'No broken bones, just a lot of cuts and some serious scrapes.'" Peter grimaced. "I didn't require stitches like you did."

"Yeah. Guess I was too close to the door. I shouldn't have gone back. My papers are gone now, anyway."

"I'm glad you didn't get inside. Papers are replaceable." He sighed. ""Oh, well. We're both going to be pretty sore for quite awhile. What a way to remember lunch."

Stephen turned to look out the window. After a moment of silence, he said, "You know, Peter, this is really unusual. It was too big a blast to be aimed at just one person." He paused. "Organized crime hits are more personal. They want to send a message when they do something, not like this. This is more like a terrorist act of some type."

"You mean like the bombing at the Boston Marathon?"

"No." Stephen shook his head. "Even that was more limited. This was a larger effort. It's more like what you experience in the Middle East."

"Don't forget, we've had a couple of pretty big attacks here in the last few years."

"Yes, I guess you're right." He took a deep breath. Shaking his head, he added, "But it doesn't seem right." Stephen appeared to look beyond Peter. "The explosion happened right after the Israelis entered the place, like some Palestinian terrorists planned to kill as many Israelis as they could, all at once."

Peter frowned. "But this is New York, buddy. That was not a sidewalk cafe in Tel Aviv." He retrieved his cell phone off the table beside the bed. "Stephen, if what you say is correct, there may be a whole lot more problems coming our way, and soon." He started to dial. "There are some people I think we need to talk to."

"And who might that be?" Olivia asked as she and Sheryl entered the hospital room.

Peter pressed the off button on the handset and returned his phone to the bedside table. Olivia walked around the bed and up beside Peter, while Sheryl moved to Stephen. Both women gave their man a hug.

"Ouch," Stephen jumped. "Not so hard, sweetheart. Save that for later, when I'm well."

"Okay, sorry." She tilted her head, giving him a mischievous look. "But just remember when it's time, you asked for it."

He smiled and nodded. "I'll enjoy it later."

Olivia put her hand on Peter's shoulder. "You sure you're all right? You're not hurt?"

"Yeah. You guys have bandages, bruises and scratches all over," Sheryl chimed in. "You both look terrible."

Peter looked at Olivia and said, "I'm all right, honey." She pulled a chair up close to the bed, and Peter continued. "The doc said I had a little concussion. There shouldn't be any complications or lasting problems as a result." He managed a small smile. "Besides, you know me. I'm too hard-headed."

Olivia nodded. "I discovered that fact already." She looked at him questioningly. "Sure you're okay?"

"Yes, dear. I'm okay. I'd show you all my cuts and bruises, but I'd better wait till we're home alone."

Sheryl glanced at Stephen. "Do I get to see yours later?"

"Later."

"I think you two were rather lucky," Olivia observed. "According to the news, this whole thing was pretty horrible. They don't think anyone inside the restaurant could have survived."

"We had just left the restaurant," Peter announced. "Our timing was good." He paused a moment. "We really wanted to see you ladies again. That's better than any lunch."

""I'll say," replied Sheryl. "It's too early in any of our relationships to end now." She made a funny face. "There's too much good stuff still to happen."

Olivia sat back in her chair. "So, any idea what this was all about?" She glanced at Peter. "You were about to call someone when we entered. Who was that?"

Stephen looked at Sheryl. "Peter is advisor to the Senate Intelligence Committee. He knows all sorts of people. FBI, CIA, NSA." He waved his hand through the air, "CBC, XYZ, ABC and a lot of other secret types." He grinned. "We can't tell you who they all are."

"I know," Sheryl responded. "If you told us, you'd have to kill us, right?"

"Only with laughter." Olivia eyes twinkled as she smiled.

"But," Peter lifted a finger in the air to make his point, "the people I know are friendly. Some other people I know are friends with terrorist types."

"What can I say," answered Stephen. "They've been good to me, and sometimes a real help." He shrugged. "They just grew up on the wrong side of the tracks."

Peter shook his head. "Right."

""So who were you going to call, Peter?" Olivia inquired.

"Stephen thinks this might have been the work of some foreign activists." He glanced over at Stephen. "Not his friends." He turned back to his wife. "He has some good reasons for that idea. I was going to call some people in Homeland Security, so we could share his ideas."

"Can't it wait till you're better?"

"I don't know." Stephen shook his head gently.

"If he's right," Peter added, "there may be a lot more trouble headed our way. We can't take the chance."

Stephen retrieved a chair for Sheryl and they both sat down. "It may be nothing, but there's something very different about this bombing. Peter and I need to discuss it with someone more knowledgeable than we are."

"We'll make an appointment a little later," Peter added, "and see them in a day or two."

Sheryl reached over and took Stephen's hand. When Stephen turned to meet her eyes, she implored, "Please tell me this is not another one of those big, crazy events in your life like your last adventure. It isn't, is it?"

"No," Stephen snickered. "You don't have to worry. I won't do anything like that again."

CHAPTER 9

"Thirty-eight people killed and a dozen injured or missing."

"And that's just what we know so far," added the Fox News anchorman conducting the interview.

"Yes. So far." The man leaned forward. "The entire building was demolished, totally gone, and several surrounding buildings were damaged, some rather significantly." The Israeli gestured, pointing his finger at the TV news man. "This is the worst terrorist act to occur here in your country since the 9-11 attack."

"I agree," said the Fox anchorman. "Oh, I know there have been other attempts, such as the planned bombing of a shopping mall in Cleveland, several bombs found planted along a Martin Luther King parade route in Spokane, and the bomb at the Social Security building in Casa Grande. However, none of those resulted in any loss of life. Of course, people were hurt at the marathon bombing in Boston, but this one here in New York was a big incident not stopped in time."

The news anchor stopped for a moment while the Israeli drank a quick sip of water. "You said you were almost killed, yourself, in connection with this incident. Would you explain what you meant by that, Mr. Ambassador?"

"Yes." Inhaling deeply, he continued. "Myself and some members of my staff were scheduled to meet for lunch at that restaurant with three American businessmen. They wanted to discuss the possibility of opening a branch of their company in Haifa. There are half a million people living in and around the city of Haifa, so it is something of large importance to my country."

The Israeli Ambassador to the United Nations, Daniel Shavit, a former colonel with the Mossad, studied the ground, remembering. "They said they were from Brooklyn." He returned his gaze to the newsman. "I no longer believe that." Leaning forward in his chair, his voice became stern, almost harsh. "I believe they were Palestinians. Terrorists. They used that line to lure us to the restaurant for a fake meeting. They intended to kill all of us."

"Fortunately for me," he leaned back in the chair, "your Secretary of State had to change her plans in order to meet with the President yesterday afternoon. She came by to meet with me earlier than planned." Suddenly he looked old, waving his hand across in front of him. "I stayed at the UN and sent my assistant and other staff in my place." He put his head down. "I did not know they would be killed."

"Mr. Ambassador, you say you think they were Palestinians?"

"Yes, that's true. And if I were you, I would try to reach them while they can still comment about it. It's now their turn to worry."

"Is that a threat, Mr. Ambassador?"

"No, of course not." He visibly clenched his jaw. "People in our part of the world know you cannot attack Israel and expect to get away with it. There would be some type of retaliation."

———————

Kamran Khan stood up and turned off the television. "Too bad the Colonel was not there for our little present." He turned to the other two people sitting there with him in the motel room, watching TV, Rana Saleem and Leena Wateeb. "We must get to work planning our next move."

"We will go back to Baltimore now?" Saleem asked.

"No!" Khan was firm. "We have to plan how to eliminate ..." he changed his voice to a lilt, "Mr. Ambassador."

"You will use the sniper rifle now?" Saleem inquired.

Smiling, Khan replied, "Yes. And I think I know how to make this all work."

———————

"Yes, sir," Khan said speaking into the phone. "I'm with WNYC-TV." He smiled at the other two people in the motel room listening. "I don't know if you heard the Israeli UN Ambassador. He was interviewed on Fox News. He said your Palestinian delegation is nothing but a bunch of terrorists, and that you are responsible for bombing the restaurant yesterday and killing many people, including several members of his UN Staff."

"Just a minute."

Khan overheard several voices talking in the background. He could tell the phone had been handed to someone else, then a new voice came on the line. "Who is this?"

"I told the other man, I'm with WNYC-TV. The Israeli UN Ambassador went on television accusing your delegation of bombing the restaurant downtown and killing a lot of people, including members of the Israeli staff. Do you have anything to say about this?"

Khan held the phone away from his mouth, but where he could hear the angry response. He grinned. "So you deny everything." Again he held the phone away where he could still hear, and almost laughed.

After a moment, he pulled the phone closer so he could speak. "Yes, sir. May I quote you?" Khan continued, holding the phone, shaking his head yes. "What is your name?" Still grinning, he said, "Would you spell that, please?" He wrote the name down on a slip of paper. "Excellent, Mr. Al Hakam." He listened. "Yes, sir, I will."

Beaming, Khan remained quiet, listening. "Yes ... Sir, I know it is not my place, but may I make a suggestion?"

Following the conversation, an excited Khan hung up the phone and danced around the room like a child getting ready for a birthday party. The others cheered and clapped their hands, keeping time with the imaginary music for Khan's dance.

As they tired of the celebration, Khan fell onto a lounge chair, still smiling, catching his breath. "We have much work to do." He turned to Wateeb. "Leena, get the maps we purchased on our way here. We will need the one that shows the details for Manhattan. We also need the maps for the farm land to the north of the city. Please spread them out on the table so you and I can examine them."

"Rana," he turned back to Saleem, "I need you to call several sporting goods stores. Start with those closest to us. We need bullets for the sniper rifle. 338 Lapua Magnum. Try not to answer too many questions. See if they stock them, and how many we can purchase. Some stores impose strict limits. I want the 265 grain polymer tip hunting shells. Next choice is the 285 grain hollow point shells. But write down whatever they have, in case we must choose a different bullet." He paused a moment, thinking. "They are both 20 rounds to a box. We should get at least two boxes, but I would like four."

He stood up. "While you are doing that, I will make tea for all of us."

A half hour later, sitting around the table, Khan explained his plan. "You both heard what I said to the Palestinians, but here's the full plan. The Palestinian Ambassador, Mr. Hadar Al Hakam, will release a statement denying that any of his people were involved in the bombing. He will claim it's a plot by Israel to increase U.S. support for their cause and diminish the Palestinians in the eyes of the entire non-Muslim world. He will challenge the Israeli Ambassador to a debate, where each one can present their side of the argument and all the dividing issues they face. They can pose questions to each other." A huge grin displayed itself and he rubbed his hands together, signaling his excitement. "This must take place in a public forum so people can attend, hear the arguments and questions. This way, more people will hear the Palestinian side and support them. The media also needs to be invited. I suggested the perfect location would be Central Park."

A cunning smile spread across Khan's face. "We will choose the right spot for a sniper, then I will suggest an appropriate set-up to the Palestinians, so we can have our targets facing in the proper direction." He snickered. "They are such pushovers." He closed his eyes and shook his head. "They will make it easy. When the time comes, I will shoot this Jew Ambassador Daniel Shavit. He will not get away this time."

After spreading several city maps across the table, it was easy to find the proper location. "Here," Wateeb said, pointing to a large, open area in Central Park. "Right here. This is a good spot for a large crowd to gather. They could build a small, raised platform for each Ambassador over here."

"Ah, yes." Khan was pleased. "There is lots of room. They could even have a platform for a moderator." He reviewed the entire park area, moving his hand over the map. "Yes. Perfect, Leena, perfect."

Tapping the area on the map with his finger, he said, "This large area here between Central Park Driveway and West Drive. It's called Sheep Meadow. The note over to the side says it's the largest open lawn area in the park without any ball fields."

"What's this over here?" His finger traced a line on the map. "Yes. It says 'Neil Singer Lilac Walk,' here along the north edge of the area." He beamed. He stood up straight and inhaled deeply. "This is perfect."

"Now, the sniper location," said Wateeb. She pointed to the row of buildings on the west side of the street bordering the park. "Where would you pick, Kamran? What would you look for?"

"I will be part of the team," Saleem spoke up. "Let me tell you what we would want."

"First," interrupted Khan, putting his hand in the air. "Leena, would you get the laptop? Let's look at Google Earth. It will give us more of a three-dimensional view of these buildings."

Searching for the area in Google Earth was easy. Once they found Manhattan and enlarged the view, they could examine different angles from the satellite image of the buildings and get comparisons of the building heights.

Khan remained quiet and let Saleem do all the talking. Saleem examined the buildings then, sweeping his hand across the screen back to the park area, pointed and said, "We could have them set up the speaker platforms over here, toward the east end of the area. Then they would be facing west, looking toward the buildings back here. The trees on the west side of the opening would not interfere with the bullet path if we stay within this area." Drawing his finger from the speakers' locations to the west, back to the buildings, he said, "Here. One of these two buildings. This one would be better for a sniper. It's high enough so the trees would not be in the way, but not as high as the other building. It would be quicker to get away from there and avoid the police after the shooting." He nodded as the others watched. "Yes, this is the building. Here on the corner of 67th and Central Park West. Zoom in on the picture. There, see. Notice where the door is for access to the roof, and over here," he pointed the northeastern corner of the building, "this raised ledge will make a great rest point for the rifle. It is good."

Khan was pleased, and it showed on his face as he regarded the other two people. "Good job, both of you. Your pick of the building is excellent, Rana. It shows good thought. I like it."

Turning back to the table, Khan said, "Now let's look at the other maps. I need a place in the country, some open farm land where I can sight in my rifle safely without being bothered. When the time comes, I want to be sure that I will shoot straight and kill that proud Jew."

CHAPTER 10

Sitting in his favorite chair, a soft leather recliner in his living room, Stephen closed his eyes and put his head back, listening. Music coming from stereo speakers floated into the air, surrounding him with relaxing tones. The easy listening cable channel of satellite music featured one of his favorite melodies, 'A Summer Love'.

Holding his glass up to the light from the windows, he gently swirled the red Shiraz. He smiled as he examined it, then took a small sip. The tantalizing flavor of wild black currents with overtones of black pepper spice and roasting meat brought superb pleasure to his pallet. The abundance of fruit sensations was complemented by warm alcohol and gripping tannins. The toffee notes came not from the fruit, but from the wine having rested in oak barrels.

After again examining the dark red liquid in his glass, he took another, larger sip. He closed his eyes again. Holding the wine in his mouth, he moved his tongue around, permitting his taste buds the full realization of enjoyment before swallowing. "Ahh."

The center of the shelf on the bookcase against the wall to his left remained open. No books. One item held a special place there. Inside a silver, 5 x 7 frame was a single photograph. Sheryl Hauser displayed a happy, almost gleeful smile as she looked back at him. It brought a smile to his face. He felt warm, appreciated and, yes, loved. She told him she loved him in very plain language that could not be misunderstood.

Studying her photo, he thought of their first kiss. He pictured it in his mind. Nervously he stepped up to her and put his arms around her. He recalled feeling the adrenaline rush through his body as he pulled her to him. He felt alive as she melted against him, the curves of her body fitting into his. Excitement built within him as he brought his lips so very close to hers. He saw the willing anticipation in her eyes. Then their lips touched.

A pleasant smile spread widely across his face. Everything felt so good that night, so right.

He brought his glass up again for another sip of wine. It only increased the pleasure of his remembrance.

"What is it that makes two people so attracted to each other?" he asked himself. "Whatever it is, Sheryl, it certainly exists between you and me." He grinned. "That attraction became huge when I held you and kissed you. You felt so good against me."

He told her that he loved her too. And, he had to admit to himself, he did. It felt good to be with her, no matter what they might be doing. He imagined the two of them being together for dinner later that evening. He could hardly wait. Checking his watch, he thought, *It's early yet, but it wouldn't hurt to start getting ready.*

Stepping out of the shower, he dried off, tied the towel around him and moved to the sink to shave. He retrieved his razor and shaving cream, then turned the hot water faucet on. He sprayed a dab of shaving cream into his hand, put the can down, and looked up into the mirror.

Samantha Sorkin stared back at him!

Closing his eyes tight, he shook his head and looked back again. She was still there.

"What are you doing here?" he asked out loud. "You're gone. You went away."

He blinked hard a couple of times, but she remained there. He rinsed the shaving cream off his hand, leaned against the sink and put his head down. He felt disgusted, both with himself and with her. "I loved you ..." He was quiet, then he shouted, "And you went away!"

Peering back up at the mirror, her face remained.

He shook his head. "No!" He wanted to stamp his foot, hit the wall, kick the cabinet, anything. "I *did* love you — but you had to go away. You had to find yourself. Remember? That's what you said." He paused, out of breath. "That's what you did."

He pointed his finger at her. "Well, I got over you. I don't love you anymore."

He turned his back, then spun around to face the mirror once more. "You are not part of my life anymore, so get out of here." He flipped his arm through the air, motioning. "Go away."

He took a deep breath and swallowed. Still staring into the mirror, he uttered, "Leave me alone so I can love somebody else." Turning away, he threw his arms out to each side. "I've finally found someone else I can love. She's wonderful. She loves me ... and I love her." He turned back to the mirror. "So go find yourself and leave me the hell alone."

He turned and walked away into another room.

———————

Sheryl took another drink of the chilled white wine, enjoyed the full-bodied taste, regarded Stephen over the top of her glass for a minute, then set it down on the table.

Stephen had ordered an unusual but delightful wine: Gewurztraminer. With its heady, aromatic scent of rose petals, grapefruit and spices, it was a nice complement to the Chilean sea bass they devoured for dinner.

Pleasurable but general conversation had turned flirtatious, until Stephen mentioned seeing Sam in the mirror.

Sheryl became quiet, and the look on her face told Stephen she was not amused. She continued to look down at the table for a very long moment, then, lifting her head slowly, her eyes met his. With their eyes locked, she remained sullen, almost withdrawn.

Stephen knew he'd screwed up. *Damn it*, he thought. *I should never had said anything.* He felt the euphoric feelings they had been sharing shatter and fade away. He could see the disappointment in her lovely face.

"I'm sorry." He realized the hurt caused by careless words was something that may never heal completely. "I should not have said that. I'm sorry I brought her up."

Small tears began forming as Sheryl continued staring straight into his eyes. She didn't move her head. She offered no smile. Stephen noticed a small tremble on her lips.

She moved her wine glass back out of the way, reached over to the side and took hold of Stephen's hand. She squeezed it very lightly. Wet eyes looked up at his. "Stephen ... "

He could feel the effort it took for her.

She glanced down, then back at him. "Stephen ... " There was a minuscule shake of her head no. "I told you I love you." Slowly rubbing her hand back and forth over his, she continued. "I do — really love you." She stopped, took a breath. "I hope that our love has a chance to grow." She paused again.

Stephen knew this was not the time to say anything. Not yet. He forced himself to wait silently.

"You said you love me. I believe that, Stephen, and I hope this special love of ours does grow." Her head nodded slowly, agreeing. "That can only happen — if you are willing." Silent tears crept down her cheeks.

"Sheryl," he waited a moment. "I do love you."

"Stephen, I believe you do." She inhaled deeply. Then shaking her head no violently, she half cried, "And I believe that you don't love Samantha anymore. I felt that — completely — when you kissed me. I know she does not live in your heart anymore." She lifted his hand and put her second hand under his, continuing to hold the top of his hand with hers.

"But she's still in your head." Dropping her head, she stared at the table. It seemed like an eternity before she continued, pleading as she looked back at him. A larger tear ran down her cheek, and a quiver chilled her voice. "Can't you forget her? She has to go. Otherwise, we're not going to make it, and I want to, Stephen. I want to."

"We will, Sheryl. I told her to go away." He shook his head slightly.

"It's going to take more than that, Stephen. Lots more."

Leaning toward her, he said softly, "I will make that happen. There's no room in my life for her anymore." He paused. "Only you, Sheryl. No one else."

"I hope so. That's what love is — or can be. You and me. *Just you and me.*" She half smiled, staring into his eyes, appealing with every emotion she possessed. "Please?"

The smile left her face as she sat back in her chair. She was quiet for moment, then pulled her hands back away from his. She lifted her face till their eyes met, and her mood seemed to change. She spoke in an ice cold, matter-of-fact voice. "This is not the evening for dessert. That will have to wait until another time. Take me home, please."

CHAPTER 11

"Hi, Stephen. It's Peter. Jamie, your new assistant, said she thought you were at the library."

"Yes. That's where I am. Catching up on a little research."

"Well, either Jamie's got your number or you need to teach her more about her job. You *do* understand that one of the reasons for an assistant is to help with research, don't you?"

Stephen put his head back, laughing. "Yes. I guess you're right, Peter. It's just that ever since Larry Newcomb graduated, I haven't had the same assistant long enough to teach them about the job."

"Where is Larry, by the way?"

"He started teaching at Framingham State this year."

"Near Boston?"

"Yes. That's it." Stephen smiled. "I hope he's doing well. I miss having him here."

"Well, I know those other three people didn't last long. You'd better get Jamie started right, or you'll be getting a reputation—and it won't be a good one."

Jamie Sims had been Stephen's teaching assistant for just over two months, working on her graduate studies at the same time. Since she enjoyed her association with Dr. Grant and the other professors in the International Affairs and Political Science Department at Columbia, the petite blond could easily remain Grant's eager associate for at least two more years.

"I don't think I need to worry about that, Peter, but I guess you never know."

Peter inquired, "By the way, what are you doing in the library? Don't you know about the Internet? It's this amazing new thing. I think some guy named Al said he invented it. Now you can do research without leaving your office."

Laughing again, Stephen replied, "You're right, as usual." He put his head down and covered his mouth, trying to stifle his laughter. "I'd better be quiet before they kick me out of here. I'll start working with Jamie on these things. But what about the— what did you call it? The Internet?" He continued laughing.

"Yeah. It's brand new, you crazy nut." Peter laughed also. "So which library are you in?"

"My favorite: Low Memorial. But I'm done here now. What's up?"

"If you can stand putting your reference books down, how about meeting me outside there, over by the statue of Alma Mater? Say five minutes?"

"See you there." Pushing the off button on his Blackberry, Stephen snickered and muttered, "Put my reference books down."

Alma Mater is literally the mother soul of the college/university. In the context of Columbia, Alma Mater almost always refers to the bronze sculpture by Daniel Chester French that graces the east side of the steps leading into Low Memorial Library. It's actually a sculpture of the goddess Athena from ancient Rome. It was a gift in memory of Robert Goelet, Columbia College Class of 1860, presented in 1903. The statue has become a symbol of the university and a repository of its lore.

Bright sunshine nearly blinded Stephen as he walked out of the library on the center of the Columbia University campus. He used his hand to shield his eyes, saw Peter talking with another man wearing brown slacks and a tan sport coat with an open-collar yellow shirt standing beside the Alma Mater statue, and walked toward them.

"Dr. Stephen Grant, I'd like you to meet Randy Osborn." They shook hands. Peter added, "He's with the FBI."

Osborn nodded. "With the counterterrorism unit." The agent's close-cropped blond hair gave him a youthful appearance, but the look on his face and the knowing blue eyes said he was a seasoned professional. Stephen guessed the man stood about five feet ten inches tall, and from the way he moved, was in excellent physical condition.

Born the only son of a young Philadelphia attorney, Randall James Osborn had been prepped for law school by his father during all of his four years at Yale. Next came law school at George Washington University, and finally the bar examination, which he passed on his first attempt.

Then, to his father's chagrin, facing a promising, brilliant law career and seventeen job proposals, he joined the FBI.

His drive to become one of the best FBI agents ever had been derailed when his father committed suicide two years later. That was twelve years ago. Now he stood tall again, this time as Supervisory Special Agent in Charge of the FBI Counter-Terrorism Unit, including running the elite team at the National Counter-Terrorism Center.

With a pleasant expression, Peter asked, "Can we go over to your office, where we can talk a little more privately?"

Stephen led them away from the library around the corner to the east, down the walkway between the Philosophy building and St. Paul's, and across Amsterdam Avenue to the International Affairs building.

After entering Stephen's office on the eleventh floor, the FBI man closed the door and pulled a small metal object from his pocket. He walked around the office, waving the item in front of the windows and around Stephen's desk.

Looking at Peter, Stephen uttered, "Shades of déjà vu."

Peter grinned and motioned with his finger in front of puckered lips for Stephen to be quiet.

When the agent finished, he pushed a button on the small metal object and put it back in his pocket. "It's okay. Everything here is clean. No one outside this room is listening."

Motioning for the two men to sit, Stephen sat down in a leather swivel chair behind his large oak desk. As he sat, Osborn motioned to the empty desktop. "That's one of the cleanest desks I've ever seen for a college professor."

Stephen nodded acknowledgement. "I hope that's an indication of my organization." He smiled. "You said you're with the FBI Counter-Terrorism Unit?"

"Yes."

"I told Peter this is like déjà vu. Next thing I know, you'll be saying you're here because you need my help."

The FBI agent stared back at him. "Actually, I *am* here to say we need your help."

Stephen glanced up at the ceiling. "Oh, boy."

"Wait a minute, Stephen." Peter raised his hands in the air. "We do need to talk." Dropping his hands, he continued. "Remember I said I was going to call some people? Well, they put me in touch with Randy, here. Let's give him a chance."

"Okay." Stephen leaned back in his chair, "But this better be good. The last time this happened, I was almost killed. Several times, in fact, and so were several other people. I don't want to go through that again."

Osborn crossed his legs and clasped his hands over his knee. "I read the reports about your last, uh, shall we say adventure. Sounds like quite a time."

Stephen nodded. "It was."

"Well, this should not be as involved or anywhere near as dangerous as last time." He looked directly at Stephen. "We do need your help for part of this."

"Okay," Stephen sighed. "Tell me about it."

"Peter said you think there was something different about this restaurant bombing here in New York. You mentioned foreign terrorists. Why?"

Stephen explained his reasoning, answering several questions along the way. Finally Osborn shared, "We also think it might be the work of foreign terrorists, for many of the same reasons." He nodded. "Have you listened to the news lately, about the Israeli and Palestinian UN Ambassadors accusing each other and denying all responsibility themselves?"

"Yes, and it scares me."

Osborn nodded. "Rightly so. You never know what either of those factions might do. And with the recent bombing, tensions are pretty high. Have you heard some of the rhetoric going back and forth?"

Stephen nodded his head. "I'm worried about some zealot stepping in and really causing problems."

"That would certainly expand the situation rapidly," Peter added.

The FBI man motioned with his hand in the air. "If this is the work of a terrorist group of some sort, there are several unanswered questions that we must consider."

"Such as what?"

Osborn uncrossed his legs and leaned forward in his chair. "What was their real goal? And did they achieve it? If not, there could be a lot more havoc to come. Where? And what are they really after?" He paused a moment.

The two other men could see Stephen was deep in thought, staring at the floor and nodding his head. Without looking up, he asked, "How do you think we could help?"

"After three days of BS going back and forth on the news, the Palestinians have come up with a proposal. They want a public forum where both Ambassadors could present any accusations and explain their side of the story. Each could question the other and be able to respond publicly on the spot. The press would be there to televise the event for the whole world to watch the results."

"Interesting idea."

"Each side has submitted a list of conditions. The list has been combined, and both sides have agreed to each condition."

"For security reasons, the event will be held four days from now in a large, open area in Central Park. Both sides feel that an indoor setting would be placing them in a trap. In the event of an attack, there's no place to go. Escape becomes much more difficult. There is also a much greater danger with the crowd pressed far too close to the Ambassadors. Then, even the smallest handgun would present a death threat to the Ambassadors and their staff."

"The area will be fenced off with metal detectors and guards at the entrances. It's a pretty fair distance to any point that an experienced sniper would use around the park, so we just need to be extremely vigilant and watch the trees."

"Anything else?"

Osborn continued. "Yes. Two conditions. Raised podiums are to be provided for each Ambassador, so he can be seen by the crowd. Microphones will be provided with speakers placed around the site for everyone to hear."

"What's the last condition?" Stephen asked.

"The Israeli Ambassador has one special requirement. The Palestinians have agreed."

Peter spoke up. "What is that, Randy?"

Agent Osborn shifted in his chair and turned to face Stephen. "The Israeli Ambassador will agree to do this if — and only if — this event is moderated by Dr. Stephen Grant, Special Assistant to the UN Secretary-General."

CHAPTER 12

"I got it! I got the job!" He came bounding into the house, gleeful as a child on Christmas morning.

"Oh, Tariq. How wonderful. Please, tell me all about it." Umara Abbas became as excited as Tariq. She turned the stove down, moved the cooking food aside so it would not burn, and sat on a matching chair at the kitchen table.

"It's amazing that I was hired." He shook with excitement. Sitting down on a kitchen chair, he continued. "Even from another country, especially Pakistan, they still hired me! This is so good. It fits perfectly into our plan. Kamran will be pleased, no?"

"Yes, he will." After spending so much time together, she had become enamored with Tariq. "The papers, they were okay?"

"Yes. Yes. They were good. Mr. Schuster looked them over and said they were fine. He said," Tariq nodded, "I was smart to get a green card when I applied for my visa. He said it didn't matter what country I was from, as long as it wasn't Iraq, Iran or Afghanistan, and since I had my green card, it was no problem for him to hire me." Tariq was breathing so hard, he had to stop to catch his breath. "He said they need extra help for the conference coming up. There was just enough time to train me."

Umara smiled, very pleased. "This is exactly what Kamran planned." She shook her head yes. "It is happening, Tariq."

Although beginning to calm down, a still-excited Tariq could hardly believe his good fortune. His chest heaved with his heavy breathing. "I still have to qualify with a handgun." He looked at her. "I do that on Thursday, three days from now."

Umara's eyes widened. "Can you do that? Can you shoot good enough to pass their qualification test?"

"Of course, woman. I think I should do that easily. You will see. They even provide the guns for their guards to carry, so they will all be the same. It's a Sig Sauer P226 9mm semi-automatic. The magazine holds fifteen rounds of ammunition." He shook his head again. His speech slowed as he got his breath back. "This is so perfect. I can't believe it."

He looked up at her. "I even get a uniform, Umara."

She folded her hands in her lap. "Tell me about it."

"It's a light brown shirt with long sleeves, and those things up here on the shoulder." He motioned.

"Epaulets."

"Yes, that's it. The shirt is lightweight and very smooth. Very nice. The pants are dark brown, and so is the leather belt and holster. I will have to get my own brown shoes." He smiled again. "After I pass the shooting test, Mr. Schuster said he would order the uniform and a name tag to go over the top of the shirt pocket. Then I can start working. It will be about six days from now."

"Will you work every day?"

"It is six days a week to start, until I learn about what to do and where everything is. Jack will even be my trainer."

Jack resulted from an extensive search completed online by Tariq and Umara to discover who worked as security personnel for the center. Once they found the names, they searched background information on each one, until locating someone who lived reasonably close to their house.

"It worked like Kamran thought," Umara uttered.

The plan first involved becoming friends with the other couple, then after a little while, letting the man know Tariq needed a job. As a foreigner, he did not have great prospects for a new job. His only work experience had been for a firm providing security for humanitarian aid shipments to his country.

They discovered Jack Williams had been s security guard for the Baltimore Convention Center for over four years. He and his wife Jennifer lived only about nine blocks from the house where Tariq and Umara had taken up residence. Tariq arranged for he and Umara to keep running into them so they could get acquainted. After becoming friends, Tariq let slip his work problem. Jack quickly said he would put in a good word for him at the Convention Center, and now Tariq had been hired.

"I look forward to telling Kamran about our good fortune."

Nodding her head yes, Umara said, "You will have a lot to learn, and only a short time to do so. The conference is only two weeks away. Is the President still scheduled to speak there?"

"Yes, he is. And I know I do not have much time to prepare." Tariq smiled broadly. "Do not worry. I will be ready. I will be there for my part of the plan."

CHAPTER 13

The phone kept ringing. Four times. Five times.

Leaning back in his chair, he put his feet on the corner of his desk and gazed out the window. From his office on the eleventh floor of the International Affairs Building on the campus of Columbia University, Dr. Stephen Grant could see most of northern Manhattan. The view to the south was blocked by the rest of the building, containing a large administrative area and offices for several other professors.

The receptionist said she was there, he thought, frowning. It was unusual for her not to answer. Seven rings. Eight rings. *She must be with a patient and doesn't want to be interrupted.*

There was a click. He listened. He was about to hang up when he heard another click, and her special voice. "Dr Hauser."

"For a moment I thought you must be tied up."

"I was. It's been a very busy day. Just had a five-year-old who is acting up at home." He listened to her long exhale. "Turns out he has a fever and may be on the verge of pneumonia." In his mind he could see her shaking her head. "Some parents don't have a clue. I'm glad I don't have too many of them these days."

"I bet you are."

"Yeah." There was a pause. "So, what can I do for you?"

His expression changed to a scowl as he was taken aback. "That's an unusual question from you, sweetheart. Is everything okay?" He pulled his feet down off the desk and sat up.

"I'm having a bad day, and I don't want to talk about it. I don't have time. Is there something special you want?"

"I'm sorry it's not a good day for you." Pausing, he took a breath. "I have some interesting news. Would you like to have dinner tonight?"

"What's the news about?"

He held the phone away and stared at it. His mind tried to analyze what was happening. He shook his head and brought the phone back to his ear. "It's, uh ... for the UN. They want me to moderate a meeting — or rather a debate, between the Israeli Ambassador and the Palestinian Ambassador. I thought we could talk about it over a nice dinner tonight."

It was quiet on her end of the phone. Finally, she spoke. "I can't. I'm busy tonight."

She had never turned him down before, no matter how busy she had been. *But then*, he thought, *I've never asked if she was busy. I just always thought she would be there — for me.* He put his head down and glared at the floor.

"I'm sorry, Stephen. I can't do it tonight. I'm really busy."

"Of course, Sheryl. I ... you usually have everything handled and closed for the evening," he spoke slowly, "except for emergencies. I do understand that those are part of your business, your career. That's part of being a medical doctor."

He tried to make sense of this. It was totally unlike her, and he didn't know what to do next.

"Listen, Sheryl. We can make it later — after you're through with everything. We can have a late dinner. We've done that before. Would that be okay?"

"No. I'm sorry, Stephen. I'm really busy tonight. I just can't make it."

"All right. How about tomorrow night?"

He could sense her hesitation. "I don't know. Uh ... we, we'd better not plan anything right now."

"Okay." He felt confused, unsure of himself — or her — all of a sudden. It was as if his heart skipped a beat. He'd missed something, and he had no idea what it was. He was lost and didn't know what to say. Stuttering, he managed, "Are you sure, Sheryl?"

"Yes."

"Is there anything I can do?"

"Not right now."

"You're okay?"

72

"Yes, of course." She became short. "We should talk in a few days."

"In a few days?" *What was she talking about?* He was perplexed. "Are you sure you're alright?"

"Yes, Stephen. I'm just ... fine! Now you go do your thing, and I'll do mine."

He became aware of a strange, empty feeling in the pit of his stomach. Almost breathlessly, he asked, "Sheryl? What is your thing?"

He heard a big sigh over the phone. Then before hanging up, she said, "I'm having dinner with someone else tonight. And maybe tomorrow night, too."

CHAPTER 14

The wine in his glass tasted stale, sour, acidic. Without conscious thought, he observed the dark red liquid as it swirled around the edges of his clear tapered glass, almost cresting over its sides. A grimace swelled across his face as he raised his head to look out the large, twin living room windows of his apartment. Blinking stars decorated the black midnight sky over the river to the west. Though fairly bright, their twinkle seemed dull tonight.

She had never declined a date with him before, never said she was unavailable, never turned him down. Never. Even when they met late because of a patient, she always found a way.

It wasn't just saying no. There was something about her voice. The tone was different — first impersonal, matter of fact. Then it became cold. Icy cold.

His view dropped to his glass. The wine had become lifeless.

He slowly walked to the kitchen. Leaning over the polished black granite counter, he dumped his wine from the glass into the sink and watched as it blotted out his reflection, ran across the polished surface and down the drain, never to appear again. Staring at his now-empty glass, he felt that he had just emptied his life.

It had been a long time since Stephen Grant felt this way. He didn't know what to do. He walked back into the living room, switched off the lights, and stared out the large twin windows at the empty black sky. He couldn't see the twinkling stars. They were gone.

How did I ever get to this point? He thought back ... remembering.

Life with his wife, Becky, had been a beautiful, bright spot in his history. She was more wonderful than life itself. She

74

brought a special meaning to every element of his life—the sparkle in her eye, her soft sexy smile, even the way she tipped her head to the side and whispered those words so softly, the words he would never forget, the words he came to treasure: "I love you." They all said how very special she was, and how she cherished Stephen and his love.

Her love gave him strength and self-confidence. With her by his side, nothing was impossible. He could walk with the lions, kill a dragon with a single blow, and eagerly walk straight and tall into a college class filled with freshmen. She made him feel like he was the king of the world.

Her unexpected death stole that happiness, tearing it away from his life. Following that time, a deep depression kept Stephen floating around a vast emptiness for over a year. Staring down at the floor, he started slowly shaking his head. He knew that was probably the worst time in his life. He wanted to forget it, put it far behind him.

Thankfully, his best friend Peter grabbed onto him and pulled him to safety, and back to life.

He recalled the feeling of being able to breathe again, almost like starting a new life once he got his head out of that murky water. Heeding Peter's advice, he started dating again. Then along came the CIA and Dr. Samantha Sorkin, all at basically about the same time.

A sad smile crept across his face as he thought about those events. Sam aroused his attention and captured his heart very quickly. He did not think it was possible to find real, true love twice in his lifetime, yet there it was.

He closed his eyes and pictured Sam, remembering how he felt while with her. A tide of memories washed into his mind, bringing back some wonderful moments. But they shared bad times also. He remembered how the painters in her office building tried to shoot both of them. In fact, they had shared danger more than once and survived. He recalled lying in a hospital bed at the end of that adventure, dreaming of a new future with her.

But that was not to be. It ended, almost as fast as it started. Samantha felt compelled to go on a soul-searching journey to find herself and discover what she really wanted in life — what would make her happy. And she needed to complete this journey by herself, without him.

Opening his eyes, the blackness of his thoughts remained, surrounding him.

That had happened just over two years ago. Again, it was Peter who provided resuscitation and helped guide him back to life.

Stephen found his way through the now-dark apartment to the sofa and sat down. Thinking about his friend brought a happier smile to his face. He had known Peter a long time now, and he dearly loved him.

Peter met a woman who brought a special love to his life, and he was not going to let her get away. He married Olivia and their love blossomed. Shaking his head, Stephen acknowledged to himself that Peter's new wife had also become a good friend, and he had grown to love her too.

Peter's new wife's best friend was a single pediatrician named Sheryl. Peter and Olivia played Cupid, and enjoyed seeing their best friends fall in love.

Stephen looked down at the floor. The quiet emptiness of his lonely apartment echoed in his ears. Walking back into the kitchen, he went to the sink, stared at the drain and asked himself, "How can I get the wine back into the glass?"

The foggy gloom that settled over him weighed heavily on his very being. Puzzled, he questioned, *what is different? What happened that changed Sheryl?* Turning away from the sink, he spoke aloud. "She said she loved me." He shrugged. "And I said I love her. And I do," he added emphatically.

Realizing his finger was tracing the scar on the left side of his face, he dropped his hand. "She seemed to change almost in an instant, while we were talking."

As his mind wandered and he began pacing the floor, reality finally penetrated his thinking. "Of course. That's it." He snapped his fingers. "She changed when I mentioned Samantha. How stupid of me." He shook his head. "Of course. A woman wants to be loved. That means being first. And it means if you really love her, there is no one else."

The freight train smashed into him. "Wow, did I ever blow it. Sheryl, I didn't mean that." He continued talking as if she could hear. "I do love you. Oh, sweetheart. I'm sorry."

Walking back to the twin windows, he thought, *she's absolutely right. I have enjoyed two previous loves in my life, but that's in the past. I need to live now, in the present.* He nodded, then said out loud, "I have to put all that in perspective. Those things are memories. Memories!" He started pacing again, shuffling back into the kitchen. "Happy times I've had in my life, but in the past. I don't need to forget them, I just need to keep them in the past."

It had been a couple of days since he had spoken with Sheryl. She said she could not see him. She was having dinner with someone else. Possibly the next night also.

"Well, she's had her time," he said aloud. He shook his head and pounded the counter next to the sink with his fist. "I'm not going to let her get away. Not this time."

He turned and walked back toward the sofa. *I've been respectful and given her the time and space she needed and deserved. But now it's time for me to act.*

He sat down, stared into the darkness, and stood up again. "I know. Yes." Talking to himself, he continued. "I'll be at her clinic when it opens in the morning. I'll have a dozen red roses — no, two dozen — for her. Then she'll listen."

He would tell her he was sorry. He had made a serious mistake. He wanted her. He loved her. Would she forgive him? He would not take her for granted again.

And this time there was no room for anyone else. Just them. Just the two of them, together.

CHAPTER 15

"Well, it's going on noon, Tuesday, and another pleasant day here in beautiful downtown New York City," he said as they walked into the west side entrance of Central Park at 67th Street. He sighed, "But I'll sure be happy when this one's over."

"I know *I* certainly will," Stephen replied. "I had an interesting morning," he shook his head, "and I'm glad that's over. Now I'm ready to get the rest of this day over with."

"What happened this morning?"

Stephen smiled. "I'll tell you later, when all this is over. Then you'll appreciate it."

"Okay," Osborn agreed. "If you say so."

Both men wore a suit and tie and were obviously groomed for a notable public appearance. Agent Randall Osborn's apparel consisted of a dark gray suit, light gray dress shirt, and black, red and white tie. Stephen knew the agent carried at least one gun, but it was concealed so well he could not identify its location.

Stephen sported a blue suit, white shirt and red tie with narrow, light blue stripes angled downward to the right. Dressed for business, he walked with a purpose, carrying a folder of papers in his right hand.

"That's a bad nervous habit you have there. Do you do that often?" Osborn inquired.

Stephen looked over at him as they walked. "What do you mean?"

"Fingering that scar on the left side of your face. It shows you're nervous. Do you do that a lot?"

Stephen dropped his hand. "I wasn't even aware I was doing it. Sorry."

"I recommend you try not to do that doing this debate. You want to display friendliness and confidence. You represent the United Nations."

"True." He paused. "You don't need to remind me of that."

"Just trying to help."

As they continued walking, they passed two men dressed in the uniforms of New York's finest. After saying "Good morning," Stephen commented, "I guess you probably have them all over the park."

"*All* over the park."

As they turned a corner, Stephen saw the metal barricades marked with bright yellow rope and flags that fenced off the area, then noticed the crowd waiting in line to pass through the metal detectors.

"You can see we put a lot of thought into this," Osborn offered. "We arranged for temporary seating and benches for the public. It'll make it easier to monitor the crowd. Anyone getting up or moving around can be seen easily." Osborn motioned with his arm. "There are lots of security people here, both uniformed police and several undercover agents mixed in with the crowd. They'll be continually scanning the trees for anything unusual. I think we're in pretty good shape."

Approaching a large metal detector, the FBI agent showed his badge and they were passed through. Osborn led Grant around the seating area to a spot on the east side of the large open meadow. Stephen was amazed at the size of the crowd already gathering, waiting for the event to begin. Television crews and elevated cameras, many of them from countries other than the U.S., populated a wide aisle at the back of the crowd, preparing to provide live coverage of this momentous event.

It was Palestinians against Israelis, and Israelis against the Palestinians. News crews had been cautioned not to use the words "Jews" or "Arabs." No one wanted to start a riot or a demonstration that could quickly become violent.

In the sky, all air traffic including news helicopters had been banned. Two police choppers were the only things flying, and they were required to keep some distance away unless there was an emergency, and then they required specific orders to enter the isolated air space. On the ground, uniformed police, present in abundance, shielded their face as their eyes constantly darted back and forth, watching the swelling crowd as it reached unbelievable proportions.

"They're still coming." Stephen shook his head. "What happens if there are too many?"

Grimacing, Osborn replied, "They're setting up more seating with speakers scattered all around. There are several open areas a little further up to the north. No one could have predicted this. It's like the entire Jewish population of the New York area is here, along with half the Muslims from the entire East Coast. I sure hope this doesn't get out of hand."

He turned to Stephen. "As moderator, you've got a hell of a job to do. Don't be afraid to pause the proceedings if anything — or anyone — starts to get out of hand," he almost pleaded. "Do your best to keep it all under control."

The agent pointed to the folder of papers in Stephen's right hand. "You know the rules of order, right? Better start by sharing those rules with the audience. They need to understand the process, and the limitations of this meeting." He paused, starting to breathe rapidly. "Be sure to tell them."

Osborn looked down at the ground, attempting to gather himself, calm himself down. Looking up at Stephen, he said, "The sun is just passing into the west. It will shine on you, providing lighting for the television cameras." He smiled at Stephen. "Don't let it bother you." He nodded. "You'll do fine. Just remember, when you're up there," he pointed to the moderator's podium, "you'll be acting on behalf of the United Nations, and you'll be in front of the whole world."

Reaching the small open area behind the raised platforms, Stephen smiled at Osborn. "Wow, that really makes me feel good." He shook his head. "That didn't help at all, Randy."

"Yeah," Osborn sighed, "I know. Listen, Stephen. I'm not trying to scare you, but I'm afraid of this one. In a manner of speaking, you're playing with what could be one great big monstrous bomb. Whatever happens here today is more important than either of us can imagine."

Hesitating a moment, Osborn looked up as if seeking some sort of magical signal in the sky and, not finding it, lowered his head with a huge sigh. "Those TV cameras out there, they'll be delivering this event live to homes and probably a whole lot of mosques and synagogues everywhere. Millions of Muslims in places all around the globe will be tuned in. And so will millions of Jews."

He reached out and clasped Stephen on the shoulder. "Stay in control. Ask for help if you need to. I'll be right here behind your platform. We're here to back you up." He took a big breath. "You can do this." He shook his head. "But let's be careful and not start World War III right here in New York, okay?"

As Stephen turned toward the wooden steps leading to the floor of the moderator's podium, about three and a half feet above the ground, Osborn slapped him on the back. "Break a leg."

It was one o'clock Eastern: time to start. Stephen stepped up to the microphone at the front of his platform, opened the folder of papers, and turned the microphone on. He did a quick test, introducing himself and welcoming the audience—both those present in Central Park and all those watching from their homes around the world, allowing the sound technicians to make one final adjustment for volume throughout the park.

After the welcome, Stephen introduced the Israeli Ambassador and his staff about twenty feet to his right, and then the Palestinian Ambassador and his staff about twenty feet away on his left. Each Ambassador had a separate large podium with microphone, and a seating area with four chairs located behind the space for the Ambassador when he would be speaking. Each staff had been seated, and each Ambassador stood when introduced.

Skimming quickly through his notes, Stephen announced, "I want to start by reviewing the rules of order for conducting this event, rules which have been agreed upon by both the parties here today."

"The purpose of this event is to address grievances regarding the recent bombing of the Midtown Steakhouse Restaurant here in New York City, which killed twenty-eight people and injured over thirty more, in a public arena, that would allow us to hear any specific accusations and the responses to those accusations, in a manner that reveals the information to the public and offers an initial step toward the resolution of such grievances. Please let me emphasize, this is an initial step. It will certainly require many more meetings and considerable effort to reach full resolution. But let me state clearly, our purpose here today is not to resolve the entire Israeli-Palestinian conflict. That is much more involved than what we can do here in one day."

"For today's event, the UN Ambassadors, Israeli and Palestinian, will be the only speakers representing each side. Each Ambassador will have six opportunities to speak, for up to twelve minutes each time. They can present any accusations, pose questions to the other Ambassador, make statements and reply to accusations explaining their side of the story. Although each Ambassador will be the only speaker for their side, they will be allowed to confer about the issue under discussion with the attending personnel seated on the podium for up to three minutes before answering each question. UN representatives stationed at the bottom front of each podium platform will act as official timekeepers. The questions and statements to be presented today have not been shared with the public or press ahead of time. This is the first time they will be revealed publicly."

He looked to each side. "Are we ready, gentlemen?"

Both Ambassadors stood, walked up to their microphone and nodded approval. Stephen told the audience, "We flipped a coin to see who would go first, and the Israeli Ambassador won. You may begin, sir."

Stephen stepped back from the mike. The Israeli Ambassador opened the folder in front of him, glanced at his papers, looked up at the audience, and began to speak.

No one heard the gunshot.

CHAPTER 16

Earlier that morning, Dr. Sheryl Hauser ended her morning reverie, pulled into the small reserved space in the parking lot behind the medical office building on East 73rd Street, put the car in park, and pushed a button on the dash. These actions comprised her usual morning routine, a thoughtless process of delivering herself to work. But this time, she had no idea of the surprise awaiting her inside Manhattan Pediatrics.

Only one item had changed in this entire process during the last seven years she had been driving to work, and that happened just over a month ago. She bought a new car — at least, new to her. And with the new car came the button on the dash.

While waiting, she removed her sunglasses and placed them inside the case in her purse, looked in the mirror to check her lipstick and makeup, and shook her head to make her hair fall straight. She so enjoyed driving to work on these beautiful, sunny mornings, listening to the light beats of soft, easy jazz, feeling the air rush around her, the wind kissing her cheeks, her hair floating in the wind. And it was all because of the button on the dash.

She removed the key and stepped out of the vehicle. She couldn't help but give one last admiring glance at the car. She now did this every morning. But that was understandable. This was her dream car.

When she first began her practice with Manhattan Pediatrics, one of the senior doctors said she could have his reserved parking place. He had been taking the bus for some time, and there were no plans to change. The old Chevy she drove since before med school fit the space perfectly, and she had no plans to change anytime soon. That old Chevy needed to be painted one color instead of sporting the multi-color, peeling paint look it possessed. It also needed new seats, floor mats, a mirror for the passenger door, and a trunk lid that would stay closed. But it had seen many good old days, and it was always there for her. It started, and it got her to work — even though her colleagues always kidded her about her beautiful jalopy.

Just over a month ago, another one of the senior doctors said he had a special friend, another doctor, in Connecticut, who was going to retire. "He and his wife have dreamed of the time when they could have a new pickup with a crew cab and travel the country with a fifth wheel. They'd like to see all of the national parks, and perhaps even stay with their kids now and then."

Her friend in the office told her this doctor had a car to sell that he thought would be perfect for her. He drove the car to work every day for nine months, but he only lived six blocks from his office. The neighborhood mechanic informed him to "take it out for a drive on the freeway once a month, just to keep the engine cleaned out and running properly." The doctor did just that. Her friend gave her the doctor's phone number and told her the car was a "beaut," and that she should go see it.

Standing there, admiring the 2004 Mercedes 500 SL luxury touring convertible with its gleaming metallic desert sand color and cashmere leather interior, she appreciated it even more. It was perfect for her. The car just turned 40,000 miles and was in pristine condition, with all the bells and whistles: 5.0 liter 302 horsepower engine, seven speed automatic transmission, chrome wheels, parking sensors, heated seats, navigation system, Bi-Xenon headlamps, side skirts, and high performance tires.

And it had that button on the dash. It was for the retractable hardtop, transforming the roadster into a water-tight sport coupe in just 16 seconds—or you could go the other way and enjoy the convertible with the top down, which she now did every morning the weather allowed.

Smiling, she turned and walked into the office building.

"Good morning, Angie," she greeted the receptionist. "How are you this morning?"

"Great."

Sheryl couldn't help but notice the huge smile Angie tried to hide. She started to ask about it, but decided not to. She nodded and started toward her office down the hall.

"Oh, doctor," Angie said. "There is a new patient waiting in your office."

Sheryl frowned. "Did I have an appointment this morning that I forgot about?"

""No. This is a brand new patient." She motioned with her head, "In your office, waiting."

She hurried down the hall, put a smile on her face, and opened the door. Walking in, she saw the back of a man in a sport coat and slacks seated in front of her desk. As she started to speak, she froze. There on each end of her desk sat a crystal vase. Each vase held a dozen red roses. She forced herself to take some more steps and stammered, "Good morning. I'm Dr. ..."

The man turned around to face her. His face revealed solid character, a light tan, and a firm, stubborn chin. At the same time, his blue eyes were soft and kind. A warm smile spread quickly across his lips as he stood up. "Good morning, Sheryl."

Hardly able to speak, she had to fight to find her voice. "Stephen." She labored to catch her breath. "What are you doing here?" She turned partway and motioned to the door. "Uh, Angie said ..." Her mouth felt full of cotton. Dropping her arm to her side, she shrugged. Her eyes darted toward the door and back to Stephen. "You can't be a new patient. You don't have any kids."

"But I'm here to see the doctor." He took a step toward her and smiled.

She melted. She couldn't help it. She opened her mouth, but no words came out. She shrugged again and walked up to him.

"Sheryl," he looked directly into her eyes, "I've been an indecisive, stubborn fool." She could sense him looking into her inner self, her soul. "I love you."

Did he really say that, or did she think it?

"I've been confused, miserable, in denial, lonely, and stupid." He shook his head. "I have so enjoyed the time with you, all the things we've done, and I don't want them to end. I have discovered a wonderful love with you, and I guess I needed to face the possibility of losing it before I realized how important and totally fantastic it is."

"Listen, Sheryl." He moved up to her, reached out and took hold of her arms. "I know now how important you are to me, and I know that I do love you. I don't want to lose you."

She melted into his arms. "Oh, Stephen." She began to cry. "I love you, too." She pushed her head against his chest. It felt so good there. It belonged there.

She stepped back and shook her head. "Stephen, I need to confess." She glanced up into his soft blue eyes. Standing there, he looked so attractive. She had to tell him. She couldn't take it anymore. "Stephen, there never was anyone else. No dinner, nothing. I'm sorry. I just needed you to make up your mind and be clear on what you want. I needed to know that you want me, that you truly do love me." A tear formed in her eyes and she lowered her head.

He placed his hand under her chin and raised her head up to look at him. "I have made up my mind." That huge smile appeared again. "Those roses are red — for love. For you. I love you."

"Oh, Stephen." She pulled her arms tight around him, and he with her.

They shared their embrace for several minutes. Then Stephen pulled back just a little to look into her face. "There's only room in my life for one woman from now on, and that's you."

They shared a smile and looked into each other's eyes. A warm, awesome feeling of oneness flooded over them.

"Sheryl?"

"Yes."

"Will you marry me?"

CHAPTER 17

The pain hit him hard in the shoulder, twisting him to the left as if he had been slammed by a sledgehammer. Daniel Shavit slumped and stumbled backward for a couple steps trying to maintain his balance, grabbing his left shoulder. The surprised look on his face showed he was asking "What was that? What happened?" As he pulled his hand away from his shoulder, he saw it was painted red with blood.

Four or five people seated near the front, also surprised, jumped up trying to see what was wrong with the Israeli Ambassador to the United Nations.

As Shavit tried to raise up and turn back to face the audience, the hammer hit him again, this time in the center of his chest. Catapulted backwards into the air, he landed on the staff members seated behind him, where surprise had frozen them in their chairs.

More people in the audience jumped up. A woman's voice shrieked. Someone shouted, "Oh, my God, no!" Screams and wails blared from the crowd as many of those toward the front started running to the side, some throwing folding chairs out of their way while others shoved them aside trying to get away from the stage. Loud screams multiplied in volume as their discordant sounds erupted in chaos across the open area.

Dr. Stephen Grant took a step back from the moderator's microphone and turned toward the Israeli delegation, ready to listen to the Ambassador. The red splash exploding from Shavit's body was clearly visible. He saw it spray the seated staff, and watched the Ambassador's body launched through the air, landing on the surprised staff members who shouted and frantically tried to jump out of the way.

The swelling crowd noise became deafening as screams, shouts, and obscenities filled the air, mixed with the sounds of a wild stampede pushing and shoving as they bolted toward the aisles, the exits, the back of the area, anywhere away from there.

Not sure what to do, Stephen started to his right toward the Israelis when Osborn appeared, standing on the ground next to his platform. He heard Osborn shout, "Stephen," and he motioned with his hand, "Down!"

Without thinking, Stephen dropped to his belly in a prone position. As he hit the floor of the platform, the left side of the podium holding his notes exploded as a bullet shattered the wood stand. Stephen gasped for air and quickly swallowed.

Television cameras already filming caught the initial part of the event, then the pictures momentarily went wild as the cameras swung around, trying to see what caused the turmoil. Suddenly the pictures being televised around the world spun rapidly to show an empty sky as horrified news crews leaped from their positions and scrambled for cover.

Intense shrieks, screams, and curses permeated the air as the entire audience was now on its feet—terrified people running, jumping and pushing, trying desperately to escape in every direction, to reach safety anywhere they could.

Stephen cranked his body around to look at the Palestinians. The Ambassador shouted, running toward the back of the stage that his frightened staff was abandoning. His voice quit immediately when the heavy sledge hit him in the center of his back. A splash of red preceded him as he was lifted into the air, arms spread wide to the sides like a swan dive, and he was thrown several feet beyond the platform.

"Get down here!" Osborn shouted, "On the ground behind the platform."

Stephen rolled toward the FBI man as fast as he could, over the edge of the deadly elevated position, and dropped three feet to the ground. Lying there, trying to catch his breath, he noticed that two more FBI agents appeared beside him with guns in their hands, heads turning quickly, searching everywhere for the threat.

Osborn raised his arm to his face and spoke into a microphone at his wrist. "Any more shooting? Anyone else hit?"

Although he could still hear screams and the sounds of panicky people running, Stephen thought the crowd noise seemed to be less intense, moving away from where he was lying on the ground. He rolled on his back and looked up at the FBI leader.

Osborn nodded and spoke again. "Good. Those shots came from the west. While they're checking the trees, let's get some people to check out those buildings across the street over there, facing Central Park West." He looked around as he talked. "We didn't hear shots. There must be a sniper team over there somewhere. Let's find them!"

Uniformed police came running and the FBI man shouted orders, dispatching them. "Some of you check on the Palestinian delegation," he motioned. "The rest of you see about the Israeli delegation. I know both Ambassadors were hit. See if anyone else was." He shouted, "And get medical help out here now!"

He knelt down beside Stephen. "Were you hit by any of the shots?"

"No, thank God."

"You're not hurt? You're okay?"

"Scared shitless, but I'm okay."

Osborn stood up and spoke into his sleeve again. "Are we finding anything?" He paused. "Okay. Hurry, people. Let's not let them get away."

He glanced down at Stephen, who was looking toward the Israeli delegation's location. He shouted into his sleeve again. "Where's those medical people? We need them now, not tomorrow."

Stephen closed his eyes to rest for a moment and gather his thoughts. His mind was racing at a hundred miles an hour to comprehend what had just happened. He remembered hearing Osborn say the word 'sniper.' He thought of the Army, people in uniform, a couple of men carrying a long rifle and a bag of gear over their shoulder. He felt the sun on his face and heard voices in the distance. Maybe the Army was just behind that hill and would be here soon.

He felt hands pulling at him. He opened his eyes and saw two men in suits bending down over him. One of them spoke. "Let us help you up. Are you sure you're all right, not hurt anywhere?"

Stephen glanced around as he stood. The two men gently relaxed their grip on his arms, then let him stand by himself. "Yes." It took a moment to get his balance. "Yes. I'm all right. Thank you." He brushed himself off and looked for Osborn. Seeing him off to the side, about ten feet away, talking with some other men, he managed to stumble toward him.

The FBI leader dismissed the others, turned to Stephen and nodded. "Are you sure you're okay?"

"Yes. I'm better now. What happened?"

"Not sure, but the paramedic said you were okay. He thought you just shut down and went to sleep for a few minutes. That happens to people once in awhile. He said you'd be okay. He didn't see any reason to take you to the hospital, but wanted to be sure we checked you out before letting you go."

"Wow." Stephen dropped his head, then looked back at Osborn. "I've never done that before."

"It's a bodily reaction, similar to going into shock. It's not that unusual. There doesn't seem to be any side effects or reoccurrences, just individual episodes."

Stephen nodded, indicating his understanding.

Osborn smiled. "Walk with me. I'll take you back to the car, then to your apartment."

"The school will be fine. I'll get a ride home with Peter later." They continued walking slowly. "So tell me, Randy, what do you think happened here?"

Still glancing all around as they walked, the FBI man said, "We had a sniper." He took a deep breath. "We had everything checked out, so it was a real surprise." He looked at Stephen. "This guy is really good. He knows what he's doing. Probably had a spotter with him." Shaking his head, he continued. "He was very accurate. He hit the Israeli Ambassador twice. The first shot hit him in his left shoulder, but the second shot was squarely in his chest. He's dead. So is the Palestinian Ambassador—shot in the back, but it hit his heart."

Osborn stopped and turned to Stephen. "You are mighty lucky, my friend. The shot meant for you splintered the podium in front of where you were standing. You could be dead right now." He clasped Stephen on the shoulder and squeezed his arm. "You are very fortunate."

As they neared the park entrance on West 65th Street, Osborn stopped and held up his hand. Again he spoke into the mike at his sleeve. "You caught them?" He pushed his earpiece to his ear, then spoke to Stephen. "They caught the sniper team." He paused a moment, then spoke into his mike again. "Okay. I'll meet you outside the main entrance to the building."

He turned to Stephen. "They caught two men. According to their ID, they're Israeli. They're screaming 'diplomatic immunity' and not saying anything else. They were on the roof of the building on the northwest corner of 65th and Central Park West." He had a questioning look and shook his head. "It doesn't quite make sense. Israelis?" He shrugged. "Let's go see if you know them."

Emerging from the park, they waited for traffic to clear, then crossed the street. As they reached the sidewalk, Osborn held up his hand again and said, "Wait a minute." He listened intently to what was said in his earpiece. "You're sure?" He paused, listening. "Okay, bring them down. We're almost there."

He turned to Stephen. "Their gun hasn't been fired recently." He raised his eyebrows. "This is going to be interesting."

They took only a couple more steps until the FBI chief stopped again. "What?" He looked at Stephen. "More of my men just caught a second sniper team in another building — across the street from this one. I guess they had to shoot one of them, the shooter, but they've got the other one, the spotter. It seems the only words he knows in English are 'Palestinian,' and, of course, 'diplomatic immunity.' He has credentials from the UN."

Osborn held up his hand again. "Are you certain of that?" Giving Stephen a stunned look, he breathed a loud sigh and said, "His gun hasn't been fired either."

CHAPTER 18

"Okay, officers, they're all yours. Two of my men will accompany you to help with the booking process." Upon being informed of FBI agents capturing the snipers, Supervisory Special Agent Randall Osborn called for uniformed NYC police to meet him at ground level, near one of the building entrances.

He turned to another FBI agent dressed in a dark olive suit. "Bob, how about helping with the interrogation? Even with diplomatic immunity, we can hold them for a short time. I suspect the two governments wanted to protect their interests, but see if one of these guys is willing to give us anything. This whole thing is totally crazy. Take Jay with you."

The two sniper teams had been discovered and captured on the roofs of buildings across the street from each other, facing 65th Street along Central Park West. Neither team seemed to have any knowledge of the other team, and neither had fired their rifles. Both teams said they were busy monitoring the situation in the park in case they had to act, and did not hear any gunshots anywhere.

"Fred, take some of the men and search other buildings for possible sniper sites. The shots came from this direction, and," looking around, he pointed down 65th, "probably from a building a little further back. But check out all the possibilities. They're gone by now, but maybe somebody saw something."

He turned to Stephen Grant, reached out and patted him on the arm. "Let's go back to the car. We can talk on the way."

Stephen and Agent Osborn walked to the corner, then followed the sidewalk along Central Park West toward Osborn's car, three blocks to the north.

"Are you sure you're okay?"

"Yes," Stephen replied. "I'm all right. A little shaken up and still scared, but," he made a face, "I'll be okay."

"Quite a day, huh? Listen, I'll be in touch as soon as we learn anything more. Hopefully the search will turn up some information. And we're still questioning people at the park. Who knows? Maybe we'll get lucky. We'll find something. This is too big an affair, we're not about to let it go. This one already has international attention."

"Thanks to those television cameras," Stephen replied. "Think one of them might have caught anything to help?"

"Naw, they were focused on the speakers, facing the wrong direction. But then again, you never know what could turn up. We'll have someone check it out." He turned to Stephen. "If any of them did catch something, it's all over the Internet and network TV by now."

"What're your thoughts on this crazy thing? Who could profit from it?" Without waiting for an answer, Osborn continued. "At first, I thought it was probably a Palestinian group. But their Ambassador was killed too." He shrugged and raised his hands in a questioning gesture. "It doesn't make any sense." He glanced at Stephen. "Any ideas?"

"No, not really." They kept walking. "It has to be a third party of some kind, but I have no idea what they hope to accomplish. You don't just ..." he stopped walking. Stephen turned his head to Osborn, frowning. Raising his hand, he pointed up with one finger. "Just a minute." He glanced around. Shaking his head, again he said, "Just a minute," and walked to the rear of the shiny, maroon-colored SUV parked beside the sidewalk. The custom Kansas license plate read PRECHR.

He took a couple of steps back toward the sidewalk, then stopped, put his hand out and leaned against the rear corner of the car. "This is a new Tahoe, right?"

"That's right." Osborn nodded.

"This is my brother's car," Stephen said.

"Oh. Maybe he was here in the park for the big event."

"No, not my brother."

"Then he must be inside one of these places on business. Do you want to look for him?"

Stephen stood up straight. "He doesn't live here. He's in Kansas." Stephen turned and glanced at the street in both directions. With a stern look, he carefully scanned the sidewalk.

Osborn shrugged. "He must be here on a trip or vacation."

Stephen walked over to the FBI agent. "You don't understand." He spread both hands out to his sides. "His car was stolen while he was on vacation."

"Here?" Osborn asked.

Stephen shook his head and looked down at the sidewalk, thinking. "No. He took his family to see Disney World in Florida."

"Let me call it in," the FBI man said, pulling out his cell phone. He dialed 911, identified himself, and gave them the information about the car. He told them they would wait beside the vehicle until an officer showed up. He motioned to Stephen, "Let's step over to the side by the building and wait for the officer. It should only be a few minutes."

As they moved to the side, Stephen continued examining the sidewalk traffic in both directions. "They were on their way here, to see me." The look on Stephen's face displayed both surprise at finding the car, and exasperation. "They stopped for a night at a motel along the way." He put his hands in his pockets and turned to Osborn as he continued. "In South Carolina. The car was stolen sometime during the night."

The FBI man stood there with his mouth open, staring at Stephen. He swallowed and asked, "South Carolina?"

"Yeah, a family motel in Fayetteville. Whoever took the car left a old, battered gray Chevy in its place."

Osborn turned his head to the side and looked off into the distance. He began shaking his head. Peering back at Stephen, he said, "One of the things you learn in this business is that very few events are a coincidence." He lowered his voice to a hushed whisper as other people walked past them on the sidewalk. "Some fishermen found a half-sunken luxury yacht in an inlet along the coast of South Carolina three days ago." He moved closer to Stephen and continued his whisper. "The yacht had been chartered out of Havana, with a captain who was nowhere to be found. Someone tried to scuttle the boat, but the water at that particular point was too shallow. The boat only went down about halfway. But there's more," Osborn said. "Harbor officials in Havana confirmed that the yacht had been chartered by a group of four. They thought they were all Arab, or at least from some part of the Middle East. One of them spoke English, but the others were talking in an Arabic type language."

Stephen raised his eyebrows. "Really. That's interesting, isn't it?"

"Yes, but there is still more. We found a body on the boat. A male, early to mid twenties, shot three times at close range. We think he was Pakistani. And get this, we found tire tracks in the mud close to where the boat was. Someone met them, or left a car for them. The tire tracks were matched to a stolen gray '59 Chevy that was abandoned in a Best Western parking lot in Fayetteville."

Stephen let out a whistle. "The car's here now. Do you think this could somehow be tied to the shooting today?"

"I don't know, but we're going to wait here awhile to see what happens." He nodded to Stephen. "Let's move back a little ways, and we'll just watch." They settled in a shaded spot in front of a small neighborhood grocery, a little over forty feet from the car.

The sidewalk traffic in New York City is always busy and hurried. Today was no exception. The afternoon crowd included busy shoppers, some obvious students, a few businessmen, and some mothers with strollers. A man with a cane hobbled along at a slower pace while three young giggling girls skipped along the sidewalk in the opposite direction. Two men went by, passing out flyers for a strip club, and another man with long, tangled red hair and a knotty beard handed both Stephen and Osborn a home printed page citing their need for redemption, as the end of the world was approaching.

Stephen nudged Osborn and pointed to a young man wearing a hoodie and blue jeans coming their direction at a fast walk. As he neared the car, he slowed, then stopped beside the driver's door. Turning toward the car, he dug down in his jeans front pocket for something, then pulled out his hand, smiled, and put a Life Saver in his mouth. He glanced around and resumed walking away.

Tense, Stephen relaxed and slumped his shoulders. He let out a deep breath.

Osborn stood up on his tiptoes and looked in both directions, seeking the police car that should be arriving.

Stephen elbowed him and nodded toward a woman approaching the car from the direction opposite them. She slowed, jerking her head around as if searching for someone. As she got even with the car, she stopped short of the driver's door and put her purse on the hood. She searched frantically in her purse, becoming visibly irritated. With a grimace, she promptly raised her arm, holding keys in her hand.

At that moment, a police car pulled up on the street side of the car, stopping with the front of the police car even with the front passenger door. Stephen noticed the startled woman jump and drop her keys as the policeman got out of his patrol car. The patrolman obviously saw the woman there and walked toward the front of the car. She jammed her hand back into her purse.

The officer began to speak. "Lady, is this your ..."

With his left hand, Osborn pushed Stephen back and started toward the car.

The woman dropped her purse and raised her arm toward the policeman. She held a small snub-nosed revolver in her hand.

Osborn broke into a run around the people on the sidewalk as he shouted, "Officer, look out!"

Thunder from the gunshot echoed over the area as sound bounced off the building walls. The uniformed officer was thrown back a step, spun to his left and knocked to the ground.

Screams pierced the air. Shopping bags dropped to the ground, spilling their contents across the sidewalk. People started running in every direction. A man grabbed the woman walking beside him, pushed her down behind another parked car and fell to the ground beside her. One young woman tried desperately to run in her five-inch heels, lost her balance and fell into a new mother, knocking her over. She pulled on the stroller she was pushing and turned it over, spilling out her newborn child.

The woman swung the gun around to face the direction where the warning had been shouted. She saw the FBI agent dodging people and running toward her. The gun echoed once more.

Osborn ducked down as the gun fired. A gray-haired man behind him grabbed his stomach, doubled over and fell to the ground.

A loud baby cry drowned out the sounds of pushing and shoving. A middle-aged couple quickly put an arm around each other. They stumbled toward the building wall to their side. Another man trying to run slipped. He fell face-first onto the concrete sidewalk.

The woman saw Stephen a little farther back, just standing there staring at her. She recognized him from the event earlier. She swung the revolver toward him.

Suddenly, it seemed to Stephen like everything was happening in slow motion. He saw the wrong end of the gun barrel swell into a cannon as it pointed at him. The gun bellowed its ear-shattering thunder again, and the plate glass window of the neighborhood grocery behind him exploded, spraying a thousand glass shards around the area.

A second policeman's voice could be heard from the patrol car shouting into the radio, "Officer down. Officer down."

Stephen looked up in time to see Osborn reach the back end of the maroon SUV. He jerked his right hand forward, holding his own gun.

The woman tried to swing her extended arm with the revolver back to her left so she could shoot the man charging her. As she brought it on target, two shots clamored through the air as the last pedestrian there stumbled and rolled onto the ground.

The woman was thrown back against the car as the thunder of one last gunshot split the air. A strange look of disbelief showed on her face. She slid down against the front fender of the SUV, then fell over with her face to the concrete.

After checking on his partner, the second policeman remained crouched and, with his gun drawn, moved quickly around the front of the car.

"FBI. FBI," the agent shouted.

The officer carefully peeked around the corner of the Tahoe and saw the woman on the ground. He ducked back. Then, very slowly and cautiously, he looked again. He saw Osborn on his knees, holding up his badge in his left hand, his right hand down by his side holding a gun.

"FBI," Osborn said. "Agent Randy Osborn." He was breathing hard. "Under control. The shooting's over." The agent slowly rose to a standing position, but stood still, waiting.

The police officer carefully stood up, watching everyone in the process. He saw the gun on the ground beside the woman, kicked it away, and kept his gun pointed at Osborn. He walked over to the revolver and picked it up.

Osborn raised his hands and spoke. "Let me put my gun away." Very slowly, he brought his right hand down, pulled back his suit coat and holstered his weapon. He walked over to the officer and let him examine his FBI credentials.

Stephen started walking up to them. The officer turned to him and asked, "Who are you?"

"It's okay, officer, he's with me. How is your partner?"

"Wounded, but not bleeding badly." Walking over to the woman on the ground, he reached down and checked for a pulse. He shook his head no and stood up. "Ambulances are on the way." He holstered his weapon. Looking at Osborn, he said, "Want to tell me what happened here?"

After describing the incident, Osborn informed the officer he was the one who phoned about the stolen car. He introduced Stephen and described the situation. The policeman told them they needed to go to the precinct house to give a written statement.

Osborn replied, "Of course. We'll be happy to. Why don't you go help your partner? While we're waiting, I want to see what else this woman had in her purse."

Examining her purse, they found many of the usual items carried in a woman's bag, then discovered two passports. One had been recently issued to a Marie Ul-Bashar in Mexico. It had her picture in it. The other passport belonged to a Leena Wateeb and also contained her photograph. The second passport was from Pakistan.

The FBI agent nodded, looked at Stephen, and said, "There is definitely something going on. We have the boat, the body," he started counting on his fingers, "the stolen car, the restaurant bombing, the shooting in the park today, and now this."

A cruel smile crossed Stephen's face as he said, "And this may just be the tip of the iceberg."

CHAPTER 19

While many parts of the country were experiencing severe weather problems, such as an inordinate amount of rain, flooding, and tornadoes, it was warmer than usual in New York City. The two men carrying a long, heavy brown leather travel case down 68th Street walked close to the buildings to remain in the shade.

When they reached the intersection with Columbus, Rana Saleem stepped to the corner and looked in all directions, searching. "This is where Leena was supposed to meet us, but she is not here."

"You don't see her coming down the street?"

"No, Kamran." He shook his head. "She is not here, anywhere." Turning back to Khan, he added, "I think we should wait."

Khan agreed. "Yes. There might be a problem with traffic. We will wait, but only for a few minutes. It is not safe here."

Both men moved back beside the building to wait in the shade. Khan carefully placed one end of the case on the ground and leaned it upright against the building. He moved to stand in front of it, using his body to shield it from obvious view of anyone who might walk or drive by them.

He leaned back against the building himself, breathing hard. "This thing is heavy. Too heavy to carry very far."

The long brown leather case contained the sniper rifle. The Savage Model 110BA by itself weighs over 16 pounds and is more than 50 inches long. Then add the weight of a bi-pod, 6-24x50 tactical super-telescopic sight, over six pounds of ammunition, plus the weight of the case itself, and you have a package weighing well over 25 pounds.

While both men wore blue jeans, they each had a loose, baggy shirt because of the weather. "It sure is hot and muggy today," Kamran uttered. He used the long sleeve of his green shirt to wipe the sweat from his forehead. "It gets hot back home, but not like this. Not very often."

"Kamran," Saleem started. "Why did you change spots where you shot from? The first building seemed good."

"It was, Rana. But that is where the police would search for us. It was too obvious." He wiped his face with the other sleeve. "The other place was farther away and not quite in a direct line. But we still had a good view to shoot from, and a smaller chance of getting caught. This was much better."

"We did not see any police, Kamran."

"Because they looked in the wrong place. By staying in the first building we chose, we would probably be in jail."

"Or dead," Saleem added.

"Yes." He paused, then spoke with urgency. "Turn away. A police car is coming. Lean back against the building and light a cigarette. That will make you look normal."

The blue and white patrol car containing two uniformed officers approached the intersection and slowed. The two officers inside the car were constantly turning their heads, searching everywhere.

"It's okay to look at the car, but then look away slowly, like you are disgusted with them. They will ignore you."

Reaching the intersection, the patrol slowed almost to a stop. The two officers continued looking in all directions. The car crawled through the intersection, turning south on Columbus. As the patrol car inched its way down the street, the officers looked directly at Khan and Saleem. The car hesitated as the officer on the passenger side pointed at them and said something to the officer driving. He leaned over and looked out the window at them, then shook his head and continued driving as the car gradually moved away.

Whew! thought Khan. He shook his head.

"They were looking at us, weren't they, Kamran?"

"Yes. They must be looking for the snipers. They did not know it was us. I guess we must not look guilty. They did not see the case behind me, or I think they would have stopped."

Saleem's questions were not over. He inquired about the shooting. "Kamran, I know why you shot the man from Israel, but why the others? Why did you try to kill the Palestinian?"

"I did not try — I did kill him."

"Yes, I know. But...but why?"

"I don't know. I just felt like it. I missed the American, so I shot the Palestinian. It felt good."

"Well, he was not important, anyway. And a good thing." Saleem stood up straight. "With both Ambassadors dead, no one will know *who* did the shooting — or *why*." He shook his head. "One Israeli and one Palestinian."

"Yes," Khan said. A large smile spread across his face. "Now that's a pair. And *I* did it, didn't I?" He slapped Saleem on the shoulder. "*I* did that." He stood up straight, tall and proud, nodding his head. *"Me!"*

"Yes, Kamran. You did that."

Suddenly Rana Saleem felt very nervous. He looked at Khan, studied him, and wondered what else might happen. He remembered Saboor Rajput, on the boat they rented in Cuba. Khan had shot and killed him when no one else was there. Now this. The way he was acting, Saleem wondered, *would he shoot anyone else? Will he shoot me?*

Saleem understood from the beginning that he might die on this mission. He was prepared to give up his life for Allah's sake. But until now, he never thought his friend Khan might be the one to do it. Would he actually do it? Saleem would like to be alive to see and know that he was part of the group that killed the President of the United States.

Khan interrupted his thoughts. "I think we'd better go."

"What about Leena? There's no sign of her."

"I think she would be here if she was coming. Something happened. I don't know what." He checked his watch and turned to face Saleem. "Something must be wrong. There has been enough time to get the car and come here." He shook his head. "We need to go." He picked up the leather case and slung the strap over his shoulder. "This thing is so heavy." He motioned to Saleem. "Hurry. Look for a taxi."

"Will we go back to the motel?"

"No, I don't think so. It would not be wise to stay there. Already we have been at the motel too long. Someone may have seen us. They could tell the police, and they will think we might be the killers. They will come after us. We'd better not go back."

"Where will we go? How will we get home?"

"We will take a train. There are lots of them here. The taxi can take us to a station where we can catch a train."

"What about Leena?"

"She will understand. She will know that we went ahead and returned to Baltimore. She would do the same."

"Will we meet her there?"

"Yes — if she's not dead."

CHAPTER 20

The next morning

"Yes, I'm at the United Nations now." He set his cup of coffee down on a coaster at the side of the desk, leaned back in his chair and swiveled to face out the window. From his office on the 46th floor, Dr. Stephen Grant looked across the East River at the traffic on the Queens Midtown Expressway. "I'm usually here in the mornings and spend the afternoons at Columbia." He turned back to his desk. "What can I do for you, Agent Osborn?"

"Do you have me on speaker?"

"No. I'm here alone in my office, so I'm using the handset. Do you have any news?"

"How are things there at the U.N.? I bet there's a lot of talk about the shootings."

"Yes. You've got that right." Stephen shook his head. "That's all everyone is talking about. I've been getting hit with questions everywhere I go, so I decided to take a break and stay in my office for awhile."

"Good idea." He paused. "I would bet you haven't shared a lot of your own ideas on this with others yet, right?"

"That's right."

"Good. Let's keep it that way for now. I want to get your thoughts on this first. In fact, I'd like to discuss several ideas with you."

Stephen heard Osborn sipping a drink. "Are you a coffee drinker?" Stephen asked.

"Yeah. Why do you ask?"

"I heard you sipping a drink. Thought it might be coffee."

"Yes, and I drink too much of the stuff. Listen, if you can get the day off this Friday, I'd like you to meet some of the people I work with at the National Counter-Terrorism Center. There's a bunch of us that all work together: FBI, CIA, NSA, and DIA."

"Sounds interesting, but I'm not so sure I can contribute much to your conversations."

"Hey, you're an expert on the Middle East. We could use your insight."

"Aw, I don't know. You fellows are the experts. I'm just a teacher here."

"Come on. Don't give me that. You could use a day away, especially after yesterday. We'll spring for the trip. What do you say?"

"I don't know, Randy."

"We really could use your help."

"Yeah. The last time I heard that, you also said this wasn't going to be as dangerous as the last time. Let me remind you that someone shot at me, too. That bullet didn't miss by much."

"True. But no one should be shooting at you down here."

"Well," he paused. "Actually there's another reason. I just got engaged. That's what happened yesterday morning."

"Yes, you were going to tell me about your morning, but with everything else happening, it was easy to forget. But you can't forget that, can you?"

"No, that's for sure. It was — is very special."

"Good for you. Congratulations."

"Thanks. I'm supposed to go shopping with my fiancé this weekend. We're looking for a ring."

"Okay. Then I have a suggestion. Bring her with you. With Friday off, you can have a long weekend. You two fly down in the morning. I'll pick you up at the airport. You come with me. We'll get a rental car for her, and she can spend the entire day shopping to see what she can find. We'll put you up in one of the nicer hotels, and even pay for a special dinner for the two of you. You can go shopping with her all day Saturday and fly home Sunday. What do you say?"

"Well, I suppose it might make a pleasant weekend for her."

"Sure it would. So it's a done deal. The FBI will pick up the tab for the whole thing, and you two lovebirds can enjoy a special weekend."

"All right," he sighed. "I'll guess there's no use arguing. I'll convince her it will be a special time for her, and a great weekend getaway for the two of us."

"Good."

Both men sipped their coffee, then Osborn spoke. "When you get here, I'll go over what we have found out so far. We really want your input on this, Stephen. We found a possible target. Remember, I said in this business there are very few coincidences. Well, next week the national convention for Homeland Security is being held in Baltimore. It's the only major event scheduled for the eastern part of the country any time soon."

"Yes, that would make sense. But you should remember not all terrorist attacks occur around a major event. A lot happen at places where people gather, such as a shopping mall or subway station."

"True. And that's even harder to predict. It depends on what you can learn about a particular group and their goals. That's one of the reasons we'd like to have you down here. We could discuss all sorts of possibilities, including whether or not this is a new terrorist threat. We believe it is. And we need your help evaluating some options."

Again, Stephen leaned back in his chair. "Perhaps I can offer some insight, but I can't promise anything. I'll call Sheryl, my fiancé, and make sure she can arrange her schedule. I should be able to talk her into it."

"Stephen, we're pretty sure if there is an attack soon, it will be during this convention. It starts next Monday and runs through noon Thursday. There will be a lot of dignitaries present, along with people from all over the country—some first-responder types and community leaders who would deal with disasters, even a bunch of private security people. A large crowd in a relatively small area. It would be a perfect target for a terrorist group, especially one that wants to make a name for itself."

"Sounds like it."

"Here's the kicker. The President will be there for opening day. He's the keynote speaker. The Secretary of Homeland Security will conduct the official opening of the convention, then after lunch she will present the Secretary of State, who will say a few words and introduce the President. All three of them will be on stage at the same time."

Stephen set his coffee down. "Now you've got my attention."

"Thought so," Osborn nodded. "I don't want to say much more on the phone. You understand. Hold on a second."

Stephen heard him talking to someone else. "Could someone get me some coffee, please. Yes, just black."

He returned to Stephen. "I'm going to have you fly into Baltimore. It's only 40 minutes from here anyway, by car. I'll have a place set up in Baltimore where we all can meet and talk freely, without fear of being overheard. It'll be screened and secure. That much I can promise."

"Sounds good so far."

"We'll get — what's her name, Sheryl?"

"Yes." Stephen hesitated and smiled. "But I've been known to call her other things, too, all good."

"I won't go there," Osborn replied. "We'll get Sheryl all set up first—rental car, shopping map, directions, that sort of thing. We'll make sure she's comfortable before we leave her, okay? Do you think she might like a female companion to go shopping with?"

"Naw, that's not necessary." He laughed. "Nice idea, but uh, she's a New Yorker — big city girl. Give her a map and point her in the right direction. She'll be fine."

"All right, if you say so. We'll send her toward Tiffany's, Sach's, and all those other cheap places. Just for you."

"Yeah, thanks. I'll owe you one." Stephen drank the last of the coffee from his cup. "So you'll arrange everything, including the transportation?"

"Are you crazy? You think I'm a travel agent?" Osborn laughed. "I'll have someone take care of it all. They'll be in touch with you to pass on all the details."

CHAPTER 21

Islamabad, Pakistan
The next day

He questioned why. This was extremely unusual. In fact, he had never heard of it being done before. Two blocks off the main highway through town, he hurried to the corner, crossed the street, turned left, and quickly walked north another two blocks.

Islamabad, the capital city of Pakistan, is one of the most beautiful cities in the South Asian region. Wide, tree-lined streets adorn the various sectors and zones of the city, making it easily accessible and spectacular. It is a region-wide symbol of progress, innovation and architectural marvel.

Now studded with tall, futuristic style buildings, the city did not begin development until the 1960s. Initially government servants and employees of the federal administration settled there. Today, the population of the fastest growing urban settlement in the country has swelled to over a million inhabitants.

Islamabad has a humid subtropical climate. Although this is the rainy monsoon season, this day is sunny with a temperature of 28 Celsius, or about 83 degrees Fahrenheit.

After passing a huge-six story hospital, he saw a large open gate in a six-foot block wall fence, back about 30 feet from the sidewalk. There were no signs or other identification visible anywhere, just the narrow concrete path from the sidewalk to the gate and beyond.

A man wearing an open collar white dress shirt and slacks stood at the opening. His sport coat, open and pulled back to the sides, revealed a holster and semi-automatic pistol.

A second man, similarly dressed, stood to the side, leaning up against the fence. Neither man smiled.

Approaching the man at the gate, he showed his ID card.

"Hammad Malik?"

"Yes, that's me."

"You have business with ISI?"

With a single nod of his head, he answered, "My ID shows I am a member of ISI."

The Inter-Service Intelligence agency, or ISI as it is called, is the largest intelligence agency in the world, with over 10,000 employees and staff. The exact number has never been announced or confirmed, so no one is exactly sure.

There are three primary wings in the organization, under which eight divisions execute several functions. Although the Internal Wing oversees counter-intelligence activities, the agency itself is primarily concerned with matters outside the country and its government. Included in the Covert Actions Division is the recruitment, training, coordination with and sometimes supervision of terrorist groups, including the Pakistani Taliban and Al-Qaeda.

"Here is the summons I received." He provided a letter to the guard. "I am to appear before the Director-General."

"Yes, I see," said the guard. "We were told to expect you." He pointed behind him to his right. "If you would proceed to those soldiers, please. Their dogs will sniff you. They are looking for weapons or explosives. Once they clear you, you may proceed."

He stepped back and continued speaking, still without a smile. "Make your way around the barriers to the line of buildings. The third one, the tallest, is the one you want. The Director-General is on the top floor. Someone will meet you as you enter the building."

"Thank you." Malik walked to the soldiers, where he received a cursory search by a corporal, then passed the sniff test by two dogs.

Walking around the concrete barriers alternating across the pathway, he admired the orderly layout of the compound. He had been here many times before, but never to meet with the Director-General.

The complex consisted of various adobe buildings separated by smooth green lawns and sparkling fountains. The neatly tended complex reminded him of a well-funded private university.

As he approached the central building, the door opened and a slightly plump, balding older man in an army uniform stepped out. "Major Hammad Malik?"

"Yes, sir," he answered, saluting.

"I am Brigadier General Mehr Tonali." There was a slight nod of his head, almost like a bow of some sort. "I am Deputy Director of the Inter-Service Intelligence Agency in charge of the Analysis and Foreign Relations Wing. Welcome to ISI headquarters." He opened the door wide, stepped back and motioned for Malik to enter. "Your Division Chief recommended you for special assignment. He said you were well qualified for this particular job."

Malik walked through the doorway. "I hope so, sir. I am ready to serve as you and the Director-General see fit."

Immediately upon arrival at the top floor, they were ushered across a large, round, echoing lobby into the Director-General's office.

"Ahh." The general rose and walked over to greet them. "You are Major Hammad Malik?"

"Sir." He nodded. "You requested to see me." He stood at attention.

"Quite right. I did, yes. Do you know who I am?"

"Yes, sir. Lieutenant General Omar Khawaja, ISI Director-General."

"Good." He turned and pointed at two chairs in front of his desk. "Please, be seated."

They all sat, the director behind the desk. "General Tonali and I have been discussing a special assignment. Your Division Chief says you are a perfect match for this."

"I hope so, sir. I am ready to serve as you deem fit."

Khawaja waved his hand, dismissing the comment. "Let me first ask you a few questions. Have you ever been to the United States?"

"Yes, sir. I went there for training with the American CIA."

"And you have worked with members of the American CIA, right?"

"Yes, sir. I have."

"How closely?"

"Very closely, sir, and for long periods of time, both in Afghanistan and Indonesia."

"Are you familiar with the United States political system and justice system?"

"Reasonably."

"Good." He smiled for the first time in their presence. Malik noticed General Tonali relax his posture slightly.

"Would you like a drink?"

Once each man had a small glass of straight Scotch with ice, Khawaja said, "We have a serious problem happening in the United States." He looked directly at Malik. "A very serious problem." He took a sip of his drink. "I'm afraid we need to interfere — and we must do this without the United States government officially knowing that we are involved."

Khawaja sat back, crossed his legs, and asked General Tonali to provide the details.

"We have invested a considerable amount of money and time developing reliable, dependable intelligence sources inside both the American and Israeli governments."

Malik raised his eyebrows. "Israeli too, sir?"

"Yes. Some people believe Jews and Arabs can live side by side, harmoniously. They are willing to provide inside information to help bring that about. And they have proven extremely valuable, giving us early information and keeping us informed as various situations develop. It is vital that we maintain these sources and the flow of information. In fact, it is crucial to our country's well being."

"I can appreciate that, sir."

"Well, a former member of the ISI is threatening to destroy that flow of information. We have learned through reliable

111

sources — friends of the family — that he has formed a small band of activists, now in America, and they are causing chaos. They killed the Israeli UN Ambassador yesterday."

Tonali continued. "Some time ago, our agent and his brother, also a member of ISI, were assigned to attend a meeting in Ramallah, in the West Bank Territory. The nature of the meeting is not relevant. What you need to know is that a Mossad team raided that meeting, killing everyone except for our man. After we identified the leader of that team, our guy wanted to go after him. We denied his request because the Mossad man was important to our intelligence sources. We had no choice."

He made a face. "Our man's name is Kamran Khan. Are you familiar with him?"

"No. Never met him, as far as I can recall."

"Well, he became so obsessed with getting revenge, he resigned from our agency to pursue this Israeli on his own. He spent some time recruiting help, and apparently conducting training. We know at least six people are in this group, maybe more, we're not sure."

"We didn't think too much about it until two days ago. That is when they killed the Israeli Ambassador."

"Was he the Mossad man who led the raid?"

"Yes." He shook his head. "We did some quick checking and discovered this group has gone to the United States. We did discover that they sent two people earlier, a man and a woman. We believe they went through Mexico and probably obtained false papers allowing entry into America. This is a good place to start tracking them down. We will provide you with a list of people receiving visas while in Mexico during the recent past."

General Khawaja leaned forward. "These people are doing irreparable harm. Our Israeli contacts are screaming." He threw up his hands. "More of this chaos, any more killing, and our sources are gone, dried up." He spread his arms with hands in the air. "Vanished!"

Khawaja stood up. "Not only must we placate the Israelis, but this is happening in America. We must placate them too. We cannot allow any of those stupid American infidels to be killed, either."

The general walked around toward Malik and sat on the side
of his desk. "Major, listen to me. Next week, American
Homeland Security is holding a convention in Baltimore,
Maryland. The President of the United States will be the guest
speaker. We think this group may be plotting to assassinate the
American President during the conference. It's their way to get
back at the Americans for backing Israel. We cannot let that
happen. Our sources are already becoming shaky, not sure they
are willing to continue cooperating with us. We must stop this
threat and maintain our secret flow of information. It is vital. We
cannot be without it."

"I understand, sir. I can appreciate the importance of this."

"Part of our problem is we can't let these guys be captured,
either. They will think we sent them, the ISI. The whole world
will think we've lost our ever-lovin' minds, and we're sending
death squads out to take down governments."

The general shook his head, stood up and walked back
behind his desk. He remained standing. "You understand we
work closely with many groups of freedom fighters. Hizbul
Mujahideen, Lashkar-e-Taiba, Al-Qaeda, and Jaish-e-
Mohammed. But we cannot allow this new group to continue.
They must be stopped."

General Tonali again took over.

He leaned to the side, toward Malik. "We want you to go to
the Unites States, find this group and eliminate them — all of
them, by any means necessary. And it must be done quickly."

Khawaja spoke again, firmly. "This must be strictly a covert
operation. Others will not, must not, know about this mission.
That is imperative."

He continued. "I am assigning Lieutenants Ali Bajar and
Fazil Virk to your team. They will meet you downstairs in the
briefing room in one hour. A file has been prepared for you to
review with all the information, at least as much as we know. It'll
be on the table waiting for you, along with a video tape of the
shooting. Television cameras recorded the killing of the Israeli
Ambassador, and it has been broadcast all over. The Palestinian
UN Ambassador was also killed, and an American was shot at. A

Dr. Stephen Grant with the UN was moderating this meeting. Somehow he escaped alive."

Tonali again spoke. "We have airline tickets there for you also. You will leave at four o'clock tomorrow morning on Qatar Airlines and fly to New York. You will be traveling as diplomats of our government. Official passports have been prepared. Your luggage will be allowed to pass through customs without being searched, so you should pack your weapons and anything else you may need in your bags. Special tags are available for you to identify them."

"When you arrive, Lieutenant Virk will go directly to our consulate on 65th Street. In case he is followed, no one will be suspicious. Have him check on this Dr. Grant. Our people at the consulate may be able to help. Some of them may even know him, since he is with the UN. Find out if there is any special involvement we should know about."

The general handed a paper to Malik. "Here is the contact information for our embassy in Washington. You and Lieutenant Bajar will fly to Washington and go directly to our embassy on International Court. You never know, you could be followed too. If you go straight there, again no one will become suspicious."

"Your contacts at those locations will be expecting you. They have been instructed to provide whatever help is needed— supplies, cars, information, whatever. They do not know why you are there, and they have been instructed not to interfere with your assignment. They must never know that information."

"Go ahead down to the briefing room where everything is ready. Review it all, then complete your briefing and work out your strategy." Khawaja again walked around his desk. He approached Malik and held out his hand. "Good luck." He shook his head. "There isn't much time."

They all stood up and shook hands. Major Hammad Malik reassured both generals. "We will get the job done, sir."

"Oh, Major," the Director-General added. "I'm afraid there's one last thing."

Malik stopped and turned back to see a scowl on the Director-General's face. Khawaja said, "Under no circumstances can you allow yourself or your team members to be captured. The

American government and the public must never know about this mission — ever!" He paused, then took a step toward the Major. "Do you understand me, Major? You know what this means."

Major Malik sucked in a deep breath and looked at the general. He nodded. "Yes, sir. I know what you mean." He turned and walked out of the office.

CHAPTER 22

"I'm glad you *did* call last night, Stephen."

"I didn't want you to be worried."

"I wasn't. Worried, that is." She pushed the switch on her leather power recliner and the foot rest raised up. Scooting to one side of the large tan chair, she moved the cordless phone to her left hand. "I was concerned. Anytime you try to mix those two cultures, you can expect problems. It's like oil and water."

"You mean oil and vinegar."

"Whatever." She shrugged. "When you called, you sounded out of breath and all excited. Hearing your voice was good, but I couldn't imagine what happened. I knew something was wrong from the way you sounded. I had no idea."

"I'm glad I was able to call you before you heard about it or saw it on TV."

"Thanks for that. If I had seen it first, I really would have been worried. I thought the United Nations was dedicated to peaceful resolutions."

Stephen sighed. "Yes, it is. Didn't work that way this time, did it?"

"No. I was shocked when I saw it on television. I never expected shooting and killing."

"Neither did anyone else. It shocked the whole world, especially being broadcast live on television. We're not used to watching live assassinations in our living rooms."

"We're not used to watching assassinations, period. And I don't want to."

"No." Stephen shook his head. "Let's hope we never get there, Sheryl. That's not a place I want to be."

"Anyway, I'm glad you called me before I saw it on television. I would have been a total wreck."

"Fortunately, the shooter missed me. But that was too close."

"Yes, indeed. Far too close, You are okay, aren't you?"

"Yes, I'm fine. Still a little shook up, but I'll be okay. Kind of a funny thing, though. I didn't get scared until afterward."

"When it was over?"

"Yes. At the time, I just reacted. Afterward, when I talked with Osborn, *that* was when I became scared. I guess thinking about it brought it closer to home. The reality of it was not pleasant."

"Well, thank God you're all right. I don't want to think about losing my fiancé before we even get married. There is too much to look forward to."

"How right you are, Sheryl." He smiled. "We have a whole lifetime together to think about. And that doesn't include anyone shooting at us."

"It better not. That's not in any of my plans."

Stephen laughed. "Not mine either, sweetheart."

"But you do seem to have a way of attracting serious problems, from what I understand."

"Not to worry." Stephen looked at the floor and shook his head, still smiling.

"So this is all over. I don't have to worry. You're not involved anymore with the FBI or CIA or anything, are you?"

"Well ..."

"Stephen! Tell me now. I'm not going anywhere, we're together. But if you're involved in more of this, I need to know. People can get hurt, and I don't want that for either of us."

"Nor do I, Sheryl. I love you, and I don't want anything to happen to you — or to me, either." He took a deep breath and wished he had a drink. The concoction he and Peter made up of vanilla vodka and chocolate liqueur over ice with a cherry sounded really good right now.

"Hold on a minute." He walked into his apartment's kitchen to see what he could find. He grabbed a beer out of the fridge, returned to the living room and sat down. "This is not like that. It's not like what I did before having you in my life. And I'm no

James Bond or Dick Tracy or whatever. But I am considered an expert in Middle Eastern Affairs, and the FBI has asked for my help."

"Help how?"

"They want me to meet with them in Washington, at the National Counter-Terrorism Center."

"And do what?"

"Just talk. They think a terrorist group may have sent some people here. They could be responsible for the restaurant bombing last week and the shooting in Central Park. They want to get my input on the ideas they're considering."

"As long as your input is just talking, give all the advice you want. Like you said, you're not some sort of secret agent and, Stephen, I need you to be here with me, not off on some crazy mission to save the world again. Please?"

"You're right, Sheryl. And Osborn promised this would not be as dangerous. They just want to discuss things. My input may — or may not — help them evaluate various possibilities. What they do from there is up to them. My part will be done."

"Well, okay. I want you alive so we can have a wonderful life. We both have waited long enough for this, let's not spoil it now."

"I won't." He paused, sipping his beer. "Sheryl, I have a proposal."

"What? I already said 'Yes.'" He could see her smiling. "Is there more?"

"How about going with me down to Washington? I'm meeting with them on Friday during the day. Let's take Friday off and make it a special weekend away, just the two of us."

"Well, I could probably arrange to have Friday off. What are you thinking? Tell me more."

"I told Agent Osborn about us and that we were going shopping for a ring this weekend. So he suggested you come with me, and we'll make a weekend of it. He said the F'BI will pay for everything—rooms in a nice hotel, meals, airline, everything. While I'm in the meeting on Friday, you could do some shopping. Then you and I could enjoy a special dinner that night, and shop for a ring on Saturday. We could fly home Sunday. What do you think?"

"I think that's a great idea. It sounds like fun. What do you think?"

"I think it would be a wonderful time. I love you, Sheryl."

"I love you too. Now, how do I get around in Washington to go shopping?"

"They'll pay for a rental car. Osborn offered. You'll be okay shopping for the day by yourself, won't you?"

"Oh, I'll be fine. That'll give me a chance to look at a lot of rings, and maybe shop for some clothes also. I look forward to it. I've never been to Washington."

Stephen sucked in a deep breath. "Well, it's not exactly Washington."

"What do you mean?"

"It's Baltimore. We're going to Baltimore."

"Baltimore? What on earth for?"

"Have you ever been to Baltimore?"

"Nnnoo." He pictured the expression on her face as she said it. "Why are we going to Baltimore?"

He took another long sip of his beer. "It's only forty to forty-five minutes by car from Washington. The people from the Counter-Terrorism Center are coming there to meet with me."

"Again, Stephen. Why Baltimore?"

"Because there's a convention there next week. It's a national conference for Homeland Security. Everyone's getting ready for that, there'll be a lot of people there."

Sheryl nodded her head. "And what does that have to do with us?"

"Okay, but we can't talk about this with anyone else."

"Stephen, don't say if you tell me, you'll have to shoot me."

"All right, I won't." He laughed. "That's the trouble with not being a secret agent, isn't it?" He paused and took a breath. "The truth is the President and some cabinet members will be attending the conference. These guys think that may be the target for the terrorists. They want to examine all the possible ways that could happen, and look at other potential targets also. We're going to be busy with this, but it should only take one day."

"Promise?"

"Yes, dear. I promise."

"Good. I want to go shopping with you on Saturday, even if it's Baltimore. Oh, and another thing, Stephen."

"What's that?"

He could feel her excitement through the phone. "Let's just get one room at the hotel."

A huge grin sprung across his face and he spilled his beer. Pulling out his handkerchief, he quickly blotted his clothes. Smiling, he said, "You got it, honey."

Then he heard a change in her voice as she said, "Bal-ti-more?"

CHAPTER 23

Tariq approached the two men in the driveway, placed his left hand over his heart and extended his right hand. He gave them the traditional Pakistani greeting, "Assalamu alaykum." (pronounced salam aLAYkoom, meaning 'peace and health.')

Kamran Khan provided the usual Pakistani response, "Wa allayk salam." (meaning 'may peace, mercy and blessings of Allah be upon you.') He shared a brief embrace with Tariq.

Turning to Rana Saleem, Tariq again put his left hand over his heart and extended his right to shake hands. Saleem nodded, "Salam," and shared a brief embrace.

Pakistanis always shake hands using their right hand. The left hand is considered unclean. And when you are extended a greeting, it is custom to reply with an even better greeting.

"Kamran, Rana." Umara emerged from the door of the house they had rented outside the city, in Baltimore County. "Assalamu alaykum." She approached the men with her left hand over her heart and extending her right hand. The each shook hands. It is not proper or polite to embrace a member of the opposite sex unless you are married or family.

With a big smile, Tariq said, "It is good to have you both back here with us."

Khan replied, "It is good to be back." He turned his head to look at Umara and back to Tariq. "Have you heard anything from Leena?"

Umara shook her head, and Tariq replied, "No, not a word. Nothing from any of you since you left, until now when you arrived. Why did you use a taxi? Where *is* Leena? Is she bringing the car?"

Khan suddenly appeared sad. "We don't know. It may be unfortunate news." He glanced back at Saleem, then turned to Tariq. "Let's go inside. We can use a cup of tea while we talk about things. There is much to discuss. But first we should clean up. It has been a long trip back here."

A little while later they each held a cup of tea, sitting in the living room to discuss what happened on the trip and what had happened in Baltimore while they were away.

Umara said, "We have been watching the television as you suggested."

"Yes," Tariq verbalized. "We learned about the restaurant explosion and the shooting in Central Park. It has been on the news every day. They have people on TV offering their ideas for why these things happened and what it means."

"You have seen all this?"

"Yes." Tariq nodded. "There are many ideas why and what to do about it. No one can agree. They said the FBI thinks some terrorists may have caused this, but many others do not believe that. They have been disagreeing on whether or not the restaurant bombing even had anything to do with the shootings. They are all mixed up with too many ideas."

Umara spoke up. "It is true. There are too many ideas. They do not believe like we do. They see life differently."

Khan nodded. "Yes, Umara. They do not think about what is important to us, or to other people. The corrupt Americans only care about themselves and their possessions. They believe everyone else thinks just like they do."

"That will be their downfall. It will lead to their destruction," offered Saleem. "Right, Kamran?"

"Yes," Khan responded. "They are infidels. They do not know or seek our truth."

"I am glad we are here," Umara proffered. "We will show them they are not so invincible. Their arrogance will help bury them."

"So obviously," Tariq looked at Khan, "the restaurant bomb did not kill our Israeli friend Colonel Shavit. That is why you shot him in Central Park, yes?"

"Yes." Khan looked down at the floor, then back up at Umara, then Tariq.

"Kamran had a brilliant plan," uttered Saleem. "The Israelis blamed the Palestinians for the bombing, so Kamran got them to agree to hold a public debate. It worked beautifully. The sniper rifle you provided Kamran was the perfect weapon. He not only killed the Israeli Ambassador, but the Palestinian also."

"We saw that." Tariq sipped his tea and leaned back in his chair. "But you missed the American. He is still alive. Much has been said about that on television also. They talked a lot about the American with the UN, Dr. Stephen Grant. He is assistant to the Secretary-General. He is also a college professor at Columbia University."

Umara chimed in. "They said he specializes in Middle Eastern events, cultures and relations. The newscasters claimed rumors exist about links to the CIA, but no one knows for sure if he actually works for them. Most of the stations don't think so, since he has a special position in the United Nations."

Tariq added, "They did report that the FBI asked him to help with their investigation. He has not commented on that part himself. Do you think he will find out about us?"

"Not until afterward. Then it will be too late."

"Good."

"What happened with Leena?" Umara asked.

Khan put his cup down on a small table beside his chair. "We are not sure. After the shooting, she left to get the car and drive to a meeting location. Then we could put the rifle and our stuff in the car and not have to carry it." He nodded. "It's heavy. Anyway, we waited where she should meet us, but she never came. We have not seen her since then."

"Do you think that she is still alive?" Umara asked.

Khan shook his head. "I don't know. She did not meet us, and she knew enough to not let herself get caught. They would torture her, and she would tell them our plans. She wouldn't let that happen." He gazed at the ceiling a moment. "If she does not arrive here in the next two days, then we will know she is dead."

Silence filled the room. Each person avoided looking at the others. Tea cups rattled as they were set down on tables or on the floor.

Finally, Tariq spoke. "Several things have happened here too."

"Yes. Tell us."

Tariq continued. "I am now a security guard at the Baltimore Convention Center." He pointed toward Khan. "It was just as you said, Kamran. Umara and I discovered that one of the security guards lives only a few blocks from here. We arranged to," he motioned with his fingers, "bump into them. We saw them a few times and started becoming friends. After we gained their confidence, I told him how difficult it is for us with me not working, and that I needed a job. My only experience was with security forces back home — just like you said, Kamran. He helped me get hired. Now I have uniforms and everything. And I carry a gun. I had to qualify, but that was no problem."

"Excellent," Khan responded. "Good for you. That is perfect for our plan. We must work out details. It will take some more planning. We will work on it."

He leaned back in his chair and placed his hands behind his head. "Did you get the list of items I gave you?"

"Yes. And I made sure to purchase them in different stores, like you said.

"Good. We do not want anyone to pay too much attention. They would if you bought all the items in one place. Where are they now?"

Tariq leaned forward. "I rented a storage unit down by the docks, not far from the convention center itself. I rented an end unit by the gate. That way we can load the stuff and leave without anyone seeing what it is we are loading. Besides, I have everything boxed except the black plastic conduit. No one can tell what we have."

"What is the black conduit for, Kamran?" Saleem inquired.

"We will stuff the plastic explosive into small pieces of the plastic pipe. After the igniter wires are connected, I will use plumber's putty to seal the ends of the pipe and coat it with epoxy. Once the seal is dry, the bomb dogs used by the American Secret Service will not be able to detect the bombs."

He lit up as he smiled. "We will prepare them ahead. They will be ready. All we need to do is connect a cell phone to the switch and put them in place."

He took a breath. "I am using black pipe because the speakers' platform at the conference is black. Using an adhesive, we can stick these to the bottom of the platform against the braces, and no one will see them."

"Good plan," said Saleem.

Taking a deep breath, Khan continued talking. "I want to get a hotel room close to the convention center. This place is good, but as we near the time for action, I want to be close. Not right next door, but close."

He looked around at each one of them. "I want us to get there quickly when the time is right. Okay? I'll take care of that and let you know where that will be."

Khan continued. "Since Tariq is a security guard, he will find a way to let us into the center early so we can plant the explosives." He turned to Saleem. "Rana, you hide somewhere. Tariq will find a spot. Later, you come out, call the cell phone number and set off the bomb."

"Where will you be, Kamran?"

"I will be sitting down toward the front, close to the speakers." He shrugged. "There will be some people who do not show up. I will use a fake ID tag. I will wait until the last minute, then walk down front and sit in an empty chair like I belong there. No one will know everyone who is there, so it won't make any difference."

He beamed as he spoke. "After the bombs explode, everyone else will be running for safety. I will stand up, pull out my secret gun and shoot anyone from the speakers' platform that is still alive."

"You will probably be killed."

With a big sigh, he explained, "I am ready to die a martyr's death for Allah. If it is his will, I will be ready."

"What will I do?" asked Umara.

"You will go into the center with us and help plant the bombs. Once we are ready, Tariq will let you outside. You get the car in position and be ready to get us the hell out of there as soon as we come out."

"If we come out," Saleem said.

"I think we will. Allah is with us. He will protect us, or we die as martyrs and enjoy our rewards with him in heaven."

"So, Kamran," Tariq began, "I am to let all of you inside early the day of the conference, then let Umara get out without being stopped when she is done."

"Yes, that is correct."

"And I need to find a good place for Rana to hide until he is ready to come out."

"Yes."

"And a place for you also?"

"Yes, a place for me too."

"Will I tell him when it is time?"

"It would be a good idea to check on him." He turned to Saleem. "But Rana, you will calculate the proper time, and then come out. Tariq will help you be on time."

Khan paused, looked from one to another, and smiled again. "When the President stands up, moves to the podium and starts his speech, that's when you call the cell number and —" he motioned with his hands, "Boom!" He clapped his hands for emphasis.

"When the bombs go off, there will be lots of screaming and shouting. People everywhere will be running for safety. I will stand up," he stood, "pull out my gun," he motioned as if drawing a pistol, "and shoot everyone from the platform that is still alive."

He looked at Saleem. "As soon as the bombs go off, get to Tariq, and both of you get out of there." He nodded toward Umara. "She will have the car waiting with the engine running, ready to go. If I'm not there by that time, get out of there fast and don't stop for anything."

"If they try to stop us?"

"Keep going. You need to get away."

He paused, realizing he was so excited he was out of breath.

"I will send a timed email message to arrive after we are finished to others in our home country, telling them about what we did. Allah will see us through this," he nodded with a huge grin. "We will get the glory for Allah. It is his will."

CHAPTER 24

The hotel phone rang twice. "Hammad."

He remembered their instructions to use only first names. No last names, no military rank. That made it more difficult for anyone trying to identify and track them. Instructed to use cash whenever possible, all three men also carried specially prepared fake credit cards in case they were needed for hotels and transportation such as airlines. The first names on the cards matched their real identity, the last names did not.

"Fazil," Lieutenant Virk replied. "With the humidity, the weather here is warmer than at home." He had to memorize several coded statements. This one meant he was not under duress, no one was listening and it was clear to talk.

"Praise Allah, the humidity is not like here." Virk recalled this response indicated no duress for the responding person either. They were clear to speak as they needed.

"I've been checking on our Dr. Grant. It seems he is a well respected professor at Columbia University here in New York. He's a specialist on the Middle East, including cultures, politics, and economics. He has given several presentations to the public on the structure and policies of different governments, including Iraq and Iran, and has also spoken about various terrorist or Jihadist groups."

Major Hammad Malik just listened while Virk reported his information.

"I went to the University and spoke with his receptionist and student teaching assistant. All his classes involve Middle East culture and international relations. However," he sighed, "It seems our Dr. Grant misses class sometimes, apparently traveling. The assistant said he does some work for the government, helping with meetings, conferences, even helping write trade agreements. He was part of the American team working on the Status of Forces agreement with Iraq."

"He gets around, doesn't he?" Malik responded. "That's an interesting tie to the American government." The Major paused a moment. "It could be a cover for other operations. Any indication of how big or close that connection might be?"

"No, not yet. But I'm still digging. I know it goes well beyond the UN. Have you watched any of the news on television? They're giving a lot of time to the shooting in Central Park and possible ties to a restaurant bombing that occurred here in New York. Grant is at the center of it, with talk that he may be FBI, or possibly CIA. They did say the FBI has requested his help in evaluating potential groups who may have been responsible for the shooting."

"Yes, I've seen some of those programs. They would never put anything like that on TV in our country. It wouldn't be allowed."

"For sure. Unless we fed it to them."

"Well," Malik said, "I guess that is a possibility. But why would they announce that? I don't think that makes sense." He inhaled deeply. "But then they're Americans, don't forget. They do crazy things. What about the United Nations?"

"He *is* part of the UN. Several of our people at the Consulate know him or have talked to him. They say everyone is cautiously respectful of him and his position. He is very close to the Secretary-General."

"Okay. That's good to know."

"Also he has met with the Secretary of State, Secretary of Defense, and several elected officials, including several Congressmen."

"Very interesting."

"His secretary at the UN said he will be away for a few days. She said he will be staying in Baltimore, but will not be available. Apparently several reporters are trying to see him, but he did not leave any contact information."

"Now that's worth knowing." Malik sounded excited. "Anything else to report?"

"That's as much as I could get. What's next?"

Malik looked across the hotel room at Lieutenant Ali Bajar, who sat at a small table listening. "Ali will call around to check the local hotels for anyone with a foreign-sounding name or a Mexican passport already checked in and staying through the start of the conference."

"Good idea."

"Here in America, employers are supposed to verify citizenship and register foreign employees online. I will be checking that source for names and Mexican passports. You catch a plane down here to Baltimore and we'll meet up. There are flights from JFK airport all the time. Call me after you arrive. Remember, no cell phones."

"Okay. I should arrive before dark."

He hung up and looked around for a phone book. He had left the United Nations and walked down 42nd Street to Grand Central Station, where he had found a bank of pay phones and called his superior. The embassy had connected him to the motel in Baltimore.

Even though there wasn't much of a demand for pay phones now that everyone carried a cell phone, he sensed there must still be a high demand for phone books, because he couldn't find one. Finally discovering one at the end of the phone bank, he checked listings for airlines, found the number he wanted and called.

He had never been to the United States. He had never traveled beyond the countries surrounding Pakistan. The rest of the world was a mystery to him. He decided to see what New York was like while he was there. He had heard a lot about this place, and now he could see it for himself.

After completing arrangements for a late afternoon flight to Baltimore, he asked directions. Told to continue west about ten blocks down 42nd Street, he would pass Bryant Park on the left, and arrive at Times Square, which many considered the heart of New York. Excited about the new adventure, he left Grand Central and started walking.

The sidewalk was crowded with people rushing everywhere. He sidestepped a man coming right at him. He saw others pushing, nudging and dodging around other people walking slower. He didn't see a single smile. No one said hello or even nodded a greeting acknowledging anyone's presence. They were all going someplace and wanted to get there.

Virk had not expected such a diversity of ethnicity. *Wow. There are lots of different people everywhere, not like at home.* He observed whites, blacks, brown people, Asians, Orientals, obvious Europeans and other Arabic people. As he continued walking, he overheard people speaking Russian, Spanish, Polish, and Japanese. He thought one language was either Italian or French. He heard a few Arabic words and even some Farsi. Although several regional languages are spoken in parts of Pakistan, the official language is Urdu and English. He heard many words in English, but none in his native Urdu.

The crowd thinned a little and a young man on roller skates moved toward him. Virk's eyes opened wide in disbelief. Wearing baggy camo shorts and an old, faded red sleeveless tee three sizes too large, the young man rolled on one skate while lifting his other foot high in the air out to his side. He alternated his feet and continued skating slowly. He wore a big smile that highlighted a multitude of dark freckles. But what really shocked Virk was the man's hair. It was a ball of curly fuzz, looking like it had exploded outward from the man's head. The hair on top of his head was colored a very strong orange, while the sides were bright blue.

Virk turned to watch in disbelief as the man skated past. Shaking his head, Virk turned around to find another man standing in front of him in a long gray top coat.

Virk wasn't sure what to do, the man just stood there. The man pulled up his sleeve. "Want to buy a watch?" He had at least six different watches strapped on his arm.

Speechless, Virk shook his head no.

The man opened his coat."How about a wallet?" Somehow attached to the inside of the coat, he displayed a half dozen billfolds.

"Uh — no thanks." Virk stepped around the man and continued walking.

It actually felt strange, rather uncomfortable to Virk, to see the extreme variety of clothing people wore. There were only a few men in suits like he dressed, but not most people. One woman stumbled, trying to walk in five-inch high heels. Virk thought about the many roads in his country that were still dirt or cobblestone, and the many broken sidewalks in the city.

Three younger women walked toward him wearing tight, very short shorts and halter tops barely concealing their contents. One of the women, a dark brunette, actually smiled at him as they approached. Her breasts were so large in the tight halter top, they bounced dramatically as she walked. He couldn't help but notice the abundance of bright red lipstick and heavy dark mascara around their eyes.

Virk stepped to the side and let the young women pass, They kept on talking to each other and walking as if no one else existed on the sidewalk.

As he continued down 42nd Street, he was in awe at the huge signs over the various stores and businesses. Lights flashed and twinkled. Names on the signs blinked. This was not like Islamabad, let alone the small village where he lived.

He was surprised at the lack of police presence. He had not seen a uniformed policeman anywhere today. The UN had their own security guards, and they were all over the place. But out here, on the streets of New York, one of the largest cities in the world, he had not seen a single police officer.

As if on cue, a blue and white sedan pulled out from the intersection ahead and drove slowly past him. The writing on the car said, "To Protect and Serve." Additional writing identified it as New York City Police.

As he thought about it, he hadn't identified any military uniforms either. There must be some. *Back home*, he thought, *they're everywhere. All over the place. Where are they here?*

As he continued walking, he spied a couple over on the far side of the walk, next to the buildings. The man wearing a leather jacket had black hair sticking up like spikes. The woman was much shorter, but also sprouted black hair in all directions. She had black lips and white shading all around her eyes. As they drew close, Virk saw the man did too. And both had fingernails painted black. As they walked past, they looked at him as if to say, "What's wrong with you?"

Virk lowered his head and studied the dirty sidewalk. A few paper wrappers had been dropped and left for others. He stepped over what appeared to be a wad of chewing gum. Then he realized he couldn't keep his head down without running into people.

"Hello there, handsome." He glanced to the side, where the voice had originated. There stood a tall black woman wearing orange lipstick and a very tight, very short orange dress. Her high heels clicked on the sidewalk as she walked over to him. "You look lonely, honey. Would you like a date?"

He looked around and behind her. He saw no dates, no pomegranates, nothing. There wasn't even a vendor's stand of any kind. Confused, Virk replied, "You don't have any dates."

The woman frowned at him. She started some gyrating movements and wagged her head back and forth. "How 'bout a trip round the world?"

Now Virk was really confused. He stammered but managed to say, "I don't think I have time."

The woman tilted her head down and looked up at him. She raised her eyebrows questioningly. "Are you for real, son? Are you sure you're all right? You hit your head or something?"

She put her hands on her hips and stood upright, thrusting her breasts in his direction. She leaned toward him. "Tell you what." She smiled. "How about a quickie? You've got time for that, don't you? Come on, let's have some fun. Only a hundred bucks." She continued to smile at him.

"I ... " Virk turned back in the direction he was headed. "I'd better be going." He started walking again.

Wow, he thought. *This New York place sure is different. Americans are crazy. No wonder they're all infidels. They must not believe in anything. Anything but money, that is.*

As he walked, he nodded. His thoughts went wild. *How can they have families? How can they please Allah like this?* He shook his head in disgust. *How can they please themselves like this? They must not all be this way.*

A man bumped into him hard, knocking him slightly to the side, forcing him to stagger a step to maintain his balance. As the man moved away from him, Virk felt the man's hand pulling out of Virk's coat pocket. The man hurried away without saying a word. He turned and watched the man continue, hurrying down the sidewalk, away from him.

Turning back, Virk felt happy he had nothing in that pocket. He smiled as he resumed walking. He had experienced New York. It was time to go to the airport.

CHAPTER 25

Tyson's Corner is located in Fairfax County, Virginia, just off the west side of the Capital Beltway, southwest of McLean, Virginia. Liberty Crossing is a modern complex recently built there, which houses the U. S. National Counter-Terrorism Center. In the Operations Center on the second floor, FBI Supervisory Special Agent Randall Osborn pushed back from his desk and stood up. "That's enough for me today." He flexed his arms out to his sides and stretched.

"Mike," he looked over to the next desk, "I'd like to have you go with me in the morning to meet Dr. Grant, all right?"

"Sure. Be glad to." Special Agent Michael Borns was one of seven FBI Special Agents assigned to the FBI Counter-Terrorism Unit that worked with the Center. Under the office of the National Director of Intelligence, 16 different government agencies combined their intelligence efforts to help protect the country from foreign and domestic terrorists.

"Good. Get us a car from the pool. A nice one. Not a limo, but a nice one. Then you can pick me up in the morning, okay?"

"Okay, boss. What time do you want me there?"

"Pick me up at six. That'll give us time for breakfast and to talk about the day before we drive up to Baltimore. We'll meet the rest of the guys up there."

"Six o'clock. You got it."

"Remember, Grant is bringing his fiancé with him. Her name is Dr. Sheryl Hauser. A pediatrician." He made a face. "I had to offer a bribe to get him here. We're putting them up in the hotel there for a couple nights."

He waved his hand, as if dismissing the thought. "She'll go shopping while we meet with him and the others. Bill over here," he turned to the desk on the other side of him, "reserved a rental car for her at the airport. Right, Bill?"

The man nodded his head once. "All ready to go, boss."

He knew they all loved to tease him about being team leader since he had been promoted four months ago. He let it go, realizing it would only get worse if he made a big deal of it. Actually, he was proud of how well the team functioned, working so closely together day after day. Each member had several years of field experience and readily contributed to each assignment, regardless of whether dangerous or menial. Perhaps their teasing was a way of dealing with the pressure, who knew? At any rate, he was proud of the team and happy to be their leader.

"And Jimmie ... " he raised his hand in the air, then pointed to a man sitting at a desk in the next row over, "Jimmie over there, our youngest team member, has prepared maps and driving directions for Miss Hauser to go shopping for wedding rings. Right, Jimmie?"

The man shook his head yes and stood up. "I have a packet of information all ready to go for her, boss. Everything but prices." He did a mock bow, acknowledging the recognition. "What? No applause? Please." He bowed again and everyone clapped.

"Evelyn?" Osborn raised up on his tiptoes to look at the tall blonde sitting at the end desk down from Jimmie.

She smiled, waiting.

"The Secret Service? They'll be there?"

"Yes, sir. Nine o'clock sharp at the hotel." She stood up. She was tall, about 5' 11". She never told anyone her weight, but it was not a concern to anyone but her. Osborn thought she had the figure of a Playboy model, and the looks of one as well. And everyone on the team knew that this tough cookie would not permit any of them to touch her other than in their dreams. So no one ever tried.

She glanced around the room at her fellow teammates. "They'll probably be late. They usually are when they're not with the President. But then, they're always late then, too. So," she shrugged, "they'll probably be late."

Osborn grinned. "Okay." He also looked around at each team member. "Everyone have a good night. I'll meet you all there at the hotel at nine tomorrow morning."

———————

Virk set his luggage down and extended his right hand. "Hammad, thank you for coming, but you did not have to meet me at the airport."

Malik replied, "I know. I wanted to. I want to talk about what is happening before we get into the city. You just have the two bags?"

"Yes, that's all. But I can manage them. It is all right. Please do not be concerned. Where do you want to talk?"

He motioned to the side. "When you fly from one city to another in America, you don't have to clear customs, so let's just sit down over here, by ourselves."

They moved to a row of seats by a back wall along a terminal concourse. It was quiet. No one walked anywhere close to them.

"What is it, Hammad?"

"Tell me, what did you think of New York?"

Virk nodded. "I now know why America will lose its future. I knew they were all infidels, but I did not know how bad it is here. Crazy people walk the streets. They're everywhere. Oh, I saw a few people who were not as bad — some businessmen and a few women who were dressed decent, by Western standards of course. I saw the same thing in Kabul. Near the University, the young people dress like they do in the west. The women have no covering. They wear short, tight clothing that shows their bodies. They color their faces and paint their fingernails. Then they stumble around in awkward shoes. Why do they do that? It makes no sense."

"I know, Fazil." Smiling, he continued. "It doesn't make any sense." His face changed to show he was serious. "But the Western world is rich, has technology, and they enjoy endless toys. They are all absorbed with themselves. They seek only their own pleasure and do not even try to understand the rest of the world." With a smirk, he added, "You are right. It will be their undoing."

"Hammad, some of the women barely conceal themselves. They walk down the street that way. Is that what a streetwalker is?"

"No. The women you saw show their bodies to draw attention or to get sex. A streetwalker is a prostitute who charges you for sex."

"I think I met one." He paused, glanced away then back. "A tall black woman wearing only part of an orange dress. But I did not understand her. She asked if I wanted to go around the world with her." He shook his head. "I told her I did not have time."

Malik laughed. "Fazil, she was asking if you wanted to have both oral sex and intercourse."

"I'm glad I didn't have time."

"Yes, me too." Malik shifted his weight on the uncomfortable chair. "Fazil, you did excellent work in New York. That gave us a good look at this Dr. Grant."

"That is my job."

"Yes. And it continues here." Malik looked around. "Ali called the airline and got the flight information for Grant."

"They gave it to him?"

Malik smiled. "He pretended to be Grant. He told them his travel secretary was to make arrangements, and he just wanted to confirm that everything was ready. They gave him the flight information. And they said there were two tickets. He's bringing someone with him."

"Yes. The student assistant at Columbia thought he may be taking his new fiancé on a trip."

"Then it is true. It could be good. That might keep a man in love distracted, no?"

"Yes, true. But we are not after him. If he does work for the American government, he will be trying to stop the same people we are."

"However, Fazil," Malik held up a finger, "he might lead us to them and make our job easier."

"I should have thought of that."

Again, Malik nodded. "Now, Fazil, I have a job for you. You see those big boards over there with the airplane information?

They tell you all about each flight, when it is scheduled to arrive, if it is on time, and which airport gate it will use."

"Okay. Yes, I see that."

"Here is the information about Grant's flight." He handed him a piece of paper folded in half.

Virk opened the note and read the information. "All right."

"You saw him on television. Do you think you could recognize him in person?"

He nodded. "Yes, I can. It would not be a problem."

"Excellent. I want you to be here tomorrow and watch for him. I want to know when he is here. I also want you to follow him to see where he goes."

"I will do that."

"Good. It is important that you are not seen. We do not want him to know he is being followed. Understand?"

"Yes, sir."

"I want to know who he meets and where he goes. You can reach me on this cell phone."

"A cell phone? I thought we were not to talk on cell phones."

"It will be all right to use this one. It cannot be traced very easily."

He handed Virk a prepaid cell. "Be brief. Just tell me the information. Do not discuss anything unless I ask. Is that clear?"

"Yes, sir. I will do that."

"Try to read this little book about the phone. I want you to take a picture of his woman so we all can see it. But, again, do not be obvious. If the time comes to surprise this Dr. Grant, we will do so. Until then, we do not want either of them to know you are there."

"Are you all packed, sweetheart?" Holding the phone to his ear, Stephen anticipated a wonderful weekend for the two of them. "I know I have business to start with, but that won't last all day. I'm really looking forward to dinner and our evening together tomorrow night."

"Me, too, Stephen." He could just imagine the gleam in Sheryl's eyes. He could tell she was smiling.

"Stephen, there is a nice restaurant in the hotel, isn't there?"

"Sure is. The hotel is a four star. It has several restaurants there in-house, including a fine dining restaurant featuring French food."

"Sounds delightful. Now I know just what to look for while I'm out shopping."

"What's that?"

"A beautiful, sexy cocktail dress. Probably black, but—well, we'll see. I have something special in mind. You'll like it, believe me. And you don't even have to wear a tux, just a nice suit and tie. But not the one you wear all day. It should be a fresh one, just for tomorrow night."

"Okay. I can do that. I'm getting ready to pack now. Let's not take too much, okay? I don't want to go broke tipping the bellman."

"Well ... all right. I'll limit my bags to what one car can hold."

"Yeah," he laughed. "You do that. I'll meet you at your place about 6:30. We'll take a cab to the airport."

Before starting to lay out his clothes for the trip, he had decided to relax with a glass of California Cabernet and call Sheryl. He enjoyed hearing her voice. They talked each evening now, sharing the day's events and expressing their love.

"I'll be sure that you're all set with everything you need tomorrow before I leave you. Do you want to go to the hotel first, or just shop till you drop, then find the hotel to recover?"

"I think I'll go shopping right from the airport. I'm eager to see a bunch of ring choices. I'm going to be choosy, you know. Then I have to find just the right dress."

"Sure you're up to it? Wandering around in a strange city all by yourself. There's a lot of guys out there that will be ready to help you, to give you a lift, to buy you a drink, to — do whatever they can."

She put her head back and laughed loudly. "I guess I'll just have to fight them all off. It'll be hard, but I think I can manage."

"I sure hope so. But then, you've had a little practice at that, haven't you?"

"Watch it, buddy. I'm not wearing your brand yet. If you'd get that ring on my finger fast, I wouldn't have to evade all those men. Without a ring, they'll all be crowding around me, you know."

"Don't I know it. I know how lucky I am, Sheryl. You don't have to candy coat it."

"All right. Just so you know. Oh, Stephen. Speaking of rings — what should I be looking for? Anything special?"

"I don't know, my darling. Do you want a big solitaire or something more fashionable?"

"Oh, that was put nicely." She was smiling. "As I think about it, perhaps one large solitaire —shall we say ten carats, or five? Or perhaps you just want a gazillion small chips glistening all over the platinum ring?"

"I think little carats are fine. I was thinking more along the lines of some twinkle, not a whole galaxy."

"Well, I like the whole galaxy, but — I suppose I could settle for just part of the Milky Way." She laughed again, playfully. "Seriously, what should I look for?"

"My most wonderful sweetheart, I would settle for whatever comes in the box of Cracker Jacks."

"Oooh. You're going to be sorry."

"Gold," he said firmly. "White or yellow, I don't care. You choose."

"And what if I like a colored diamond?"

"Sheryl, my dear, our love is pure — and clear. But if you want to add some color, then add it to the list. I just get to review the options before we choose. Okay?"

"Spoiled sport."

He broke into laughter. He loved her sense of humor. It made her that much more attractive. "Let's just make it a lot of fun. You find some you like, I'll narrow the list, then we can choose together. It'll be easy, just like choosing Chinese takeout for dinner."

"Yeah, sure. Just don't forget the soy sauce."

"Okay, my darling." He felt warm all over, thrilled with the love they shared. "I love you, Sheryl. I'll see you in the morning."

"Good night, Stephen. I love you, too. Just keep thinking about tomorrow. It will be a night you will never forget."

He sipped the hot tea, "Ahh," and leaned back in his chair. Like most Pakistanis, Kamran Khan enjoyed his tea. He found it relaxing and energizing at the same time. He closed his eyes and enjoyed the moment. Quiet, peaceful, he felt in touch with the blessings of nature all around him that Allah had provided.

Tariq, Umara, and Rana had gathered with Khan in the large living room of the home on Cedar Garden Road just outside Baltimore. It felt very open with a tall ceiling and light colored walls. Sunlight flooded the room. Along with the light gray carpet, it gave them a feeling of warmth and comfort.

Khan set his tea cup down on the small table beside his chair. "It has been long enough." He looked at Saleem, then Tariq and Umara. His dark, penetrating eyes appeared soft. "We know Leena will not be coming back." He bowed his head. "It is unfortunate that she must have died." He looked up at the others. "Otherwise she would have been here."

Using his thumb and forefinger, Khan stroked the sides of his bare, pointed chin. All the men had shaved off their beards and cut their hair before leaving Pakistan. It would help them blend in with the American crowd and not draw attention to themselves.

Reaching for his tea cup, Khan wore a sad smile. "I will miss her."

Turning back to the others, he proclaimed, "She was a good soldier. She died in service to Allah." Khan stared at them a moment, then shouted, "Allahu akbar!"

"Allahu!" the others replied in unison.

Silence filled the room as they sat there, remembering.

"We should continue with our plan," Khan announced. "We are here for a purpose." His mood seemed to change. He smiled. "The American conference for their Homeland Security starts Monday. We must be ready."

Everyone clapped their hands and cheered. "We will be!" Umara shouted.

"So," Khan said. "Everyone agrees. We continue."

Lowering his head, Khan studied the floor for a moment, then raised his head to look at the others. "As I said earlier, I want to be closer to the conference when the time comes. I will get a hotel room for us near the convention center and let you all know where it is. We will be moving everything there. It will be easier for us."

He continued. "Tariq, you rented a storage unit to hold our equipment. Is our stuff still there, ready to go?"

"Yes, Kamran. We still have to cut the plastic pipe and make the bombs, but everything else is ready. I rented an end unit next to the gate, so it will be easy to load our things. The storage area has a chain link fence around it. People can see through that fence, so I put everything in boxes. I will have to get a small truck or maybe a large pickup to have only one load."

"Good. You and Umara get our things tomorrow and take them to the hotel. I'll let you know where. Call Rana when you get there, and he will help you bring everything into the hotel room."

Saleem nodded.

"After I check into the hotel, I will walk around examining the convention center access points and other things. You and Umara wait there with Rana until I return. Then we can finish our plans."

Umara asked, "Do you really think all this is going to work?"

"Of course," Khan replied. "We just have to work out some details. We will review everything in total later." He pointed. "Tariq now works there. He will get us into the center. We will hide and wait until the proper time, then we will join the crowd."

He nodded enthusiastically, looked each one of them in the eye, then lowered his voice a little. "There will be three guest speakers for the conference Wednesday afternoon. The place will be filled with American dignitaries and community leaders. There will also be many people from the media. Television and radio will be broadcasting live."

He took a breath, and his eyes glazed over. He continued talking, staring into the distance. "Three special Americans, in their eyes, will talk to everyone. The Secretary of Homeland Security, the Secretary of State, and the President of the United States. When the President stands to give his speech, he will have no idea that it will be his very last speech ever."

A wide grin spread across his face. "This will be a perfect opportunity for us. All three of them will be on the stage at the same time, and we will kill them all."

CHAPTER 26

Osborn waived his hand above the airport crowd and called out, "Stephen, over here."

Dr. Stephen Grant smiled, nodded, and directed Sheryl in the proper direction.

Osborn extended his hand in greeting. "Good morning, Stephen. Glad you're here. Was the flight all right?"

Stephen shook his head. "Naw. It was pretty bad. I think we'll go back and do it over."

Osborn looked at him questioningly.

Stephen slapped him on the arm. "I'm just kidding. It was fine. Randy, I'd like you to meet my fiancé, Sheryl Hauser. Sheryl, this is Agent Randy Osborn."

He smiled and nodded toward her. "Nice to meet you, Miss Hauser."

"Call me Sheryl."

"Okay, Sheryl." He pointed to the man beside him. "This is agent Mike Borns." Osborn glanced at Stephen. "He's babysitting me for the day."

"Pleasure to meet you, Mike." Stephen laughed and shook hands.

Sheryl nodded and smiled. "Nice to meet you."

"Let's get away from this crowd and sort things out." He saw that Stephen carried two bags and Sheryl managed a smaller carry-on. "Is that all your baggage?"

"No." Having picked up his bags, Stephen motioned with his head toward the area behind him. "There's twelve porters back there somewhere, bringing the rest of hers."

Sheryl smacked Stephen on the arm. "There are not." She grinned at the FBI man. "There are only five."

Borns spoke up. "I can see what kind of day this is going to be." He nudged Stephen as they walked. "Is she always this way, Dr. Grant?"

"No." He shook his head. "Only during the daytime."

"I'm not going to touch that one."

"Better not," Sheryl responded. She reached over and took Stephen's arm with her free hand. Shaking her head, she said, "I'm better sometimes, aren't I, sweetheart?"

"Yes, dear. Sometimes you only require three porters."

They all laughed.

Osborn motioned to them. "Let's get back away from the crowd. Everyone's after their baggage right now."

They moved a few steps away. Stephen set his bags down, raised up and stretched his shoulders. Two men wearing sport shirts and slacks rushed from the crowd and bumped into Stephen, knocking him back a step. One of the men looked up at Stephen and shrugged. Both men hurried on without saying a word.

Stephen looked back at the crowd only a few feet away. Another man in a green, short-sleeved shirt approached, looking behind him as he walked, talking on a cell phone. He stopped about two feet from running into Stephen and turned to look forward. He immediately lowered his head, mumbled, "Sorry," stepped around Stephen and kept walking.

Another man in a red plaid shirt emerged from the crowd toward them, snapped his fingers as if he remembered something, then abruptly turned and headed back into the crowd of people.

Osborn said, "We better move further on down, away from everyone."

About twenty feet from everyone, Osborn spoke again. "Sheryl, we have reserved a car from Hertz for you. We'll all go with you to help you get settled. When you're all set, then we'll go on to our meeting. We'll be at the hotel where you are staying. There are directions for everything in this packet." He handed a brown envelope to her. "Do you have your cell?"

"In my purse."

"Great. And Stephen, you have yours?"

"Yes."

"So Sheryl, if you experience any problems, just call Stephen." He turned to Grant and smiled. "He might not be much help, but at least it's someone to talk to." He laughed.

Sheryl picked out a gray Ford Fusion, placed her carry-on bag in the trunk, studied the information packet with directions, asked a couple of questions, and off she went to search for newly discovered treasures.

As she pulled away from the curb, Stephen waved and turned back to the FBI men. The two men were leaning in toward each other, having a private discussion. Osborn almost whispered as he spoke to Mike Borns. Borns nodded, asked a few questions and nodded again. He turned and quickly walked away.

Osborn turned to Stephen and said, "Something has come up. Mike has to leave for awhile. He'll join us later at the hotel. Right now he has to hurry, so I told him to take the car. We'll take a cab to the hotel."

Arriving at the Hyatt Regency Baltimore, the taxi driver gave Stephen's two bags to the doorman and thanked the two men for using his cab. Osborn instructed the door man to leave the bags at the concierge desk, and they would get them later when they registered.

Stephen was impressed with the magnificent appearance of the hotel interior. The lobby had a high, recessed ceiling with a circle of indirect lighting softening the entrance. Oversize white tile highlighted by small black diamond shapes provided a spacious, open feeling. The semi-circle hotel desk of polished oak added a richness to the ambiance. The well-dressed hotel desk clerks all paused from their business to smile graciously at the two men as they walked past the desk and down the hall to the elevator.

"There are five conference rooms on the second floor. We have three of them at one end. Our meeting will be in the middle room. We have reserved the conference rooms on each side of it for privacy."

Stephen nodded.

Osborn added, "You'll find we have taken every precaution to ensure absolute secrecy for our meeting. I'll show you."

They walked into the conference room and found three men busy checking the ceiling, walls and electrical outlets. Osborn walked up to a short man in a tan suit. "Hi, Tom. How's everything looking?"

The man glanced past Osborn to Stephen. "Oh," Osborn responded. "This is Dr. Stephen Grant, our guest." He motioned to the man beside him. "This is Tom Bradford. He's one of our security experts."

Bradford looked back to Osborn. "Everything's in place. It's clean. We've checked for everything. No mikes, no cameras, no transmitters, no bugs of any kind. And we now have our new portable acoustic noise generator here and working. It's pretty cool. It projects noise around the room's perimeter, not directly into the room itself. This allows for conversation at normal levels while preventing eavesdropping devices that rely on acoustic leakage." He shrugged. "There are no windows, so that is not a problem. We are all secure, sir. You are ready to hold your meeting."

"Thanks, Tom." Osborn turned back to Stephen. "Let's sit down and talk a minute before everyone gets here." He motioned toward the far side of the conference table.

The room itself was fairly large, with two long conference tables sitting end-to-end in the middle of the room. Tables with black marble tops glistened, reflecting the recessed lights in the tall ceiling. Heavily padded tan leather chairs lined each side of the tables, providing room for 20 people. Each chair had the seat, back and arms molded together as one piece, then covered with leather and padding, almost like easy chairs.

Sitting down, the FBI agent spoke in a hushed voice. "I didn't want to worry you earlier, but you need to know. You are being followed."

Stephen's eyes lit up and his eyebrows raised. "How do you know? I didn't see anyone."

"That's because he's good — but not good enough. We spotted him at the airport. Do you remember a guy in a green shirt with a cell phone?"

"Yes. He, uh, almost bumped into me."

"That's him. He probably picked you up when you got your baggage, just before we met. I think he pretended to talk on the cell phone so he could get close enough to you. He took your picture." Osborn nodded. "Got a pretty good close-up."

Stephen frowned. "Why would anyone want to follow me? Are you sure it's me, and not Sheryl?"

"Yes. He stayed with us rather than follow her when she left the airport. I don't think there's anyone else following her."

"I hope not," Stephen exclaimed.

"Sorry, but I didn't have enough people ready to dispatch. She does have a cell phone. We'll tell her once she's back. Try not to worry, I don't think she is a target. But you —" he pointed at Stephen, "You're a different story."

Stephen sighed. "You're sure? Sure I'm being followed?"

"Yes. I'm sorry. We watched him at the airport taking several pictures of both you and Sheryl with his cell phone. He must have needed confirmation that he'd identified the correct target."

"Why do you keep calling me a target? That's rather scary."

"Figure of speech. Just a term for someone you want followed."

Stephen became nervous. "Do you think he's here in the hotel now?"

"Not yet. But he probably will be soon. I have a man in the lobby watching for him."

"What would they want with me?"

"Damned if I know. But we're going to find out who he is and what he wants. Mike began shadowing him at the airport and has been following him ever since. We're using all our contacts now to find out who he is. Maybe that will tell us what he wants."

Swallowing hard, Stephen said, "So I'm just a sitting duck, a ... a target until he does something. Randy," Stephen reached over and put his hand on Osborn's shoulder. "I was shot at, remember, at Central Park. They missed. Maybe someone is out there who wants me dead. This guy might not miss again."

"You need to calm down, Stephen. We don't know what this guy wants. But we are following him. We will keep him in sight, and react if needed, before he can do anything to hurt you."

"So in the meantime ..."

"In the meantime, you go on with business as normal."

"I'm not sure any of this is normal. That's why we're here."

Osborn gave Stephen a knowing smile. "You'll be fine."

CHAPTER 27

"Ali, Fazil called and said they are here. Grant and his woman. He took pictures of both of them. He'll send the photos to us in a few minutes."

"He does good work."

"Yes, he does. He said the woman picked up a gray Ford rental car and left the airport by herself. Grant was met by two men in suits. One of them left. He's not sure where he went, but he's gone. Fazil followed Grant and the other man to a hotel here in town. They're at the Hyatt Regency Baltimore."

"If I remember right, from studying the map, that is close to the convention center where the conference will be held."

"Yes. I think you're right." He paused, thinking. "I think I'll tell Fazil to stay with them, or at least with Grant, and see where that leads. How are you doing on your search of the hotels?"

"Nothing so far, but I still have several to call this morning."

"Start with that hotel, the Hyatt Regency Baltimore. See if they have anything."

"Okay. I will do so. Then to call the rest, I will work off the map and call the hotels closest to the convention center first."

"Yes. Do that. I'll continue my check on the employer database. We should find something soon."

Both men used laptops to continue their searches. Malik sipped a cup of hot tea while searching. He was becoming nervous and irritable. Their searches had not discovered any promising leads at all so far.

Malik believed the American Homeland Security Conference had to be the place where the terrorist group planned to strike. It was the only time and place that made sense, especially given the timing of the recent restaurant bombing and the shooting in Central Park.

Central Park? he thought. *He missed the American. He would not have done that on purpose.* He thought about it a minute. *It was the fourth shot. Maybe the barrel on the sniper rifle got too hot. Maybe it warped just enough to make the shooter miss his target. Maybe.* He shrugged.

He kept the computer cursor moving down the screen, one line at a time. Still nothing. No one with a Mexican passport.

Maybe the shooter became nervous, he thought. *It was his fourth shot. Between being excited, and feeling the pressure to shoot and get away before being caught, might have been enough to make him miss the last shot. Now that I think about it, he did not try again after that.* He shook his head. *Maybe that was it.*

His cell phone chirped. Checking, he discovered Fazil had sent the photos of Grant and the woman. "Ali, check your phone. The pictures are here."

Malik examined the photos carefully. The pictures of Grant matched the man on the television. No doubt that was him. The woman was a very pretty blonde. He wondered why she was there. *If Grant is working with the government trying to catch these terrorists, why would he bring her along with him?*

Ali spoke up. "At least now we can recognize them when we see them. That will help if they do get close to our group of Pakistanis. Perhaps we will have an opportunity to kill all of them, the Americans included. That would be good, Hammad."

"It could happen, but our mission is not to hurt the Americans." He put his tea down.

"We must stop our brothers in arms from causing more violence that would hurt the flow of secret information to our government. Remember, Ali. Strange as it seems, our mission is against our own brothers. It is truly a crazy world."

"Yes," Ali answered. "It is all mixed up and makes no sense." He shook his head. "But sometimes governments make no sense."

"How right you are." Malik continued searching his computer.

After some time, Malik stood up and stretched. "I need some more tea. How about you, Ali?"

"Yes, I will make some more for us. How is your search progressing? I have three possibilities so far."

"That's good. I found four people recently hired with Mexican passports." He made a sour expression with his mouth. "One of them is a Lopez who was hired at a supermarket. I do not think it could be him. But that still leaves three for me to check out. You said you also have three possibilities?"

"Yes. Since we do not know what name our brothers used, it could be any of them. I will have to check on each of them. It is good we were given a picture of Kamran Khan from the ISI files. I can show that to the desk clerks. Maybe they can recognize him."

"If it *was* him and not one of the others."

"That is true. But I must check each one. We could get lucky."

"Yes. We have to. Something will turn up. You'll see." He looked back down at this computer. "What's this?"

His face showed surprise as he scanned the information on the laptop screen. He frowned and read it again. "Here is one that just showed up."

"What is it?"

Malik clicked on the listing to bring up more information. "Here is a Tariq Gorshani. It says he came to America from Mexico." He paused, continuing to read. "And listen to this. He was hired as a security guard for the Baltimore Convention Center." He jumped up. "That's it! I found him." He glanced at Ali. "It has to be him. It's too perfect." Malik bent over slightly and rubbed his hands together. "This is him."

"Good. Good. Is there an address for him?"

"Let's see." Malik scrolled down, read more information, scrolled down some more and continued reading. "Yes!" He became excited. "I've got it!" He reached for a tablet and pen and wrote the address down. "I will look this up on the Internet to see where it is." He started dancing around the room like a child on his birthday who just received his present.

"Ali," Malik tried to calm himself, "you said you have three possibilities?"

152

"Yes, Hammad."

"Excellent. Go to those places. Take the picture with you and see what you can discover."

Jubilance overtook him. "We are going to get these guys, Ali. We're going to get them and stop them." He shook his head. "They won't be killing many more people here."

"Kamran, I rented a cargo van."

"Excellent. I'm happy you did not steal one. If the police are looking for a stolen vehicle, they might see you with it. We don't want their attention."

"Yes," Tariq nodded. "That's true. Okay, Umara and I are on our way to the storage unit."

"Good. Rana and I just checked into the hotel. We have two adjoining rooms at the Embassy Suites Downtown on St. Paul Place. It should be perfect. Both our rooms have a small kitchen with a stove, microwave and refrigerator. We can stay here and be very comfortable. It is just five blocks from the convention center It will be easy to go back and forth."

He paused, taking a breath. "We're on the fourth floor, but it is only two rooms away from the elevator. Let us know once you're here. I will wait until you arrive. I can go out to examine the convention center access later."

"Oh, Tariq?"

"Yes, Kamran."

"We will come down to help you. There are a couple of luggage carts in the lobby We can use those to bring everything up to our rooms."

"Okay. It will take some time to get to the storage unit and load everything into the van. I'll call you when we get there."

Excited, Khan held the phone to his ear with his shoulder and rubbed his palms together. "This is so perfect. We are going to do this, Tariq. We are going to do it. No one can stop us now."

CHAPTER 28

"Evelyn, you were right. The Secret Service is late, as usual. Would you wait outside in the hallway for them?"

"Sure, boss."

"Just bring them in when they get here. Don't knock or anything, just come on in. There are others out there to take care of security."

"Will do."

Osborn turned to Stephen. "I'd like to have you sit next to me near the middle of the room, so everyone can hear what you have to say."

"Be happy to."

Osborn raised his voice slightly. "Please, everyone. Get your coffee or juice and sit down. We need to get started."

After everyone was seated, the introductions started. Five of the FBI team were present. Osborn and Bill Anderson sat at the table, and three others sat in chairs back along the wall. Evelyn waited outside the room and Mike was on assignment. Osborn told Stephen before the meeting that the man following him was in the hotel. He also told Stephen that Agent Borns had that man under surveillance.

Seated at the table were people from the Defense Intelligence Agency, National Security Agency, Central Intelligence Agency, Homeland Security, one person from the Department of Defense, and one from Army Intelligence. The room was filled.

Before completing the introductions, Evelyn entered the room with two men.

"I'd like you all to meet Ed Janson and Maury Gold, with the Secret Service." The three of them took chairs around the end of the table.

Gary Fuller

Osborn pointed to Stephen, "This is Dr. Stephen Grant, our special guest. You've heard me talk about him. He is considered an expert on Middle East Affairs and does ad hoc work for our government from time to time, helping with international agreements and treaties. He was part of the delegation responsible for negotiating the Status of Forces Agreement with Iraq. He does hold a top secret clearance, so we can all talk freely about our subject today."

"Thank you, everyone," Osborn continued, "for meeting here in Baltimore. We have all agreed that we may be facing a terrorist attack of some sort in the near future. Since the Annual Conference for Homeland Security is the only major event in the immediate future, and given that our President and several cabinet members will be present, we consider this event a likely target for such an attack."

He paused and sipped his coffee. "Please, each of you, take time to go over to the convention center and explore any idea that comes to mind. There is an over-the-street enclosed walkway, so getting there should not be a problem."

He took a big drink of coffee and made a face. "One day hotels will learn how to make decent coffee." He pushed his cup away from him. "First, let's discuss more about who these terrorists might be. That may help us identify how they have operated in the past, and possibly the type of attack we can expect." He glanced around the table. "Who wants to go first?"

A woman from Homeland Security raised her hand and started speaking. "I think we should look at Al-Qaeda. Everything points to Pakistan as the source. Al-Qaeda has a strong base there, and they're the obvious choice."

FBI Agent Bill Anderson spoke up. "It's true that the two bodies we have are Pakistani. But that doesn't mean the whole group is from Pakistan."

The NSA representative spoke up. "What about ISIS? Aren't they saying their black flag is going to fly over the White House?"

"Yes, what about that?" inquired a DIA man.

"Dr. Grant," the woman from Homeland Security asked, "What do you think? Could it be ISIS?"

155

Stephen shook his head. "That's a very remote possibility. They would like it to happen, but they have their hands full where they are. They're not ready to promote an actual attack here."

The Homeland Security woman continued to press. "Then what about this Khorsani group? They're Al-Qaeda, aren't they?"

Stephen took a breath. "Yes, Khorsani is affiliated with Al-Qaeda. They follow the same philosophy. They do want to unleash an attack against a Western country. But here again, they are largely a Syrian organization. I don't believe they're involved in our present situation. The two bodies we have tied to the events here that we are discussing are Pakistani."

Someone else said, "We don't even know how many people are involved."

A CIA man answered, "Most terrorist cells contain five or six people."

FBI Agent Jimmie Clark, seated in the back along the wall, spoke up. "We did have one incident with ten people, but that was unusual."

Osborn spoke up. "Let's take another look at what we *do* know." He held up one finger. "We have a Pakistani body discovered in South Carolina on a half-sunken yacht chartered out of Cuba."

He held up two fingers. "Tire tracks from there match a stolen car from Baltimore that was left in the parking lot of a motel in Fayetteville, South Carolina."

He held up three fingers. "Another car was stolen from that same parking lot, then later discovered in New York."

Four fingers. "A Pakistani woman trying to take that car and drive it, pulled a gun and tried to shoot several people, including police officers. She was killed in the shoot-out."

Five fingers. "Between the time the car was stolen in South Carolina and when it was discovered in New York, two other incidents happened there. The bombing of a restaurant, and the shooting in Central Park. Are those two items related?" He shrugged. "Could be."

Anderson added, "We now know the bullets used in the shooting were .338 Lapua Magnum. That's a special American made ammunition used for long-distance shooting. It's not popular yet and a bit unusual."

Several people shook their heads, while others just listened.

Anderson continued. "We did find two sporting goods stores in the New York area that sold some a few days before the shooting. Both stores sold only two boxes. And both stores sold the shells to the same man. A dark-complexioned, Middle Eastern man named Rana Saleem."

One of the NSA men offered, "That's a Pakistani name."

"I think it's the Muslim Brotherhood," Ed Janson, Secret Service, said, pointing his finger in the air.

"What makes you think *that*?" asked the Homeland Security woman.

"That's Egyptian," responded a DIA man.

"I read there's a lot of them in Pakistan." Janson was not about to let it drop.

Someone asked, "What do you think, Dr. Grant?"

Stephen pressed his lips together and took a deep breath. "The Muslim Brotherhood is not just Egyptian. They have followers, members actually, all over the Middle East." He looked over at Janson. "And there *is* a pretty large group of them in Pakistan."

"Yes," offered the CIA rep. "But there are a lot of terrorist type groups in Pakistan. In addition to Al-Qaeda, there's the Pakistan Taliban, the Lashkar-e-Taiba, Jaish-e-Mohammed, and the Hizbul Mujahideen."

The DIA man said, "Pakistan has one of the largest terrorist areas in the world. Pakistan's ISI helps sponsor a lot of groups we consider to be terrorists. The center of it all is the northwestern border area of the country. It's very rugged mountain terrain and provides ideal locations for training, and lots of places for seclusion and hiding. There have been more drone strikes there than anywhere else. It is even off limits to foreigners. They would be killed on sight."

"Another group," the NSA man said, "is the Harakat ul-Mujahidin."

"Never heard of them," the Homeland Security woman responded.

"They're real," the NSA man continued. "We know that their leader, Khalil, lives in an Islamabad suburb, Galra Sharif. It's situated near the Margalla Hills in the Islamabad Capital Territory."

Stephen spoke up. "They were formed in the early 1990s, originally known as the Harakat al-Ansar. Their primary goal is to unite Kashmir with Pakistan. They have not had any overt activities directly against the United States, but their new leader, Farooq Khalil, did have links to Osama bin Laden. Supposedly he signed bin Laden's fatwah calling for attacks on the U.S. and Western interests. All in all, I don't think they are really a player here."

Janson raised his point again. "What about the Muslim Brotherhood?"

Stephen responded, "I don't think it would have been them, but we cannot rule them out. The motto of the Muslim Brotherhood is, and I quote, 'Allah is our objective; The Quran is our law; the Prophet is our leader; Jihad is our way; and dying in the way of Allah is the highest form of our aspirations.'"

"Wow," offered Osborn. "That's quite a statement."

"I'm telling you, it's the Muslim Brotherhood," Janson firmly answered.

The Army Intelligence Officer added a thought. "The Brotherhood is certainly capable, but they have not been active outside the Middle East. We have no information that would lead us to believe they are ready for any activity here in the West."

"So, Dr. Grant," the Homeland Security woman said, "what do you really think? Do you have any ideas on who this might be?"

He pushed his cup of cold coffee away from him. "I've been reviewing all this in my mind while we've been discussing it. Like Randy, here, said, we need to take a close look at what we *do* know. There are some additional pieces of information to consider."

He glanced around the room, which had become very quiet. "It has been several days since the bombing and shootings in New York. No one has claimed credit for either of those events." He nodded. "That's unusual."

Several people shook their heads. One person whispered, "He's right."

Stephen waited a minute, then continued. "I think what we may have here is a small splinter group or an independent group, acting on their own. They may be trying to make a name for themselves, become known, and thereby get the recognition needed to be invited to join one of these other organizations. Or they could be seeking revenge for some unknown grievance that affected their lives. Remember, it is common in the Arab culture to harbor revenge and plan for retaliation that might come sometime later."

Several murmurs filled the air. People nodded and whispered. Osborn said, "Please continue, Dr. Grant."

Stephen replied. "They could receive additional funding from one of these other groups. They may *already* have received some financing from an organization, or from several individuals with similar beliefs."

He paused to let the others consider this. Continuing, he added, "If this is an independent group, they will not stop with their previous activities. It will not be enough. Even if their cause was revenge, they will still want one last major event — the coup d'état."

There were a few gasps and gulps, raised eyebrows and wide eyes. Everyone's attention was riveted on Grant.

"It will be big. Big enough to draw international attention. They will want the world to know about it, especially the people back home in Pakistan." His fist pounded the table. "This conference, with the President, cabinet members and various dignitaries attending, presents the type event they will be seeking. This is probably their target. And if they are an independent group, the only history we have to go on is what happened in New York."

The room was quiet for a couple of minutes. Finally Osborn spoke to the others. "So how do we prepare, people?"

Janson, from the Secret Service, offered, "We know they used bombs and bullets. We have to prepare for that. I will be sure we have bomb people and trained dogs to sniff for explosives."

The other Secret Service man, Maury Gold, asked, "So how do we control guns?"

Bill Anderson, FBI, said, "We'll have metal detectors at all the entrances. But we definitely have to control both entry and exit to the center, to the entire area where meetings will be held and dignitaries are talking. We'll need to seal off most of the center."

Janson added, "We will have people monitoring the computerized entry areas. Badges will be required to open the doors for security and staff to enter the building at the locations not used by the public. The computer system in the security office will give us a full accounting. We can identify who opened what door, when, and how long it was open. We'll need a couple people to work with building security to monitor that."

"Good." Anderson said. He turned back to the FBI men seated along the wall. "What about the loading dock area?"

Don Ellis responded, "We'll need to keep a team there the entire time. We'd better be in position well ahead of the time required. Can we get a list of any scheduled deliveries during that time?"

Janson spoke up. "That has to be controlled. No deliveries during the main hours. All required deliveries can be made before or after the conference hours. But you need your team there the whole time. You'll need to monitor those deliveries closely and be sure the docks are guarded properly when they're closed."

"Right. We can do that," Ellis answered.

"Okay," Janson said. "We already have a list of the staff and have checked everyone out. I don't anticipate any problems there, but we will have people monitoring all their activities. That's just normal protocol."

"Do you have a list of guests and the hosts that will be greeting or escorting them?" Osborn inquired.

"Yes," Gold answered. "We have that covered. We will instruct the hosts on the standard procedures and paths to use during the conference. Not a problem."

"And, of course," Janson added, "We'll have our standard compliment of agents around the President and at various locations throughout the conference area. They'll be monitoring the crowd as usual."

"Do you want any extra help?" Osborn asked. "I can have additional agents at your disposal."

"Let's keep them in reserve. Have them present, but out of the way. I'll let you know where we will need them, if we do."

"Sounds good. I'll have ten agents here before the place opens. You can use them however you think is needed."

Osborn turned and looked around the room. "What are we missing? Anything?"

Ellis asked, "What about the coordination with the convention center security people?"

Janson answered, "We've already had one meeting with them, plus a couple with the Director of Security. Their entire security force will be on duty. There are 84 officers, five shift leaders, the Director and two assistants. We will have one last meeting with them the morning of the conference. I think we're good there."

"Anything else?" Osborn took a deep breath. "This is a big one, people. With the President and others here, we can't afford to blow it. We'll take a break for lunch. Get over to the convention center and scout it out. Check everything. Make notes. Then we'll meet back here at three o'clock for a final review. Have your questions and concerns ready for that time. Okay?"

There were murmurs as people stirred.

"Stephen, why don't you have lunch with my group, then you and I can walk around the center ourselves and see what we can find?"

"Great."

"Okay. See everyone back here at three."

CHAPTER 29

"Mind if I join you two for a walk around?" Janson asked. "I'd like to go through the whole place to be sure we both understand the total picture. Okay?"

"Sure," replied Osborn. "That'll be good for both of us, and it will give Stephen a feel for everything."

The three men took the enclosed over-the-street walkway from the hotel to the convention center. Osborn described everything as they went through the various areas.

"This walkway joins the convention center on level 2. Here, as we enter," he pointed to his left, "is an elevator to take people downstairs. As all the delegates come into the center, they will be directed downstairs for registration. They will exchange their ticket for a badge to clip on their clothing, or they can use the cord and wear it around their neck. There will be several registration desks downstairs."

"How many delegates are coming?" asked Stephen.

"Eighteen hundred and fifty."

"Wow, That's a bunch."

"Yes. This is a pretty large conference. There are also ninety-two convention center security personnel, two hundred twenty staff members for the conference, plus ten convention center office personnel."

"We have all those people identified for us, right, Randy?" Janson asked.

"Yes. They are all on the lists that were given to your people and mine."

"Good. So they should all have been given at least a cursory check."

"Yes." They continued walking. "Over here to the left is the Sharp Street entrance. The lobby here will not be functioning. We will check for tickets and direct people through to the elevator over there on the right, to take them downstairs for registration."

They continued walking. "This is the mezzanine level. From this vantage point, you can see over the entire vendor area below."

"That area over there across the opening is the Pratt Street entrance. The only thing there is the elevator. Again, we'll have people at every entrance checking tickets and directing people downstairs. Further down here on the left is the Otterbein entrance and lobby, which will be closed during the conference."

"The conference center offices are further back to the left, behind those double doors. The offices will be manned, but they will not be seeing any visitors during the conference. The security office is also back behind those doors, off to the other side. There will be some traffic to the security office, but it should only be our own people. Let's go down to the first level."

Getting off the elevator, Osborn moved to the right. "This level is for registration and vendor displays. Ninety-three vendors will be displaying their wares. They have all been vetted to be sure they are legitimate dealers for the various products they will be showing. Back over here, the other side of the partition," they kept walking, "This area here in front of us is designated area A on the map. It will be one of the registration stations. To our left is the Charles Street entrance, which will be combined with this area to accommodate registering delegates. On the other end of the vendor area is the Swing Space and section F. You can see those on the map. That will be the other registration station. There's almost 100,000 square feet there, so we will have a lot of tables to help speed up the registration process."

He turned to look at them. "Once delegates have their badges, they are free to wander through the vendor area at their leisure or go directly to the third level, where the conference will be held. Shall we go up?"

As the elevator arrived at the third floor, the FBI supervisor continued his description. "This is where the actual conference will be held." The elevator door opened and they stepped out.

"All the room dividers and partitions you see will be removed for the conference. Here at the south end of the hall, tables and chairs will be set up for lunch. The President and his cabinet members will not be eating while here. This area will be for special guests and dignitaries, and a limited number of delegates selected ahead of time, who will be given special passes. Everyone else will eat upstairs in the ballroom area."

Osborn had them follow as he walked toward the north end of the building, where the room became one very large open space, narrowing slightly as it continued around a corner to their left. "You can see this area expands. This is where the main conference will take place. There will be a couple of small meetings upstairs that will only last an hour or so each morning, then those people will join the main conference here in time for the start of the general activities. All the delegates will be here for opening day, the day our President and the others will be making their appearances. This is where it will all happen."

He guided them to his left, past the service area. "This area is where the stage will be set. It will be a raised platform large enough to hold fourteen people seated behind the speaker's area. In the front will be a large podium with multiple microphones and teleprompters."

"How will the seats be arranged?" asked Janson.

"We have comfortable padded chairs for everyone. There will be sections of ten rows, ten seats across. Aisles between, in front and behind each section will be six feet wide to accommodate people moving to their seats. You can see the space is shaped like a funnel and widens toward the back. We will add additional sections back there until we have enough seats. There is more than enough room to seat everyone in here."

"Well planned," said Janson. "I like it. You did a good job."

"I wish I could take all the credit, but it wasn't just me. The people here at the center helped me design the arrangement."

"Well, it is a good job planning it all out," said Stephen. "Looks like it should work fine."

Osborn pointed to various spots around the large open area. "Restrooms are spaced all around the area, enough to support this large of a crowd."

He nodded at them. "That just leaves the dining area upstairs. Do you want to see it?"

"Yes." answered Janson. "Let's see the whole thing while we're at it."

Getting off the elevator, Osborn told them, "The only way up here are the elevators and two back stairways. There are no outside entrances."

They started walking through the area. Several tables had been set up, scattered around the open area in no particular pattern, each table prepared to seat eight people.

"Tables will be set up all though this area," he motioned, waving his hand, "but we will be seating ten people per table. This whole room will be completely filled with tables."

He paused, suddenly appearing out of breath. Looking down, he put his hand on one of the tables to steady himself. Flushed, he looked up at the other two men. "They ... they'll be much closer together, of course. We need to feed ... a lot of people ... to feed ... in a short time."

"Randy," Stephen asked, "are you all right?"

"I think I — "

Janson grabbed a chair and pulled it over for Osborn to sit down. "Here, Randy. Sit."

Osborn slid down onto the chair and inhaled deeply. He gazed up at the two men sheepishly. "I'm sorry, guys. I need a minute to gather myself."

Both Stephen and Agent Janson pulled chairs around and sat facing Osborn. Janson said, "Take your time, Randy. It's okay."

Stephen inquired, "Do you need anything?"

Osborn slowly shook his head. "No. It's nothing physical. Just an old memory overtaking me." He turned to Janson. "You said you would have some bomb demolition people and dogs here for the conference, right?"

Frowning, Janson replied, "Yes. I'll have a full crew standing by, here on-site." He turned his head slightly and looked at Osborn out of the corner of his eyes. "Why? What is it, Randy?"

Osborn remained flush and appeared to struggle getting his breath. He pressed his lips together and shook his head. "I'm sorry. Sometimes this gets the best of me."

The two men waited, giving Osborn time to catch his breath and recover.

A couple of minutes passed, then a grim smile spread across Osborn's face. He looked up at the other two men. "I know you both can understand this. Something happened, some time ago, and once in awhile the memory just hits me and knocks me for a loop."

Stephen sat quietly, and Janson asked softly, "Care to tell us about it, Randy?"

"I don't talk about it much." His facial expression became very serious. "Don't either of you say anything about this to my team. They don't need to know."

"Oh-kay," Janson replied in a low, soft voice.

"Four years ago, in Tel Aviv," he began. "I was the station chief for the FBI's small chapter assigned to work with the Israelis." He looked off to the side, into the distance, remembering. The two men gave him time, allowing him to gather his thoughts.

"There had been an incident with a member of the Knesset, Israel's legislature. He was a member of the standing Ethics Committee," Osborn forced a laugh, "and he had a big gambling debt. The man he owed the money to, an Arab, threatened to kidnap his family if he didn't pay up. They got into a fight and the Israeli shot one of the Arab's bodyguards, who was an American. I had to drive down to Jerusalem to interview everyone."

He shook his head. "I had promised my wife and daughter that I would take the afternoon off and meet them for lunch." Osborn looked at Janson, then over at Stephen. "I had been working overtime and didn't have a chance to spend much time with them."

Tears appeared at the corner of his eyes, now turning red, and started slipping down over his cheeks. "My wife wanted to share some ... magical moments, as she called them, with me and our daughter, so I promised." He paused, swallowing hard. "I was supposed to meet them at Eden House, a bistro sidewalk cafe on Yishkon Street, tucked away a little off the main road to the Tel

Aviv beach." Grimacing, he lowered his head to stare at the floor. "It should have been a quiet, beautiful afternoon."

Sitting up, he raised his head to look at them both. "I was late getting there." He shook his head, looking at them, searching for understanding. "I had to park the car a little ways away and walk to the restaurant. I remember it was so busy. People were sitting outside at tables on the sidewalk. I was hurrying to the door. I didn't see them, they had a table inside the cafe."

Looking from one man to the other, Osborn broke down. He started crying. "I just got to the door when it happened." His voice became so low, it almost left him. He could hardly speak. "The bomb exploded with a flash and a loud roar. Windows were blown out, and I was thrown backward and landed flat on the ground. I couldn't think at first. I just laid there a few minutes, then I realized my family was inside."

He stared at them, unblinking, tears streaming down his face as he spoke. "They were inside the cafe."

He stopped crying and struggled to get a breath.

"I managed to get inside, but couldn't see, with all the smoke and dust. Most everything was black and charred, tables turned over," he motioned with his hand, "parts of chairs everywhere. I can still hear some of the screams." The look in his red eyes changed as he looked up and into the distance, away from the others. "And the people moaning."

His voice drifted away and he became quiet. Pain etched itself across his face. His lips quivered. Tears appeared again in his bloodshot eyes and flooded his cheeks. And again he looked into their eyes, searching for understanding.

"I remember I started walking," he paused, sucked in air, and swallowed, "searching." Shaking his head, he tried to smile but couldn't make it. "I called out to them. Sally?" His blank look couldn't stop the tears. "Sally? Where are you? Linda, baby? Are you here? Are you okay?"

He dropped his head into hands, sobbing, losing control to the emotions, and started shaking. Stephen reached out and put his hand on Osborn's shoulder.

After a moment, Osborn regained some composure and raised up in his chair. He looked at Janson, then Stephen, and lost it again. With his head in his hands, he managed, "All I could find ... were pieces. Pieces! An arm. A hand." Raising his palms, he extended his arms toward the other two men. "Pieces of my family. That's all that was left."

The sobs continued. Then, finally, after a few more moments, Osborn raised his head to look around. "I'm sorry. Sometimes it just hits me and I lose it. I'm sorry, guys."

Stephen kept his hand on Osborn's shoulder. Janson nodded and said, "It's okay, Randy. It's okay."

Osborn managed to stand, trying to regain control of himself. "Sometimes, when I think about bombs and what they can do, I think of that damned suicide bomber and what he did to my family."

Pulling a handkerchief from his back pocket, he wiped his face and tried to smile. Janson and Stephen both nodded their understanding.

After another few minutes, Osborn stood up straight and pulled his shoulders back. Looking at the two men, he said, "Don't you dare tell my team about this. They can't see any weakness in me. They have to think I'm strong, as their leader. Understand?"

Again, both men nodded. Janson patted Osborn on the back. "It'll be our secret."

Osborn smiled. He stretched out his arm, pointing. "The kitchen is back on the left, over there." He took a deep breath. "Meals will be banquet style, of course. Most of the food will be prepared ahead of time, and be ready for serving as the delegates arrive. The staff will be ready and the meals will be served quickly."

He stood in the middle of the room with them. "Any questions?"

"No. Thank you, Randy. And thanks for sharing with us," Janson said. "You and your people have done a great job getting ready for this. It seems you have everything covered. I just hope it all goes well, without any problems." He smirked. "But that's what we're here for, right?"

"Yes. It is." Osborn shook his head.

"Indeed," Stephen added. "A superb job." He smiled. "It's just too bad I won't be here to join you."

CHAPTER 30

Although he felt like running, Malik walked through the underground parking area of the Hyatt Regency Baltimore Hotel at a normal pace. He didn't think anyone was watching him. There was no reason to believe otherwise. *No one even knows me and my team are here, so why would they?*

Finally he reached the car, opened the passenger door and slid in beside Ali. He nodded his head. "All set. Let's go."

Ali put the car in gear, eased out of the parking space and out the building exit. He turned right onto Light Street and merged with the traffic.

"You have the address and the directions?" Ali asked.

"Yes. I wrote the address down from the employer database. I got the directions off MapQuest." He breathed heavily, trying to get his nerves to relax. "Go another three blocks, then turn right and go straight. We want to get on Interstate 83 North."

"Got it," Ali responded.

The ISI men had used the American computer system for registering foreign workers to locate and track the group of people from their home country of Pakistan. Malik had an unhappy smile. "They are considered terrorists here, just because they want to kill some infidels. The Prophet teaches us that is what we should do. If we can, convert them. If we cannot, then kill them. The infidels must change or die. That is what is written."

He took a deep breath. "It is unfortunate that our job, our mission, is to prevent our brothers from doing what they have been taught, what they know is correct." He shook his head. "We are to find and kill our own countrymen, and keep the American infidels alive. What a terrible task we have been given." He sighed again. "I guess that is our job, is it not?"

"Yes, it is. But it does not seem right. Yet we do what we have been instructed to do."

"I guess we don't have to like it." Malik pursed his lips and continued shaking his head. "It is too bad we cannot let them kill the President of the United States. That would really shake everything up. Then both America and Israel would fear us. That is the way it should be."

"I told Fazil to continue watching Grant," Malik continued, looking down at his map, checking for the entrance to the Interstate. "Fazil said Grant has been meeting with the FBI and several other government officials. They talked for a long time, then went over to the convention center, apparently to check it all out. They're back in the meeting room now."

"Here's the Interstate." Ali completed the turn and merged with the higher speed traffic on the highway. "How far do we go?"

"About thirteen or fourteen kilometers. Oh, with this car, about five miles. I forgot this is America. They don't use kilometers like the rest of the world."

"America truly is in its own world, isn't it, Hammad?"

"I guess so," he replied, looking out the side window. "They have so much here, they must think they can do whatever they want. And in most cases, they get away with it."

"At least for now. The time will come that this world will change."

"I hope so, Ali. I hope so."

They continued driving for a couple of minutes, then Malik said, "Watch for Exit 10A, Northern Parkway East. When we get there, we take the exit, then have a quick turn back onto West Northern Parkway. We'll follow that for a few kilometers, or rather a couple of miles."

"Okay. There is the exit up ahead. Help me find the next turn."

"Yes." It only took a moment. "There it is on the left. See it?"

"Here we go." He made the turn and headed west. "Now how far?"

"Just over two miles. We go to York Road, or Maryland Highway 45. That'll be a left turn."

Soon they were traveling down York Road, looking for Cedar Avenue. "It hasn't been too bad of a trip," Ali offered.

"Not at all. You are a good driver for American roads. You do well."

"Thank you, Hammad."

"You did put the guns in the trunk, didn't you?"

"Yes, they are there. Loaded and ready to go."

"We'll drive by the house to be sure which one it is, and to see what we can. Let's park about three houses away from them and return on foot. Let's hope they're home."

"And let's hope no one else bothers us. I'd like to be done with this and get out of here quickly."

"Here's Cedar Avenue. Turn right and go slow, Ali. I need to see the house numbers."

"You're sure this is the right address? It seems like they are staying a long way from the convention center."

"Maybe they didn't want anyone to see them. I know we're ten miles from downtown, but maybe that was their plan. Who knows?"

"If there's no car there, will we still try to get into the house?"

"Of course. Even if the car is not there, someone could be inside the house. And if not, I want to be sure there are some clothes there, or something that tells us that is where they are staying. We can always come back later to kill them. We just need to do that before the convention to complete our mission."

"I know. But if they're not home, let's come back at night. It will be easy when we know where the house is. I'd much rather try to find and kill them in the dark, when they cannot see us so well."

"True. But they are not expecting us, anyway. So whenever we catch them, it should work to our favor."

"Slow down a little more. The houses sit back from the road, and some of these numbers are hard to read."

The car slowed and the two men searched both sides of the road. "What's the number again?"

"1381. 1381 Cedar Avenue."

"Well, we're on Cedar Avenue. It must be further ahead a little."

The car kept going.

"Nothing here. These numbers are too low. Keep going."

"We're out of road. They're not here."

"Turn right and go down a block. We'll turn and go around a block or two, and see if the road resumes on the other side of this property."

"Okay." They did, but Cedar Avenue was not to be found again. "Let's keep driving around. It has to be here someplace."

It became obvious both men were frustrated. Malik kept checking the map and looking around. Bajar kept glancing at Malik, hoping for new information.

Finally, Malik threw up his hands. "I give up, Ali. There is no such address here. I'm sure I wrote it down correctly. And this is where MapQuest said to come. It should be here."

"But it's not. I guess we'd better go back to the hotel and figure this out. Maybe the address in the database was entered wrong or something."

"Must be. I'm sure I copied it correctly." He sighed. "Okay, let's go back. We'll check it out and see what we can find."

Frustrated, neither man spoke. It was a quiet drive back to the hotel.

CHAPTER 31

It was a beautiful day to go anywhere you wanted in Baltimore, especially for shopping. Sheryl had enjoyed every minute of this day — until now.

She pounded on the top of the steering wheel. Twice. "Why now?" Frustrated, she pulled over to the side of the road, stopped in a marked parking spot and slammed the gearshift into park. She sat there glaring at the dash, breathing hard. "I should have picked the car with the navigation system!"

Reaching over to the side, she grabbed the map off the leather seat. "Humph." She unfolded it with both hands, pulling so hard it almost ripped. She stared at the map a full half second before she turned it up on its side. She still couldn't find her road, so she quickly jerked the map sideways in the opposite direction. Still, nothing jumped out at her. With a huge sigh, she turned the map upside down.

The day had started pleasantly enough. She looked forward to the fun of finding some wonderful items in great stores, maybe even on sale. She left the airport with enthusiasm, eager to get started shopping.

She would spend most of the day searching for two items. The first: a wonderful wedding ring set. She had all sorts of possibilities in her head, and she was open to different styles. Stephen had said, "Gold. White or yellow, I don't care. You choose." *Well, it all depends on how the rings look. Yellow is nice with the color contrast to the diamonds, but white gold blends so well, presenting a rich-looking appearance.* Either way was fine with her, as long as it was beautiful and conveyed their feeling of love. She was sure it would.

A lovely solitaire diamond would be nice, maybe even with some smaller diamonds around it. Holding her left hand up to examine it, turning her hand around in the sunlight, she thought, *of course, the wedding band has to match somehow.* She knew there would be a lot of choices, and more than a few sales people trying to convince her they had the best choice.

The second item of her search was a sexy, cool looking cocktail dress to wear that evening when she and Stephen went to dinner. She wanted the evening to be special for both of them. *I want Stephen's total attention — undivided.* She wanted him looking at her, smiling at her, romancing her, wanting her — all night.

She would prefer the dress to be black. That's always sexy. But it had to be the right cut, and the right length. Not too tight, but definitely not loose. It had to show off her curves. She knew she had the right curves, she just wanted to be sure he saw them, and that he saw them all evening. It wouldn't hurt to have a little skin showing either, but just a little to tease. She would know the right dress when she saw it.

Baltimore, the largest city in the state of Maryland and the 26th most populous city in the country, is located on an arm of Chesapeake Bay. It is the second largest seaport in the Mid-Atlantic area and is closer to Midwestern markets than any other major seaport on the East Coast.

Inner Harbor, where their hotel was located, and where Sheryl did most of her shopping, was once the second leading seaport for immigrants to the United States. After a decline in manufacturing in the area, Baltimore shifted to a service-oriented economy. Inner Harbor was now filled with hotels, shopping malls, small quaint retail stores and restaurants of all types. Baltimore had now been nicknamed "Charm City."

Sheryl visited Harbor Place Mall, Lexington Market, and Towson Town Center Mall before visiting the well-known jewelry stores, including Tiffany's and Michael Kors. While Tiffany's had many absolutely beautiful wedding sets, she discovered her favorite at the store "Fire and Ice."

The engagement ring featured a sparkling Princess cut diamond solitaire flanked by a smaller, round cut diamond about one-third the size mounted on each side. Four oblong diamond accents continued down each side of the 18 carat white gold ring. The matching wedding band had a line of five small, round cut diamonds in the recessed center of the ring. Sheryl thought the set was gorgeous and would certainly meet Stephen's approval, but she selected two other alternatives just in cast. Knowing Stephen, she understood he wanted to have a choice, even if he did agree with her favorite.

She enjoyed a light lunch at a small restaurant overlooking the harbor. It was fun watching the various boats moving all around in the water. The colorful scene was serene and provided just the relaxing time-out she needed, away from her professional responsibilities and patient concerns. She enjoyed the moment so much, she never thought about the reason Stephen had been asked to come to Baltimore. In her mind, the restaurant bombing, the shooting in Central Park, discovering his brother's car and the shooting there, all these events were in the past, behind them. Now she only wanted to look forward, to her and Stephen being together, to the day they would be married.

Sheryl found the dress she wanted at Nordstrom's. It wasn't on sale, but when she saw it, she knew she had to have it. It was the perfect dress for the evening she had planned for her and Stephen.

The dress was an original double V-neck bandage dress by Herve Leger. All black, the length ended above the knee. The rayon/nylon/spandex dress was designed to provide a snug, body conscious fit. The deep double V-neckline would add an undeniable allure. It was her size and fit perfectly. She had to have it.

After an exhilarating day shopping and with her new dress hanging in the back seat window, Sheryl decided to drive around the harbor area and enjoy the sights. However, after a considerable time driving, now just after five o'clock, the enjoyment had worn off. She threw her hands up in the air and spoke out loud to herself. "Wouldn't you know it? I'm hopelessly lost. I haven't a clue where I am."

Looking out the side window of the car, she scanned the area for a street sign, which was nowhere to be found. Shaking her head, she glanced out the other side, then up and down the street.

Her expression contorted to a scowl as she acknowledged that she still had to find her own way back. No one was going to come and get her, and there was no one on the sidewalk anywhere whom she could ask for help. Nervous, she put the car in gear and pulled back onto the street, slowly moving forward.

Nearing an intersection, she finally discovered a street sign. Covington Street. The other road had no sign. She stopped the car and checked the map, but couldn't find the street. She put the map down and allowed the car to move forward.

The sign at the next intersection identified both streets: Covington Street and East Clement Street. She was about to reach for the map again when she spotted a storage rental facility just past the intersection. It was surrounded by a six-foot high chain link fence which you could easily see through to the inside. As she drove closer, she spotted a woman on the other side of the fence, loading boxes into a white van. The woman had obviously rented the end unit and was taking boxes and other things out of the storage unit.

Sheryl pulled over next to the fence, got out of the car, and moved around next to the fence. "Hello." She waved at the woman. "Hi. Can you help me? I'm lost. I need directions, please."

The woman acted as if she didn't know what to do. She looked at Sheryl, then turned to look into the storage unit, then back to Sheryl.

"Please. I really need some help."

The woman took a couple of steps toward Sheryl. "I don't know this area very well. I'm sorry."

"Please. Can you just tell me how to get back to the main roads? I want to go to the Hyatt Regency Hotel. Do you know where that is?"

The woman shook her head no.

"How about a highway, a main road, anything? How do I get out of this place?"

The woman took another few steps toward Sheryl and stood there. She raised her arm and pointed. "Down this street. Six blocks, then turn left." Her English was not very good. "You get to highway, I think."

"Thank you." Sheryl was relieved. "Thank you very much." She waved to the woman.

The woman waved back, turned and walked toward the storage unit.

Sheryl got back into the car and started down the street. Still not too sure, she drove the car slowly, watching for any sign that would tell her more about where she was. After six blocks she turned left and continued, advancing very slowly, often stopping to see if anything looked familiar. Nothing did, and she kept driving.

After a couple of minutes she reached a busy intersection with a stop sign. So many cars were moving down this street, it had to be a main thoroughfare. She found the street sign. Light Street. That sounded familiar. She snatched the map and searched. Sitting there, it seemed to take forever. *Ah, here it is.* She followed it with her finger. *Yes, I found it.* Light Street was where the Hyatt Regency was located. She pointed to her right and told herself, "It should be just down here, maybe ten blocks or so." She smiled as relief swept over her. "I'm closer than I realized." She smiled. She was happy. "I'm almost there!" she shouted, and turned the corner.

———————

Sheryl hadn't seen the man emerge from the storage unit with a questioning look on his face. "Who was that, Umara?"

"Some woman was lost. She asked for directions."

"What did you tell her?"

"I said I didn't know this area. I told her to go six blocks down and turn left. That should get her to a main road."

Tariq looked at the street outside the fence. They were in a spot where both pedestrian and car traffic were sparse. Everything was quiet. He glance back at Umara. "That may have been totally innocent, but it could have been someone watching us. They want to know what we are doing." He motioned to her. "Quick. Get in the car."

He closed and locked the storage unit as fast as he could, then jumped into the front seat of the van and pulled out the gate onto the street. He floored the gas to pick up speed, then made the left turn that Umara had identified. The speeding van covered the next few blocks quickly.

"There, up ahead," Umara shouted. "The gray car. That's her."

They saw the car sitting at the intersection ahead of them, waiting for something. Tariq slowed the van so not to approach too fast. "I don't want to come up right behind her. I'm going to follow to see where she goes, but I don't want her to know we are following her."

"Okay," Umara nodded.

"There she goes." The gray Ford turned the corner and started down Light Street. Tariq stopped at the intersection to provide a short distance between the vehicles, then turned and followed Sheryl's car.

"There," Umara pointed. "She's turning into the underground parking for the hotel."

"I see. We'll follow her, but park in a different spot. Let's see what she does, if she meets anyone. Then we'll know if we need to be careful."

"Thanks, Randy," Stephen said. "I hope I've been some help." He smiled. "You've got quite a challenge to work on. I wish you luck."

Agent Osborn offered his hand. "Thank you, Stephen. You've been a big help. We have a lot to chew on. And with the conference starting on Monday, we don't have a lot of time to prepare. We're shooting in the dark here and we don't know what to expect. Just have to watch for the worst-case scenario and pray to God that we stop these guys before they act." He nodded.

"Thanks again, Stephen. You and Sheryl enjoy your stay here. Have a good time."

"We will. Here comes Sheryl now." He pointed to the gray Ford Fusion entering the underground parking garage.

"Yeah, and there's someone else coming in for a good time." Osborn pointed to a white van following Sheryl's car into the garage.

The two men turned back to each other. "Say hi to Sheryl for me, will you? You two have a good time." He started to walk away toward his car parked somewhere in the garage. He turned back. "Bill and Jimmie are in the lounge having a drink. You might want to join them before you get ready for your night out. Tell them the drinks are on me."

"Okay. Will do." Stephen waved at Osborn.

He didn't have to wait long for Sheryl. She walked over to him, almost out of breath. "Hi, darling," he offered.

She reached up and put her arms around his neck. Still breathing hard, she smiled at him, then gave him a long kiss. "It's so good to see you. You have no idea what I've been through."

"Oh? You'll have to tell me about it."

They turned to go into the hotel. "I see you got your dress."

"Yes." The frustration was going out of her. "Wait till you see it. I told you you're going to like it."

They reached the door. "After all the shopping, I got lost, Stephen."

He looked at her and laughed.

"It's not funny. I was scared. Well, for a little bit, anyway."

Stephen put his arm around Sheryl. "Let's go have a drink in the lounge. A couple of the FBI guys are still there. Osborn said to tell them our drinks are on him. You can unwind and tell me all about your adventure."

They both turned their heads at the sound of screeching tires. The back of that same white van slid sideways, then gained its footing as it sped out of the parking garage.

CHAPTER 32

"Kamran, are you there?" Tariq pounded on the door again. "Please open."

As the door opened to reveal Khan standing there, Tariq said, "Good. You are here." He pushed the door back and he and Umara entered the room, almost out of breath. "We have news for you."

Khan stuck his head out the door and checked the hallway. The fourth floor of the Embassy Suites Hotel was quiet, no one was there. He closed the door and motioned to Tariq and Umara. "Here. Sit down. Tell me what it is." He put his hand up. "Rana, come in here. Tariq and Umara have news."

As they all sat down, Saleem emerged from the back bedroom. "You should have called us like Kamran said. We would have come downstairs to help unload."

"You still can. But first I wanted to tell you — Grant is here."

"The guy from the UN?"

"Yes. I recognized him from the television."

"Where did you see him?" asked Khan.

"He was at the Hyatt Regency Hotel."

Frowning, Saleem asked, "What were you doing there?"

Tariq put his hand on his heaving chest and waited, taking a couple of deep breaths. "We were loading the equipment from the storage unit into the van." He described what happened, and Umara nodded as he spoke. "We followed the woman into the parking garage at the hotel. That is where she met Grant. He was talking with another man in a suit. Then the other man left, and Grant and the woman headed into the hotel." He paused a moment, still out of breath. "I thought we should tell you right away."

Khan nodded. "Yes. You did good to come here to tell us." He stood up and looked over at Saleem. He made a face, turned and started pacing.

After a minute of silence, Saleem asked, "Why do you think he is here, Kamran? Do you think he could be after us? Could he know somehow?"

"I wish you would have shot him in New York," Tariq said.

Khan turned to them. "Yes. If I had not missed, he would not be a problem. Now we do not know." He continued pacing.

Quiet settled over them as everyone pondered this new information.

Khan raised his arms out to his sides. "It may be nothing at all, but I don't believe in very many coincidences. This Grant fellow keeps turning up everywhere. First he was at the restaurant. You saw him there, didn't you, Rana?"

"Yes. He was there with another man when we pulled away from the curb."

"And then," Khan continued, "he was at Central Park. Why was he chosen as moderator for that event, anyway? Anyone have any idea?"

No one had any suggestions.

Khan kept pacing. "Now he is here. Why?" He looked over at Tariq. "You say he was talking to a man dressed in a suit? At the Hyatt Regency Hotel?"

"Yes, Kamran."

"Hmm. He's with the UN. Could he be here for the conference next week? Just for any Homeland Security matter? That man could be part of Homeland Security."

"Possible," said Saleem. "Or he could be CIA or FBI."

"Yes. If it is any of those, he might be looking for something to happen during the conference." He glanced at Tariq, then Umara. "Could he know we are here, after being in New York? How would he do that?"

Tariq shook his head. Umara spoke up, "We don't know, but can we take that chance? Do we dare let it go and hope he does not know?"

"If he does know," said Khan, "or if he suspects, he may tell others. That could be what he was talking about to that other man."

Saleem motioned to Tariq. "Do you have our equipment in the van downstairs?"

"Some of it. Most of it," he replied. "We left in a hurry to follow the woman. We were not sure who she was or what might be happening. We can unload what we have and go back for the rest. Then we can decide what to do."

"Yes, Rana. You're right. Let's go downstairs and unload, then go get the rest. While we're getting it all here, we can decide what to do."

The four of them took the elevator to the first floor. Khan and Saleem found the two baggage carts while Tariq retrieved the van. As they loaded the boxes onto one of the carts, Khan instructed the others. "Let's keep all the boxes on one cart. We must be careful with the black plastic pipe on the other cart, so it does not get damaged. We do not want to dent any of it, or it won't be good for making our bombs."

Umara went back upstairs to be sure the area was clear and no other people were walking around on the fourth floor. She met the others at the elevator, informing them that the area was quiet. They moved the carts off the elevator and to the first room, two doors down the hall.

Once everything was unloaded and the boxes separated, Tariq and Umara left to retrieve the balance of the equipment. Khan and Saleem began opening the boxes and laying out the contents. They grouped the appropriate items to make the bomb assembly and preparation easier.

During the ride back to the storage unit, Umara was unsettled. "I am afraid of this Grant. I do not like that he is here, in this place, at this time. I do not like it at all. I have a bad feeling."

"So do I," agreed Tariq. "I do not think we can just hope he does not know. We have come too far for him to interfere."

"We cannot allow that," Umara stated. "We must do something ourselves. We must eliminate this Grant."

"Agreed. We will tell Kamran when we get back."

After their return to the Embassy Suites and the balance of equipment was brought into their hotel room, they discussed their ideas. Khan agreed. "But you must be careful. We must eliminate him without attracting attention."

"How do we do that?"

"Wait for him in the parking garage. Perhaps he will leave the hotel for dinner."

"If we are lucky."

"Well, he must leave the hotel sometime. You will need to wait for him. When he comes into the parking garage, force him into your van and take him away somewhere. Once you are some distance from the hotel, away from downtown, then you can shoot him and dump the body."

"He will be missed."

"Yes. But if they don't know what happened to him, or where he is, it will take awhile for them to find out. By then, we should be ready for our big event at the conference. Then no one will be able to stop us."

CHAPTER 33

"They seem like nice men, don't they?"

"Bill and Jim? Yes, they do, Sheryl. I bet they are nice men," Stephen replied. "I could have enjoyed another drink with them, but we need to get ready for our night out."

She smiled. "We sure do, darling."

As they entered the hotel two room suite Osborn had reserved for them, Sheryl raised her eyebrows and said, "Hey, this is nice." She turned to Stephen. "I'll tell you what. It's a fact women always take longer to get ready, so why don't you get ready first? Then you can relax while I'm getting ready. Maybe you could watch TV or something. Okay?"

Stephen put the suitcase on the bed and opened it. Carefully removing his other suit, he hung it in the bathroom, turned on the hot water in the shower, walked out of the bathroom and closed the door. "That'll get the wrinkles out." He smiled. "It'll be just like new."

Sheryl sat down on the sofa while Stephen retrieved the rest of his things from the suitcase. He turned to her and said, "I'll just jump into the shower myself."

"It won't get the wrinkles out."

"Funny girl. You're going to be fun tonight." He winked and gave her a huge smile. "I can tell."

Sheryl picked up the remote and turned on the TV. Channel surfing, she said, "Oh, we'll have some fun all right, so don't take too long." She blew him a kiss.

After hanging up his jacket, he removed his tie and white shirt. He kicked his shoes off, removed his socks and went into the bathroom.

After a few minutes of listening to his off-key singing, Sheryl knocked on the bathroom door and called to him. "Sounds like you're in a good mood." She added, teasing, "Better stay that way."

"Why wouldn't I?" Stephen asked, exiting the bathroom wrapped in a towel. Holding his second suit out to the side, he bowed to her. "The shower is all yours, my lady."

"Why, thank you, sir. You are so kind." She did a curtsy.

He finished dressing while she was in the bathroom. He found a TV news channel and put his shoes on. After a few minutes of TV, he glanced back over his shoulder. The bedroom door was closed. He hadn't heard her come out of the bathroom, let alone close the door to the bedroom. *I must be more engrossed in the news than I thought.*

She was humming on the other side of the door, and he heard a couple of containers click as they were set down on the counter. He turned back to the TV.

Sometime later he heard a noise and started to turn around. "Don't turn around. I'm opening the door for some air, but don't look yet. I'll let you know when I'm ready."

"Yes, my dear. Your wish is my command."

"And don't you forget that." She laughed. "You can bet I won't, and I won't let you forget either, mister." She resumed her preparations but continued humming.

Stephen sat up straight without turning around. "Are we happy tonight?"

She stopped applying make-up long enough to walk over to the door and reply dramatically, "Dreadfully, dahling." Stephen smiled and he heard her return to complete her duties.

Soon she stood in the doorway and tried to speak in a slow, sexy voice. "Stephen, my only love, would you be so kind as to help a lady with her necklace?"

He jumped up and turned to see her.

She stood there with one hand on her hip and slowly moved the other hand out to the side, holding a silver necklace. The stunning, short black dress clung to her as if painted on her body. The deep V-neck revealed just enough cleavage to capture attention. Tanned, shapely legs displayed below the dress also shared some of that attention. Her dark brown hair, styled magnificently, almost glowed as she tilted her head.

Not just pretty, she was gorgeous. Red lips shined against her light, smooth skin. Her fascinating soft brown eyes invited him to come closer. Her teasing smile beckoned him, almost daring him to touch her.

He couldn't take his eyes off her. He was speechless. He tried to walk toward her, but stumbled on his first step. He quickly looked down to see where he was walking, then back at her. With a nervous smile, he motioned with his right hand toward his feet. "I .. uh." He motioned some more. "I'm ... Sure. I'll help you."

He somehow managed to get to the doorway. She stood there. Her eyes never left his. Her smile enveloped him, caressed him. He stuck out his hand.

Still smiling, she raised one eyebrow and tilted her head down. Using just the one hand, she slid the necklace around his hand. Keeping their eyes locked as long as she could, she slowly turned her back to him.

He was surprised at the deep V in the back of the dress. He gently touched her back with his fingertips. She felt cool and calm.

Realizing he had been holding his breath, he exhaled slowly. He regained his voice. "Sheryl, you are so — so stunning. Absolutely gorgeous."

With a low, soft voice she uttered, "Thank you, Stephen."

Very carefully, he moved the necklace over her shoulder and around her neck. He was all thumbs, but managed to get the clasp fastened. "There."

She put her hand up to it and looked down. She took one step forward, away from him, and turned around. Slowly spreading both arms out to her sides, she said demurely, "I told you you'd like it."

She flashed that enticing smile again. Keeping her voice soft and low, she said, "I'm ready." She turned her head slightly and looked at him out of the corner of her eyes. She parted her lips as if to speak, but said nothing. Then she raised her eyebrows. "If you are."

"Oh, ha, ha-ha. Am I ready. Oh, to go you mean." He offered her his arm. As they started toward the main door to the hotel room, Sheryl said, "I bought you a present when I was out shopping. It's in the car. Let's get it when we go downstairs. I want you to open it before dinner."

"Okay."

"Stephen." She stopped and turned to face him. "I've been waiting for this night for a ..." she shook her head once, "long time. I know you have too, haven't you?"

"Yes." He looked into those lovely eyes. "I have longed for this night."

She moved up to him and raised up on her tiptoes. "Well, it's finally here. We're going to really enjoy this night." She wrinkled her nose. "Let's have fun tonight, Then, my darling, when we come back to our room, you can enjoy the treasure you so richly deserve. You can have all the love you need — all that you want — for the entire night."

CHAPTER 34

The elevator travelled all the way to the bottom floor. The doors opened and, as they stepped into the underground parking garage, Stephen said, "I wasn't watching when you came in. Where did you park the car?"

"Over here to the left," Sheryl pointed, "across the aisle and down about ten rows." They started walking to the car.

"So you bought me a present, huh?"

"Yes." She gave him a big smile. "It's just a little thing, but I think you'll like it." She glanced at him and raised her eyebrows. "You'll never guess what it is."

"Oh, let me see." He gave her a very serious look. "I have to think hard about this." A big grin spread across his face. "I know!" He stopped and turned to her. "I know what it is. It's an engraved paper clip holder."

She broke into laughter. "How did you know?" They started walking again. "That was a good guess."

Still smiling, Stephen responded, "I knew it. I knew it as soon as you said it."

Sheryl continued laughing. "You should go on television. Maybe have a road show. You could be famous."

They were getting close to the car. Sheryl pointed. "There it is, up there on the left."

Nearing the car, Stephen inquired, "Think I could make it on one of the late-night TV shows?"

Shaking her head, she said, "I don't know. You *are* pretty good, but ..." Sheryl stopped abruptly. Her entire demeanor changed. She did a quick turn to face Grant. "Stephen, that couple coming toward us." she nodded, apparently not wanting to point. Her voice became barely more than a whisper. "She's the woman from the storage unit. After getting lost, I saw her there and stopped to ask for directions. She acted very strange, like she was afraid of something, but she gave me directions anyway." She turned to the side, away from the approaching couple. "This is kind of creepy." She shook her head. "I don't like this."

Stephen looked over at them as they came nearer. They could have been any couple having parked their car and walking toward the hotel entrance.

Both the man and woman had a healthy tan. As they kept walking, he recognized their features as Arabic or Middle Eastern. The slender woman had long, straight black hair and wore a loose-fitting white blouse with the tail hanging out over her blue pants. She looked as if she were going to a picnic, but she wore heavy shoes, not sandals or thongs.

The man had a medium build with shoulder-length dark hair and dark eyes. He wore a long sleeve, loose-fitting plaid shirt. His sleeves were rolled up almost to the elbow and the shirt tail also hung out over his dark pants.

They walked deliberately, as if they had a purpose.

Stephen took Sheryl by the arm and guided her toward the automobile. "Let's get in the car." He opened the passenger door for her.

"Grant!" the man shouted.

Sheryl stopped, and Stephen turned to face them with a questioning look. He wondered, *who are they? How do they know my name?*

The couple were now within twenty feet of them, continuing to approach. Both the man and the woman reached behind them, then jerked their hand forward. They each held a black, semi-automatic pistol, now pointed at Stephen and Sheryl. They stopped less than six feet away.

Watching them carefully, Stephen walked to the rear of the car and stood in the aisle, closer to them. "What do you want?"

Paralyzed with fear, Sheryl stood still. She put her hands together over her mouth, but remained silent.

The couple stopped their march. The man motioned with his pistol. "You're coming with us. We're going for a ride."

Trying to remain calm and evaluate the situation, Stephen glanced at Sheryl, then back at the couple. "Why would I want to do that?"

The woman responded loudly in an angry voice. "Not just you." She took another step closer and pointed her gun at Sheryl. "Both of you. You're coming with us."

Knowing he had to get their attention away from Sheryl, Stephen started walking toward the couple. "Okay." He took four steps and stopped. "But what if I don't want to come?"

He could see the man was becoming nervous. Keeping his pistol pointed at Stephen, the man brought the gun up in front of his chest, then pulled it back down to his waist. Both the man and woman remained quiet a moment. Then, slightly stuttering, the man said, "You — you're coming with us. We," he glanced over at the woman who stared back at him, "We are taking you for a ride."

The woman spoke. "You will come with us." She walked to within a couple feet of Stephen. Glaring at him, she said, "You *will* come."

Stephen stood perfectly still, looking back at her. "Why?"

"Because we want you to!" the man shouted.

Stephen had succeeded in getting the couple to focus on him. He made them angry by not complying with their wishes. They were frustrated and now not sure of what to do next. That advantage ended when Sheryl spoke up.

"And if we won't go anywhere with you?"

Stephen's heart fell. *Damn it, Sheryl. Why didn't you get away when you had a chance? They weren't watching you.* He inhaled deeply.

The woman took three fast steps toward Sheryl. Stephen could see from the side of her face that she gave a deliberate smile to Sheryl. "Then we will kill you right here."

Wide-eyed, Sheryl turned her head to look at Stephen. The look on her face told Stephen she wanted to say, "I tried. I wanted to help. What do I do now?"

Stephen tried to mentally evaluate his options. He wasn't sure what to do next, either. He saw the look on Sheryl's face became pleading.

He turned back to the man. "You're going to kill us ..." he spread his hands out to his sides, "here? Right here? People will come running to see what happened. You'll be mobbed. You'll never get away."

The man walked up to him and stuck his hand out, pointing the gun in Stephen's face. His speech was filled with frustration. He shouted, "I'll kill you right here, anyway!"

The man had lost control. This was the moment Stephen had waited for. The man was unprepared for his reaction.

Stephen thrust his right hand upward, catching the man's wrist and pushing it away into the air. The gun went off. The loud clap of thunder from the pistol sounded like two shots as it echoed all around them.

Before the man could recover, Stephen pushed his hip into the man's body while at the same time grabbing the man's wrist with his other hand. Using both hands, he jerked the man's arm down while continuing to push back with his hip. The man's feet left the ground and he flipped over Stephen's shoulder, landing on his back.

Stephen kicked the gun out of the man's hand, then brought his heel down on the man's chest. The man let out a noise and rolled on his side. Stephen kicked him hard in the back of the head, then dove over the man and rolled away.

He saw the gun lying there on the floor in front of him. Quickly stretching out his arm and reaching for it, Stephen looked up to see what had happened to the woman.

It seemed like everything shifted to slow motion. The woman held her gun with two hands and was turning away from Sheryl toward Stephen. Pivoting around, she had both arms extended, swinging the pistol around in front of her to aim at him. Her face was contorted with tremendous anger. He could see her lips move as she emitted a strange, animal-like sound.

He focused on the black pistol in her hands. It was big and growing larger with every fraction of a second. He saw the round black hole at the end of the barrel. It was coming around to face him. He knew it would explode and send a huge bullet to blast his body, tearing him to shreds and ending his life. Any moment now, measured only in fractions of seconds.

He felt the man's gun under his hand. He clasped his fingers around the handle and jerked the pistol up into the air, swinging it hard around toward the woman. She had lined up her gun on him, ready to shoot.

Stephen squeezed the trigger. A loud noise erupted, the concussion sending a shock wave shaking everyone. With a surprised look, the woman was thrown back a step, bringing her arm up slightly. Her pistol discharged an echoing shot into the air over Stephen's head.

He pulled the trigger again. The pistol blasted its deadly projectile into the woman, knocking her backward. She fell against the trunk of the gray Ford, dropped her gun, looked up as if to pray, and started sliding down the back of the car, finally rolling to the ground and landing on her back.

Hearing a noise behind him, Stephen rolled over and sprang to his feet. He saw the man he had knocked down dash between the cars, about twenty feet away on his right. He brought the pistol up and pointed it in the direction the man had run. He could still hear the pounding feet of the man running, but he was lost in the clutter of cars, nowhere to be seen.

Stephen took a few steps in that direction, but could not see the man anywhere. He heard a car start and wheels screech. Suddenly the blur of a white van appeared at the back of the parking garage. It shot out the exit into the street and quickly disappeared.

Stephen turned and ran over to the woman lying on the ground. He picked up her gun with his empty hand, then stared at the woman. She lay on her back with one arm stretched out, staring off into the distance, not blinking. She was dead.

He turned to find Sheryl.

She wasn't there. He wondered if she got away. Perhaps she ducked behind the car door. It was still open.

He moved quickly, starting to walk, almost run, toward the side of the car. She must be there. Either that or she ran away and was hiding behind another car. But he didn't hear her running away.

As he stepped around the end of the car he saw Sheryl, sitting on the ground, legs sprawled askew, leaning up against the side of the car, against the rear passenger door.

His mouth dropped open. This couldn't be.

She looked up at him. Suddenly her eyes clamped shut, the pain written across her face. She kept them shut tight for a moment. Then she spoke with great difficulty. "I'm sorry, Stephen."

"Sheryl!" He dropped to his knees beside her. "Sheryl." He shook his head. Reaching out and taking hold of her shoulders, he could hardly speak. "Honey, ... " He saw the middle of her dress was wet.

"She shot me. I couldn't get away." Terrible pain caused her to shudder. She whispered, "Couldn't leave without you."

Scared, he couldn't find his voice. He looked back into her eyes.

She shook her head, just a little, very slowly. "I ... " She lowered her head, out of breath.

He shook her shoulders. "Sheryl, you're going to be all right." Tears formed in his eyes. "You hear me? You're going to be all right."

She raised her head and looked at him with vacant eyes. He saw them gradually focus slowly. Recognition appeared on her face. "Stephen."

Her gaze dropped over his body with a question on her face, as if to ask if he was hurt. She brought her eyes back to meet his. She spoke, but her scratchy voice sounded as if she was out of breath. "I was ... looking ... forward."

"Don't talk." He slid his arms behind her shoulders. "Don't talk, baby."

Her head seemed to bobble, tilting down, then back. Her pretty eyes widened. "To tonight." Stephen could see it took a great effort to force a smile on her face.

He shook his head quickly. "So was I, honey. So was I." He searched her eyes with his, and his tears started gushing. He sat on the ground facing her, his legs extending under the car. He leaned forward and pulled her to him. Tears became rivers flooding his cheeks. He started rocking her back and forth. "Oh, my Sheryl. My Sheryl."

Her head lay against his shoulder. She moaned and tried to move. He sat her up straight, looking into her face. "I'm sorry ... darling."

He closed his eyes tightly trying to stop the tears so he could see her clearly. They wouldn't stop. Pain erupted inside him. He could hardly move, either.

Her chest heaved and she gasped. She looked into his eyes again, longingly. She coughed. Blood began to ooze over her lip at the corner of her mouth. Stephen watched it as it slowly crept down her chin. His eyes widened with disbelief.

"It hurts.." She spoke with great difficulty, taking every effort she could muster. "It hurts bad."

He wanted to scream. This couldn't be happening. Not to her.

He cried, then managed to say, "I love you."

She tried to smile, but didn't quite make it. "Stephen, ... I don't ... think I'm ...going ... to make it."

"Yes, you are, darling. Yes. You have to. You'll be okay."

Her eyes looked at him, moving from one eye to the other. "No. I'm sorry." She paused, trying desperately to breathe in more air. Then with more difficulty, she uttered, "I'm not."

"No, Sheryl. Don't leave me. Don't," he pleaded. He held her to him again. "Don't leave me, please." The tears just kept coming, they wouldn't stop.

"Stephen." He moved her back just a little so he could see her face.

She coughed and spit blood. It started running from her nose.

Loneliness began eating his insides, leaving only gigantic pain. "No, Sheryl."

"Remember," she managed, "I ..." She seemed to stop breathing, then jerked and inhaled. "Remember, I ...."

He nodded his head.

"I ... love ..."

Her head fell forward against him. He couldn't feel her breathing anymore.

"No! Sheryl!" He shouted. "Don't leave me!"

He squeezed her tight against him and rocked back and forth. "Don't leave me."

CHAPTER 35

Running with gun in hand, he rounded the back of the gray Ford. "Stephen?"

One quick look provided him all the information he didn't really want to know. He started shaking his head. "Oh, my God. *No!*" He rushed the few remaining steps to them.

Pulling his cell phone from his pocket, he dialed 911. "This is FBI Special Agent Bill Anderson, badge #4127. There has been a shooting. I need two ambulances at the underground parking garage of the Hyatt Regency Hotel. And I need them now!"

He replaced his phone in his coat pocket and shouted to the other agent. "Jimmie," he motioned, moving his hand in a circle, "check this all out just in case. Then come help me."

He dropped to his knees beside the rocking couple next to the car. He realized Stephen was crying so hard, it was impossible for him to see who was there.

"Stephen. It's Bill Anderson." He looked up and again motioned with this hand. "And Jimmie Clark. An ambulance is on its way." He put his hand on the side of Grant's arm. "Are you hurt? Have you been shot?"

Stephen continued crying, rocking Sheryl back and forth. He held her head against his shoulder. Bill could see him attempting to look through the tears and comprehend who he might be. Bill shook his head in understanding. To Stephen, it no longer mattered who it was. "It's me. Bill. Are you hurt?"

Stephen lowered his head and laid it against Sheryl's. "Don't go." It was almost a wail. "I don't want you to leave!"

Stephen managed to pull back a little and shake his head. "I'm okay." Then he put his head back down. "But Sheryl ... Sheryl is hurt." He kept rocking, rocking and crying.

Jimmie came running up to Bill. "There's no one else here, now. They must have got away."

Bill nodded, then raised his head to look around. "Where's that damned ambulance? Isn't it here yet?"

"It should be here any minute," Jimmie responded. He reached for his cell phone. "Hey, boss. I'm glad you weren't going home tonight. You better get over here to the Hyatt. Stephen and his fiancé have been shot."

As tears formed in his eyes too, he looked up and away. "I don't know. I think Stephen might be okay, but his fiancé is hurt." He shook his head. It was hard for him to talk. His new friends who he had shared a drink with were lying there in pain, blood all over. "No. I don't know how bad. Please, just get over here."

———————

The black Chevy Tahoe rapidly entered the parking garage, followed by two more FBI vehicles. Tires screeched as the SUVs stopped abruptly. FBI SSA Randy Osborn leapt from his vehicle running. Approaching Bill and Jimmie, out of breath, he shouted, "What ... where ..."

Shaking his head, Bill Anderson pointed.

Stephen still sat on the garage floor cradling Sheryl, her back lying against him, The noise from Stephen's crying stopped, but the tears continued flooding his cheeks. He just sat there, holding her.

Two police cars flew into the parking area, followed by a few ambulances, sirens winding down. Red and blue lights continued flashing as people exited their vehicles and began assessing the situation. Jimmie walked over to the patrolmen and explained the situation.

Osborn tried desperately to piece everything together without bothering Stephen any more than necessary. Agents combed the area looking for anything that might have meaning, while other agents started talking to everyone who came out into the parking garage.

Finally, Osborn told Stephen he had to let go of Sheryl. The paramedics needed to take her body. He could see her again later.

Reluctantly, Stephen helped the paramedics take hold of her and lift her into an ambulance.

As the ambulance drove off, Osborn said, "I'm sorry, Stephen, but I have to ask. Did you get a good look at them? Had either you or Sheryl seen them before? Can you describe them?"

He shook his head no. "Oh, wait a minute. It was a couple." Stephen had a difficult time putting his thoughts together. "A man and a woman. Sheryl said she had seen her before." He told Osborn what Sheryl said, and then described what happened.

"So the white van shot out into the street and got away."

"Yes. Fast."

"Would you recognize the man if you saw him again?"

"Yes. I'm sure I could."

"Hey, boss." One of the FBI agents interrupted. "We found a woman's purse over there," he pointed to an area toward the back of the garage, several parking spots away. "We found these inside."

He held out some items in his hand. There was a wallet, lipstick, hair brush, makeup, a passport, and some keys. "Let's see that. Hmm. Mexico travel papers, visa to the U.S., uh ..." he turned it over. "This was issued in Pakistan."

He thumbed through the items and stopped, examining the wallet. "This is a hotel key." He turned it over. "It's for a fourth-floor room at the Embassy Suites Downtown, on St. Paul Place." He looked at the two agents standing beside him. "Let's go hunting. If we hurry, we might catch them. Call the SWAT team and notify the locals." He raised his voice for everyone to hear. "Okay, people. We're on our way to the Embassy Suites. We just might find our bomb makers after all. Let's move."

He turned to Grant. "Stephen, you don't have to go."

"Yes, I do. I want to catch them. Not just for what they might do," he nodded, "But for Sheryl. I can recognize that bastard, and I'm not about to let him get away."

"All right, then." Osborn answered. "Let's get to the cars. We're headed to the Embassy Suites."

"Hammad, I know you said not to use our cell phones, but I had to this time."

"What is it, Fazil?"

"I've been watching Grant, like you said. He and his woman came down to the parking garage and were walking to the woman's car when this other couple got out of a van and walked up to them. They had guns. They argued with Grant. Grant tried to wrestle the man for his gun. Grant knocked him down. It was really something to see."

"So what happened, Fazil?"

"The woman shot Grant's woman. Grant got the man's gun and shot her. The other man got away. He made it back to the van and drove away very fast. Hammad, this man and this woman ..."

"Yes?"

"I think they are the ones we are looking for. I think the man is the one hired as a security guard. He looks like the picture you showed me."

"Where are you now, Fazil?"

"I'm at the Embassy Suites Hotel. That is where the man drove to. I tried to follow him inside, but I could not get here fast enough. I lost him in the hotel, so I am not sure what room he is in. There are a lot of rooms here."

"That's okay. You did good. Where are you right now?"

"I'm in the Embassy's parking lot, on the north side of the building."

"Can you see the door if he leaves?"

"Yes."

"Good. Stay where you are and watch to see if he remains there." He became excited. "If he leaves, call me. And follow him. But if he does not leave, stay where you are. I will find you in the parking lot. When I arrive, we will figure out a plan. I'll be there in a few minutes."

CHAPTER 36

Two dark colored sedans and three black SUVs pulled into the parking lot at 222 Saint Paul Place. *Embassy Suites*, thought Osborn. *Who would have thought they'd be here, of all places?*

The car skidded to a stop and Osborn was out running for the door. Bill Anderson jumped out and started giving orders to the others.

Red and blue lights flashed and sirens wailed as several police cars turned into the parking lot, and the officers started piling out. One approached Anderson, since he seemed to be directing the others, and asked what the FBI wanted them to do.

"Put two men on each exit door, now. Don't let anyone leave without clearing with Agent Clark here." He pointed to Jimmie. "If there are too many people at once, he'll get help. But do what he says. I'm taking the SWAT team inside. Keep at least three men on the front door, plus two more inside, in the lobby."

"Got it." He moved away and started giving orders to other uniformed officers.

Osborn had already gone inside to the front desk. After showing his badge, he explained the situation and asked for help. He showed the desk clerk the key, and the clerk identified the room. He told Osborn the party had two adjoining rooms on the fourth floor. It was supposed to be a party of four people.

The clerk called hotel security. They wanted to go with the SWAT team to the fourth floor to help their hotel guests, if necessary. Osborn allowed them to go, but they had to stay back out of the way and let the FBI conduct the operation.

Osborn turned to Stephen. "Please stay here and watch all the guests coming off the elevators. See if you can recognize the man you described. If you do see him, point him out to the officers. Don't try to stop him yourself. Okay?"

Stephen nodded his agreement. "I'd love to get my hands on this guy again, but I really just want to see him get caught. He needs to pay for what he did. And besides, I'm not up to tangling with a group of four of them."

Two additional uniformed officers moved in front of Stephen. "We'll be here in front of you, just off to each side. Let us know if you see this guy. Just point him out. We'll take it from there."

"Good enough for me," Stephen replied. They moved to where they could watch the bank of elevators.

Two stairways led to the fourth floor. Osborn had men go up each stairway, while others took elevators. Reaching the fourth floor, one man remained at each stairway while the others formed at the elevator doors.

Osborn led five FBI men dressed in SWAT uniforms and tactical gear next to the first door. The discovered key would fit this door. The desk had provided a key to the adjoining room also.

One of the SWAT members listened at the door. They all could hear people talking inside the room. The SWAT leader nodded and motioned to one of the team members. He pulled out a monitor unit with what looked like a long hose attached to it. It had a silver metal tip with a built-in camera. He unrolled the hose and worked the end under the door. He checked the monitor. They were getting a picture. He moved the hose around, searching for people in the room.

They all heard loud laughter, then more subdued voices. It seemed that two people were doing most of the talking. More laughter. More talking. But nothing moved in the picture they watched.

The officer moved the hose again, pushing it further into the room. They could tell it was a two-room suite, but the hose camera couldn't see into the back room where the sounds originated.

The officer pulled back the hose and put the instrument away.

The SWAT leader reached out to Osborn and took the room key. He looked around at each member of the team to be sure they were ready. No one made a sound. He nodded his head, and slowly inserted the key.

He checked each team member one last time, then pushed the key card down into the slot. It offered some resistance and moved slowly. He hoped it would not make a loud click. Stopping before it did, he backed away from the door.

He motioned to other team members standing further back. He signaled them to group at the door to the adjoining room. He wanted to go into both rooms at the same time.

The additional team members quietly stepped down the hall to the next room. The man with the hose camera went with them. They listened at the door. No sound. No talking. He pushed the hose beneath the door, checked for a picture, and inserted hose further, turning it to see what or who might be there. There were no suspicious shadows. Nothing moved.

He pulled the hose camera back and stepped away from the door. The leader of the second group looked back and nodded. They were ready.

The first team leader held up his fingers counting silently. One, two, three, GO. Both men slid the key cards into the locks, heard the click and quickly pushed the door open.

"Police! Police!" The shouts came from the groups in both rooms as officers charged into the space and dispersed, guns at the ready. "No one move! FBI!"

Osborn stood in the hall and heard the word shouted and repeated, "Clear. Clear." He rushed into the first room. It was empty except for the SWAT members. He went to the back room. No one was there. The room was empty. The television had been turned on with the volume up, so it could be heard from the door to the hotel room. No one was there.

The officers lowered their weapons and breathed easier. There would not be a shoot-out in these rooms today.

"Okay," Osborn told the others. "I want three men in each room to go over everything. Look for anything that would tell us who was here and where they could have gone. The rest of you get out. Go back to your office or wherever."

He found a uniformed officer. "Let's keep the officers downstairs on station for a bit. These people may still be in the building. Watch for them."

He turned back to the FBI team. "Let me know if you find anything. I'll be downstairs in the lobby." He turned and took the elevator down to find Grant.

As he walked up to Grant, he said, "Well, Stephen, it looks like they made it out of here very quickly. We probably won't find anything, but I have men searching each room. I take it nothing happened down here."

"Not a thing," Stephen replied. "A few people moving around, but no one that resembles our subjects." He made a face and sighed. "No one."

CHAPTER 37

"Keep driving. Go around the block."

Ali Bajar stepped on the gas to hurry past the Embassy Suites Hotel.

"Not so fast, Ali. We don't want the police to notice us. Just go at normal speed." Malik turned in the seat to look at the parking lot as they drove by. "Wait. Slow down." He took a quick breath. "So many police cars. There are blue and red lights flashing everywhere." He shook his head. "Okay, keep going. Turn right at the next corner. Let's go around the block and drive by again. I want another look."

Bajar turned the corner and asked, "Do you think they are there for Fazil?"

"No, I don't think so. There are too many police. They would not send all those cars and police just for one man," Malik replied with a cruel smile. "Even if there were a shooting, they would not send that many. It has to be something else."

"Maybe they are after the same people we are after."

"That could be, Ali." Malik nodded in agreement. "That might be it." He pointed to the intersection. "Turn here. When we go past the hotel, slow down again so I can look. If the police do notice us, they will think we are looking at the lights like everyone else."

The car slowed as they approached the hotel. The parking area provided space for parking on both sides of the hotel and in back. The front of the hotel did have a few parking spots, but it was mostly a wide open area for guest registration and possible deliveries.

"There is a SWAT team vehicle," Malik said. "I have seen these on television before. That means there are special police units here." He pointed, even though Bajar could not see where he pointed. "There are several men in suits. One man seems to be speaking to the rest." Suddenly, he became very excited. "There's Grant! He's standing there with them. I knew he had to be involved somehow." He smiled and slapped Bajar on the arm. "That means he *does* work for the government."

"I guess so," Bajar replied.

"Ali, turn left up here at the corner. There will be another entrance to the parking lot toward the back. We will go in there."

Bajar followed the instructions and found the back entrance to the parking lot. Surprisingly, it was not blocked. Even though the evening was becoming dark, the flashing lights from the police cars provided enough light to reveal two uniformed police officers at each of the hotel back entrances.

"See the police there? Let's be careful of them." Malik pointed toward the hotel doors.

"Yes. I see them."

"Go around here to the left," Fazil said as they drove along the north side of the hotel. "I didn't see his car, but he must be here somewhere."

Bajar maneuvered the small green Chevy Cruz around the parking lot to the north side and slowed. "There he is." He pointed Virk's car out to Malik. "He has that blue Chevrolet Impala over there."

"Yes. I see it." Relieved, Malik smiled. "Park next to him. Back in like Fazil did. That way we can sit in the car and watch what is happening."

Backing in beside Virk, Bajar said, "Let's get in his car to watch and talk. It's larger." Malik waved at Virk.

Both men exited the car and climbed into the rented Impala, Malik in the front seat.

Virk greeted them and said, "They must be here after the same people we are." He looked at Malik. "I saw Grant get out of one of the cars and go into the hotel with two other men in suits."

"It must be the FBI," Malik offered.

"That's what I thought," Virk responded. "I've been right here since I called you. The police and others arrived a few minutes ago. They just now went into the building."

"We will wait and see what happens. Keep your window down a little so we can hear if there is any shooting."

They prepared to wait. Malik spoke. "Remember our orders. We cannot allow them to be arrested." He lowered his head and gazed at the floor of the car. "We *really* don't want them to be caught." He paused. "This could become a difficult situation." He looked behind him at Bajar in the back seat. "Are the guns still in the trunk?"

"Yes, Hammad. They are still there."

"Good. We may need them."

Virk jerked his head around to look at Malik. "You want to use guns? With all these police around?"

"I don't want to, but we may have no choice. Remember, we cannot allow them to be arrested."

"So you will shoot them in front of the police?" Virk asked questioningly.

"Only if we have to." He frowned. "Maybe I'll go ahead and kill some American infidels also."

———————

"Roger that," the police sergeant answered into his shoulder radio. He turned to his partner and shrugged. "We have the all-clear. Time to go." He turned and started walking toward the front of the hotel. Nearing the next hotel door, he called to the officers posted there. "Okay, guys. The excitement's over. All the big guns have gone. We can leave now."

At age 43, Sergeant Fred Jackson had been with the Baltimore Police Department for 17 years. He had four commendations and two medals for heroism. His wife, Kaye, a stay-at-home mother to their three children, did not like the fact that he still worked the streets. Fred, however, loved working the neighborhood patrols and being close to "his people." He had not even taken the detective's exam.

"Well, that helps the shift go fast. Only three more hours to go before we can have a beer." Jackson's partner, Larry Perkins, 36, newly married to Jenifer, had been with the Baltimore PD for just over 12 years. "So, Fred. Are you and Kaye coming to the police picnic tomorrow?"

"Yeah, we're planning on it. It's the last chance we have to relax until after the convention next week. You know, we're all working through that thing." He turned to his partner. "Why don't you bring the softball equipment and we can have a little game after the meal?"

"Great idea. That'll make it more fun. Everyone can enjoy seeing me hit more home runs than you do."

"Don't count on it. I'm the champion, you know."

Perkins smiled. "Yeah, but you're also getting older. Every year."

"Yeah, that's true." Jackson slowly shook his head. "But every year I still beat your ass in both hits and home runs."

"Until this year, old buddy." Perkins smiled broadly.

"Yeah, well, we'll see who can hit the ball out of there."

"You guys going on about playing ball again?" Alex Fulton and Tom Schmidt, the officers stationed at the second hotel door, now joined them walking back to the front of the parking lot.

"Larry, here, thinks he gets better every year. He's hoping he can out-hit me at last this year."

"You just wait," Schmidt offered. "One of these days some rookie will come along and outshine both of you."

They all laughed. Perkins replied, "That'll be the day, Schmitty." They continued laughing as they neared the front of the hotel. The SWAT team was putting their gear away and the FBI vehicles had already left. Only about half of the police cars remained, lights still flashing.

Jackson pointed over toward the side of the lot. "Look at those two cars over there." Shaking his head, he added, "Those idiots." He reached up and pushed the button on his small shoulder radio. "Hey, Bert."

"Yeah."

"Would you and Glen go tell those guys over on your right to move. You're a lot closer than we are. The three guys just got out of their car and they're looking in the trunk. They're in a reserved loading zone. There's a sign right behind them that says 'No Parking.' I guess they can't read."

"Okay. Will do."

Jackson and the other three officers watched as Bert and Glen started over to the two cars. As they approached, Jackson heard Bert shout to the men. "Hey, guys. You gotta move those cars."

The three men looking in the trunk of the Chevy Impala jumped, and started pushing each other. One man reached into the trunk, retrieved something and nervously stepped farther to the side, behind the second car.

"Guys, see the sign behind you? You're in a loading zone. Better move it out of there."

The two men still standing by the open trunk looked at each other. The taller of the men shrugged.

"Let's move it, guys. Now." The police officers continued toward the men.

One of the two men by the trunk of the car said, "Malik is right. Let's do it."

The second man nodded. They quickly reached in, grabbed something and then jumped back. The taller man held an AK-74 assault rifle. Using one hand, he jerked the bolt back and let it fly, sending a round into the chamber. As he raised the rifle chest-high, he pulled the trigger, shooting at the two police officers.

Having seen the men react, Bert dropped to the ground. Unfortunately, Glen hesitated and was hit by the gunfire. Three bullets pounded into him, pushing him back and to the side. Eyes wide in surprise, he grabbed his chest as he fell.

The second man raised a black, semi-automatic pistol and fired two shots in the officers' direction, then ducked down behind the car.

Jackson and the three officers with him rapidly spread out, drawing their pistols. They all carried the Baltimore PD standard issue Sig Sauer 9mm semi-automatic P226. Jackson dived to his left, hit the ground and rolled. Perkins, walking to his left, took three steps and dived to the ground. Schmidt dove to the right, and Fulton ran to the right several steps and went down on one knee.

Bert rolled and sprang up to one knee, firing three shots in rapid succession toward the tall man behind the Impala. The tall man only had a second to respond after shooting the officer and was not quick enough. Bert's bullets hit their mark as the tall man was knocked backwards, throwing his rifle into the air. The man stumbled, turned to the side and fell.

The man who had moved behind the second car, the Chevy Cruz, came around the side of that car with gun in hand and began shooting at Jackson and the three officers.

Jackson and Perkins fired back, almost together as one. Their guns blasted two shots each toward the shooter.

Bullets slammed into the side of the Chevy next to the shooter, who quickly retreated to the back of the car and bent down out of sight.

Fulton and Schmidt both fired their weapons at the smaller man behind the Impala. He made a loud shout as he ducked out of the way. Part of his head and gun became visible as he peered around the car, trying to get a shot.

Fulton and Schmidt peppered that section of the car as their guns fired another two shots each. The man ducked out of the way, then quickly came into view again, ready to shoot. Schmidt was ready and fired first. The man's head snapped back and exploded with a red spray bursting into the air.

Bert tried to move out to his right to get a shot at the remaining man behind the second car. Crouching, Bert tried to run about five steps. It was five steps too many. A gun fired three quick shots from behind the car. Bert dropped his gun, grabbed his side, and appeared to keep running. His feet slipped. He fell forward and stopped moving.

Perkins started to get up and run for the front of the car, but Jackson was close enough. He reached over and pushed Perkins back down just as the gun behind the car sounded again. Bullets struck the concrete just to the left of Perkins, who shouted, "Damn!"

Jackson clung to the ground, making himself as small a target as possible. He peered under the second car. He couldn't see the man crouching there, but he did see his legs. He brought his pistol out in front of him with his arms fully extended. He fired four rapid shots at the legs.

The man behind the small Chevy jumped and shouted something unintelligible. Jackson knew he must have hit him.

Perkins lay still and extended his arms, aiming where he thought the man would peek around the side of the car looking for another shot. He lay still, waiting. It only took about four seconds, but it seemed like an eternity. The instant the man appeared, Perkins' gun blasted two bullets at him.

The man's gun flew through the air, hitting the ground several feet behind him. But the man did not show himself.

Everyone waited.

The man dropped to the ground behind the car.

Jackson was ready. He pulled the trigger and sent two more bullets under the car into the last man there.

If Perkin's bullets didn't kill him, then Jackson's did for sure.

They all waited to be sure there was no more movement anywhere.

Other officers came running from the far side of the parking lot. Jackson shouted out, "Call an ambulance. Get several of them. We have a bunch of people shot here. Get those ambulances here now."

The officers slowly and carefully stood up. They approached the rear of the two cars very slowly, guns still ready. No one there moved. The bodies of the three men lay sprawled behind the cars. Officers picked up the guns lying around them.

Other officers ran to check Glen and Bert. One of the new officers stood up. He shook his head. They were both dead.

Jackson and Perkins examined the open trunk of the blue Chevrolet Impala. Perkins said, "Look at all those guns. There's enough there to start a war." He started to reach in and pick up one of the guns.

Jackson put his arm out to stop him. "Better let the lab guys check for prints first."

Perkins nodded. "Yeah, you're right." He pulled back and they both stood there looking at the guns, amazed. Perkins motioned to one of the other officers. "Watch this, will you? We'll get some lab guys down here to take care of them."

He turned to Perkins. "Let's wait in the car for the Captain to show." As they started walking back to their patrol car, Perkins commented, "Think this is who the FBI guys were looking for?"

"I don't know. They were sitting here. Over there," he pointed, "those two cars just outside the parking lot. They've been watching the whole time. Not a lot of help, huh? Doesn't say much for the FBI, does it?"

"Well, I hope they do better during the convention next week. With the President and other dignitaries here, they'll have to be on their toes."

"Let's hope it goes well. It has to."

CHAPTER 38

"Stephen, you don't *have* to come."

"Yes I do, Randy. I'm the only one who's seen them."

"One of them."

"Yes, one of them. But how many have you guys seen? That's why I should be there."

"Stephen, I —"

"It's not just for me, Randy." He transferred the phone to his other hand. "Sure, I want to get these guys, especially that *one*. But they're all responsible. They killed Sheryl. That's enough for me to want them captured, or even killed for that matter. But that's not why I should be there. If I can spot this guy, it will help save a lot of other people's lives, including the President and God knows who else."

It was quiet for a minute, then Osborn answered, "You're right, Stephen. Your help could be vital. Right now we're still shooting in the dark. Oh, we have some names from the hotel registry, but who knows if those are the real names, or even if they will be using those same names? That *is* all we have to go on. So I guess you'd better come on down. You are the only one to have seen one of them."

Osborn paused for a moment. Stephen could hear him sipping his morning coffee. "But I'm going to run you ragged. I'm going to have you go with some of my guys and go through the whole place. It may take several times, but it's our best chance to catch them. If we can get the one man, then maybe we can get the others before they blow the place up."

"That's right. So I'm coming." Stephen wished he had some morning coffee. He'd go by Starbucks after this call. "With everything that has happened, it's almost a sure thing that they're going to try something during the conference. And an opportunity for them to kill our President is just too much to pass up. They'll be there someplace. And you know they're going to try to do something, some sort of an attack."

"You're right. And all we have for history is the restaurant bombing and the shooting in Central Park. So we'll have to be watching for both those things."

"What about the Secret Service?" inquired Stephen. "They can help, can't they? Can't they check for bombs?"

"Yes, and they will. They will have explosive sniffing dogs checking everywhere, right before the start of the conference."

"And you said you would have metal detectors at all the entrances, right?"

"Yes, we will. And we'll have agents watching each entrance. But if they are clever enough, they'll find a way to smuggle a gun or two into the building. It's almost impossible to stop them. Which is why we *do* need you to help spot them."

Stephen shook his head. "Any idea about the people shot by the police at the hotel last night?"

"The desk clerk said they were not with the group who checked in."

"That doesn't mean they weren't on their way to join our terrorists."

"True, especially with all the firepower they had. There were a lot of weapons in that car trunk. And another thing, all three of them had fake IDs."

"So maybe that's it."

"I'm not so sure. They each had a driver's license and a couple of credit cards. The names were not real. We checked them out."

"Kind of proves our point, doesn't it?"

"Not really. All the IDs were too good. Not just copies bought on the black market. We can usually spot those pretty easily. No, these were so good, they had to come from a foreign government."

"Wow. What does that say?"

"I'm not sure." He paused. "I think it tells us they were not just additional terrorists. Or it could say that another government has a hand in these terrorist activities. We've alerted the CIA, but I don't really think that is it. I'm just not sure what it tells us."

Osborn sipped his morning beverage again, then lowered his head as he asked, "How's the arrangements for Sheryl coming?"

"Okay." He took a deep breath. "I've been pretty busy since I brought her back yesterday."

"Stephen, you know how sorry I am that this happened. She seemed like a wonderful lady."

He tried to smile, but the pain overcame him. He pictured her face, the look of love she had for him, and it only hurt more. It was all he could do to speak. "She was, Randy. I really felt that way. Of course," the tears rushed to his eyes. It became difficult to speak. He gasped and pushed back the sorrow. "I was going to marry her."

"Yes. It's such a shame. You both seemed so happy together. You could tell by the way you looked at each other. I'm truly sorry, Stephen. When will you have the funeral?"

"It's not going to be here. And that's too bad. Her parents moved to Milwaukee recently. They want to have the service and burial there, so they can be close. Apparently they have a lot of friends there, including some of Sheryl's old friends from school. Strange, but several of them ended up in the same town." He managed a partial smile. "I guess that happens."

"Are you going out there?"

"No. Since I brought her back here, I've been coordinating everything on their behalf. She was supposed to be picked up and transported today." The empty loss he felt pushed the tears from deep inside to his eyes again and down his cheeks. In less than a minute, he started crying hard and loud.

"I know it hurts, buddy. I wish I could do more. There was just no way anyone could have expected this to happen."

Stephen responded even though crying. "I know, Randy. I know. It's not your fault." He shook his head and the tears came relentlessly. He had to put the phone down and try to regain his composure. The twisting pain inside him wouldn't quit. His dreams had been shattered.

It had taken over two years for him to get past a previous love. Finding Sheryl had been a wonderful miracle to him. He didn't think he could ever really love again. And now, after discovering the wonder of Sheryl and her love, their plans for a beautiful future together had been taken from them both. The future was not something he wanted to think about right now. He wasn't sure there was much of a future for him, at least not one that could be shared.

That was the lonely part of being single—not having anyone with whom you wanted to share all those events in your life, the big ones and even the smallest of those. Now he would be alone again. He felt that emptiness grow inside him, twisting, pushing, rising up in his throat.

He swallowed hard. The tears continued streaming down his face. It became difficult to see anything clearly, with his eyes or with his mind.

"Stephen." Osborn paused. "Are you all right? Is there anything I can do?"

"No, Randy. Thanks. There's nothing right now."

"Are you sure you're up to coming here? You really don't have to."

"Yes. I do, Randy. I'll be there. I need to be there."

"Come early. I have to go to the convention center early to start getting everything ready. You can find me there. We'll talk more when you get here. I'll have a ticket for you at the airline counter. Delta Airlines."

He took a deep breath. "Listen, Stephen. If something happens and you can't make it, just call me to let me know. Okay?"

"Okay. I will. But I'll be there, Randy." Even though he tried brushing away the tears, they just kept coming. He couldn't stop them.

"I'll see you tomorrow, Randy."

"Rana, you want to pull into dock number seven."

Saleem nodded and inquired when Tariq had gone to work.

"He started at 6:30. All the security people for the convention center started working longer shifts today. He will start at 6:30 again tomorrow. That works great for us, so we can get into the center early tomorrow, before everyone else."

Khan looked over at Saleem driving their car. "Tariq said to be at the dock at 7:40. He will open the door for us. We need to get everything out of the car and inside quickly, so no one sees us. He said there should not be anyone else there until around ten o'clock today, but we still need to be careful."

Saleem drove around behind the convention center and pulled into the lower area. "Tariq said the loading docks are in back."

"Yes. Go slow. If there is anyone there and they stop us, we can act like we are in the wrong place."

Saleem found dock number seven and backed the car up to the dock. They sat in the car waiting. Soon, Tariq opened the door, looked out, and motioned for them. Both men quickly exited the car. Khan opened the back door of the car and retrieved six small boxes, three at a time, setting them on the dock.

Saleem opened the trunk and transferred four larger and heavier boxes onto the dock. He closed the trunk and looked around. No one else was in sight. Khan had already climbed up to the dock surface, and Tariq had picked up a couple of the smaller boxes. "Let's get these inside," he said. "Then I'll show you where we can put them."

Saleem walked up the six concrete steps to the dock surface and lifted two of the larger boxes. Khan smiled at him, seeing that those boxes were obviously heavier.

Once they had all the containers inside, Tariq closed and locked the door. He had a cart there they could use to move the boxes to their destination. "There were workers here, yesterday," he said. "They assembled the stage already. They just have to connect the speaker wires and adjust the sound. It is all set."

"Great." Khan was excited. He had been waiting for this opportunity for some time now, and it was finally here. "So we can place the bombs, then?"

"Yes," replied Tariq. "No one is scheduled to be here until ten o'clock. That gives us time to place the bombs out of sight under the stage."

"Excellent. Let's do it."

They wheeled the loaded cart into the elevator and rode up to the third floor. The elevator doors opened to the special dining area, filled with tables covered with white tablecloths and padded folding chairs. A few serving tables had been set up off to the one side.

"This is where officials and special guests will enjoy their lunch. Everyone else will be eating upstairs." He started walking along the tables. "Follow me. The main conference will be at the far end of the building. That is where the stage is."

Khan and Saleem moved the cart loaded with their precious items. When they turned the corner and Khan saw the large black platform at the far end of the room, he broke into laughter. "Here! This is where the surprise will take place. Wow, it looks huge."

Tariq nodded. "There will be eighteen hundred people here."

Grinning, Khan announced, "And many of them will die here. Right here," he spread out his arms in gesture, "right here. They will not know what happened." He turned to Saleem. "Tomorrow will be the last day for many of them, even the President. He will not know his speech will be the last one he will ever give."

"Come on," said Tariq. "Let's get all this in place while there is time. It will take all three of us to put the bombs in place, you know. I want to be done before anyone else comes here."

"What about the other security guards?" asked Khan.

"Most of them will be here later. Right now, there are only four of us here. Two are in the center's office. There is one more checking upstairs," he pointed. "The kitchen and tables for those not eating on this level are all up there. It is a large area. He will be busy for awhile."

The three men went to work opening boxes and extracting various sizes of black plastic pipe, filled with plastic explosive and sealed. Wires protruded from one end of each pipe length.

"Remember, spread the adhesive on the pipes and be sure they will stick to the wood. Place them in the joints where the platform and legs meet. That way they will be less noticeable."

After putting the bombs in place, Khan gave them instructions on how to connect the wires extending from each pipe. The wires had to make a tight connection so the current would flow to the explosive.

Batteries were set in place and connected to the wires, and to cell phones. Several prepaid cell phones were installed, all with the same phone number. Once everything was in place, one call would activate all the cells, sending an electrical charge to the explosives.

"Everything set?" Saleem asked.

"We are ready," Khan replied. "You will make one simple phone call, and there will be one great big bang." He clasped his hands and shook them over his head, like a professional boxer just having won the championship fight. "You do have the phone number programmed into your cell, don't you?"

"Yes, Kamran. It is all set. I am ready."

As they started walking back to the elevator, Tariq cautioned them to be quiet. "The other security guard may be coming around, so please do not make any noise."

Down by the loading docks, Tariq said, "It is unfortunate that Umara was killed by Grant. Now we will have to park our car where we can get to it quickly and drive away ourselves."

Putting his head down, Saleem commented, "Yes. That is unfortunate. I miss her."

"I miss her, too," Tariq replied. He shook his head. "She was a good partner for me. We worked together well. We even practiced being married so no one would be suspicious." He smiled. "That was a fun part of our assignment."

"Don't let her distract you, Tariq. We are at the most important part of our mission for Allah. We cannot let anything stand in our way." Khan stopped and looked from one man to the other. "We must focus on what needs to be done. We cannot fail Allah. We must not. This is a time that the entire world will notice and celebrate. It will be the beginning of the downfall of the Western world. They will not be able to overcome this event."

A huge smile crossed his face. He raised his fist in the air above his head. "Allah will have his revenge tomorrow. They cannot stop it."

CHAPTER 39

"Tariq said to be there at 6:50. He will open the door for us, but we must be on time. He cannot hold the door open. He has to close it quickly."

"Okay," Saleem answered. "He will help hide us. I know we must hide for awhile. It will not be easy just waiting."

"You're right, Rana," Khan replied. "We must be patient. It will be a little difficult, but worth it. This is a very big day."

There was no one else in sight as the two men walked up to the loading dock door and waited. It didn't take long. Tariq opened the door right on time.

"I'm happy you were here," said Tariq. "I didn't want to open the door again. Too many times could cause the Secret Service to be suspicious."

"Are they here already?" asked Khan.

"No. But they will be soon. Come. Let me show you where you will be."

Walking to the elevator, Tariq told them, "You'll be hiding on the floors away from the crowds. There will be less people using the bathroom."

"Is that where we are hiding?" inquired Saleem.

"That is where you will be — in the ceiling. You will be hiding in the overhead air duct. I'll show you." They arrived at the first floor elevator. "Kamran, you will be staying in a supplies closet. That is where the cleaning crew keeps their equipment."

Tariq pushed the elevator button and the doors slid open immediately. Stepping into the elevator, he continued. "The cleaning people worked all night getting the place ready. They finished at six and left. They won't be back again until tonight, after everyone else has left."

The elevator stopped at the second floor and they stepped off. "You can see this is a small area. The entire vendor area below is visible from here. There will probably be some FBI or Secret Service staying here to watch over the activity on the floor below. You can see almost the entire area from here."

As they walked along the left side of the concourse, Khan smiled and motioned at Tariq. "You look good in your uniform, Tariq, all starched and pressed. You look sharp, ready for action."

"Thank you, Kamran. I wanted to look extra good today."

"You do that," Saleem added.

As they continued walking, Tariq pointed out an area set back to one side with a double door and posters tacked to the walls on each side. "That's the convention center offices. Security has an office back there. We will have two people in there at all times, and the Secret Service will have at least two agents there all day also. They will arrive shortly."

He stopped and turned to Saleem. "Remember this, Rana. When you come out, you must know they are here in the area, along with at least two agents watching over the vendor area from up here. You must be careful."

He pulled a piece of plastic from his pocket. "Here, Rana. This is your security badge, your ID for the conference. You are Mr. Leon Rogers from Texas."

"Texas? Oh boy. I've never been there, but that's great, you all."

They all laughed softly. Tariq motioned with his head and they continued walking toward the far end of the floor. "There are four sets of restrooms here on this floor. This is the farthest one from the entrances, so it should be used the least."

He pushed the door open to the men's bathroom. Fairly large with several sinks, it had a row of urinals and, farther to the back, a row of toilet stalls. Tariq pointed to the ceiling. "See the air vent up here? That is where you will be, Rana. Even though the vent screen is small, the ducting is large, five feet across. There should be lots of room for you."

"It won't be comfortable, but you'll be out of the way," Khan said.

"And out of sight," added Saleem. "Okay." He turned to Khan. "When should I come out, and what time do I call the phone number?"

"The conference is scheduled to resume at two o'clock. The Secretary of Homeland Security will call the conference to order, then the Secretary of State will make a short speech. The President is scheduled to speak at about 2:30. However, these always run late." He looked frustrated. "Do you have your watch with you?"

"Yes."

"Okay." Khan smiled at him. "Mr. Leon Rogers from Texas, why don't you come down out of your hiding spot at 2:15. They'll probably be at least five to ten minutes late with the speeches, so plan on making your call at 2:35. If they go later, let the President speak for a couple of minutes, then make the call."

Khan looked at Tariq who nodded, then back to Saleem. "What time do you show now?"

Saleem checked his watch. "Twelve minutes after seven."

"Perfect," replied Khan. "So do I. Tariq, do you agree?"

"Yes. That is the time I have also."

"Then we're good." He turned to Saleem and repeated. "So, you come out of hiding at 2:15, find a place in the dining area on this floor by the elevator, or better yet, by the back stairs over there to the right. Then at 2:35 or after the President has started his speech, you make the call."

"Okay. Will do."

Saleem glanced up at the fresh air vent. "How do I get up there?"

Tariq answered his question. "I have a chair here in the third stall. I'll get it." Retrieving the chair, he wore a huge grin. "I thought this would work. We can leave it out over by the hand dryer. No one will expect anything; they'll just accept that it is here." He placed the chair under the air vent.

"Okay, Rana."

Saleem stepped up on the chair, wobbled for a minute, then gained his balance. Reaching up, he was within easy reach of the vent. The restroom had a flat ceiling only about eight feet high. That left the vent grill only a few inches over Saleem's head when standing on the chair. He pushed on the vent and the grill moved up freely. "Ah." He pushed it to the side.

He jumped up and caught himself by pressing against the sides of the metal ducting. With only a little difficulty, he pulled himself up enough to get a good hand hold on the grill frame. He pulled his legs up and found there was plenty of room to maneuver. He waved at the two men standing there and pulled the grill back into place.

"Good," said Khan. "Now move back away from the opening, so no one can see you there."

Saleem slid back about three feet. He could not see the floor directly beneath him until he raised his head about a foot. He smiled and told the others, "This is good. I will lay right here until it's time." He paused a moment, then asked, "Tariq? If you can, please come back and check on me when it is time for me to come out — just in case I am asleep or something."

"Or something?" Tariq asked. "What do you think you are going to do up there? Daydream?"

"Maybe. Really, I do not think I will do anything but lie here waiting. But please check on me if you are able to do so."

"I will."

The two men standing there looked at each other and turned toward the door. "Okay, Rana. We are leaving now. Do your job. Good luck."

They walked out and back to the elevator.

"Kamran, you will be on the top level. The closet there will be more comfortable than the air vent. The closet is only used by the cleaning crew, so you should be left alone the entire time."

Khan nodded.

"However, the Secret Service and FBI will be all over the place. They could open the door to check, so be ready, just in case."

"Yes. I will be, just in case. Is there a chair there for me?"

"Yes. I put one in the closet for you this morning."

Arriving on the fourth floor, Tariq led Khan to the supplies closet. "It is back here, out of the way. No one should bother you."

As they got to the closet door, Tariq pulled another piece of plastic from his pocket. "Here is your conference badge."

Khan looked at it, then put the cord around his neck.

"You are Mr. Derek Jones from New Hampshire."

Khan smiled. "Mr. Jones, huh?"

"Yes. Both your name and Rana's are people who registered for the conference but will not be attending. So no one should pay extra attention."

Khan put his hands on Tariq's shoulders. Looking directly at him, he said, "You have done an excellent job, Tariq. Allah will surely reward you."

Tariq asked, "Do you have your Glock?"

"Yes. It is the polymer model and should not set off a metal detector."

"But remember," Tariq said, "you don't have polymer bullets. The real bullets will set off the metal detector alarm. Try your best to avoid them." He smiled at Khan. "I don't think you will have a problem."

"I think I will be fine."

Tariq used his key to unlock the door and open it. "I will leave the door unlocked, so you can come out when you are ready."

"Good. I will come out just before two o'clock. I will stay back, but start mixing with the other people. Once everyone sits down, I will find an empty chair and take my place."

"What if someone comes in at the last minute and says that is his seat?"

"I will simply apologize, say I made a mistake and look for another empty chair."

"And then Mr. Derek Jones will join the audience and wait for the moment of surprise," Tariq said, smiling.

"Exactly." Khan walked into the closet and turned around. "Thank you, Rana, for your excellent work." He stopped talking and just gazed at Tariq. Then he walked up to him, reached and put one hand on Tariq's shoulder, and nodded his head. "Tariq, my brother. I may not see you again. If I do, that is good. But if not, remember you have worked hard and done a good job. I know Allah has to be proud."

He became very sober. "If I do not see you here again, my brother, I will see you in heaven, when we are both with Allah."

CHAPTER 40

Delta Airlines on-time arrival exceeds 79 percent. Stephen Grant's flight to Baltimore was no exception, actually arriving a few minutes early. He took a cab to the Hyatt Regency and checked in, already dressed for the Homeland Security Conference. He wore the same solid, medium blue suit that he wore the day of the Central Park shooting. He considered it his lucky suit, since the shooter that day missed him and not the others. He sported a fresh, new white shirt with a light metallic blue colored tie.

Stephen left his bag in the hotel and took the above-the-street walkway to the Baltimore Convention Center.

"May I see your ticket, sir?" the usher asked pleasantly.

"I'm here to see FBI Special Agent Osborn."

"And you are — ?" The usher remained pleasant.

Another man dressed in a suit, obviously an FBI agent, stepped up beside the usher. "Are you Dr. Stephen Grant?"

"Yes, I am."

"Do you have some identification, sir?"

"Sure." Stephen showed his driver's license.

The FBI man smiled. "Thank you. We've been expecting you. Would you follow me, please?"

He turned and started moving toward the elevator. Stephen followed. Stepping off the elevator on the first floor, the agent spoke into his wrist microphone, announcing that Grant had arrived.

"Yes sir. Will do." The agent turned to Stephen and said, "Agent Osborn is at the booth for the Central Security Group. He said he'll meet you there. It's about a third of the way to the back, on the far right side." He nodded. "Okay?"

"Thank you, agent. I'll find him."

Stephen was amazed at how many people were at the various vendor displays. It seemed like enough to populate a small town. He started threading the crowd, making his way toward the back. There, at the Central Security Group display, he spied Randy Osborn.

Osborn waved and Stephen waved back, continuing to find his way through all the people.

"Hi, Stephen. Good to see you. How was your trip?"

"Pretty good, considering."

"Yes. Well, The circumstances sure could have been better," he gestured with his hand, "but you understand. I wish you had more time before the conference started. Did you get all the arrangements for Sheryl completed? Did she get moved to Milwaukee all right?"

"Yes, everything is done. It all went fairly well, considering the rush to complete everything. But it's done and over, now. There's nothing else I can do, so my full attention is here."

"That's good. Stephen, you understand how sorry I am. I wish it could be different." He shrugged. "Life has its surprises, and this was one of them." He nodded. "At least you're here now."

Osborn motioned to a side area not so crowded. "Let's move over here a minute so we can talk."

Stephen asked, "Is there a place around here to get a cup of coffee while we talk?"

"Of course. Come with me."

Stephen followed him to an elevator and up to the second floor. "There are people I want you to meet, anyhow." They walked to the conference center offices, through the double door and back to an office in the rear of the area.

"This is the center's security office." He swung his arm around at the five men in the office. "Gentlemen, this is Dr. Stephen Grant. I've told you all about him. He's here to help us find the bad guys."

Each man introduced himself and shook hands. The last of the five was Ed Janson, Secret Service. "Hi, Stephen. We met last Friday. So sorry to hear about your situation, but I'm glad you could be here now to help."

Stephen gave a knowing smile and nodded. "Thank you."

"Still have some coffee left?" Osborn inquired.

"Yes. Fresh pot. Help yourselves," one of the Secret Service agents offered.

Sipping the hot coffee, Stephen said, "Now this is better." Everyone smiled.

"Okay," said Janson. "Here's what we have." He showed Stephen the bank of monitors covering all the main areas. "Jack here," he tapped him on the shoulder, "is monitoring these. And over here, George is monitoring the computer system tracking all the secure outside doors. They're all locked. Your security badge has to be authorized to open a particular door. The computer logs the time, how long it is open, and who opened it."

"Quite a system, isn't it?" Osborn stated.

"Indeed, it is," Stephen replied. He took another sip of coffee. "And I assume everyone has radio contact?"

"Yes," Janson said. "Both FBI and Secret Service are connected on our portable intercom system."

Stephen commented, "It looks like the registration process is going well."

"Yes, it is," Osborn responded. "We have several agents watching the process in each location. It's progressing smoothly."

Stephen turned to Janson. "I assume you have people checking the entire facility for anything out of the normal?"

Janson nodded. "The bomb people," he paused, "and their dogs, have checked the conference area, platform and everywhere, for explosives. I have two people in the kitchen with the food preparation, watching that. Others are going through the rest of the center checking everything else, including the rest rooms, closets, everything. They should be completed with their search within the next thirty minutes." He shook his head once. "Then we have to wait. Wait and watch. That's about all we can do."

Osborn spoke up. "I thought I'd walk Stephen around the place, so he might spot our terrorist." He looked at Stephen. "Let's hope he shows himself and that we can capture him. Otherwise, it's a cat-and-mouse operation."

Stephen dropped his empty paper coffee cup into a waste basket. "Let's get started."

Entering the same elevator they had used earlier, Osborn said, "We'll start at the top and work our way down."

Getting off the elevator, Osborn added, "Most of the cooking staff all know each other. A stranger or substitute would stand out. But we'll check them just to be sure." They walked back to the kitchen.

Two agents stood just inside the kitchen door a few feet apart. "Hi, boss. How we doing?"

"So far, so good," answered Osborn. "You guys remember Dr. Grant. He wants to get a look at the crew here."

Osborn started walking around the kitchen with Stephen following. They didn't interrupt the cooking activities, but Stephen made sure he got a good look at each of the people there. Walking back toward the door, Osborn looked at Stephen, who just shook his head. They went back into the open dining area. "Nothing there?"

"No," Stephen replied. "It's not any of them."

"Okay, this area is clear. Let's just stick our head into the bathrooms to be certain no one's there."

"Okay." Stephen followed Osborn to the bathroom furthest from the entrance. The FBI man pushed the door open and they walked in. No one was there. Osborn bent down to look under the stalls. Nothing. "Okay, nobody here."

They went through the same exercise at the three other sets of bathrooms, checking both the men's and women's. Nothing.

"Let's go down to the third floor and see what we can find. Or should I say who we can find."

Getting off the elevator, Osborn said, "This will take longer. Many more people are here. Most are still downstairs at the vendors, but some are here waiting. Let's walk around and see who's here."

There were three tables with people sitting there, talking softly. Stephen made sure he could see everyone's face before they walked past. He did not recognize any of the faces. He looked at Osborn and shook his head.

They moved to the conference area itself. There were several people standing in small groups, discussing various topics due to be addressed during the conference. One group of three men were talking about their good time at the bar the previous night. One mentioned a great-looking cocktail waitress with a very short skirt and beautiful, long legs. One group of women were discussing what they would wear for the banquet that night. Again, Stephen shook his head, indicating no recognition of anyone there.

They returned to the second floor, where they stuck their heads in the general office. They greeted the five people working there, saying they were just doing last-minute checks. Was everything okay? Yes? Then we'll be on our way. Thank you.

They said hello in the security office to let them know they were marking areas off their list, but still had a ways to go.

Down on the first floor, a crowd remained around most of the vendors' booths. It took awhile to work their way through the crowd. Stephen took his time, making sure he saw everyone's face before he moved on. After completing one aisle, Stephen offered, "Phew. That's a mess out there."

Osborn raised his eyebrows and said, "Only three more aisles to go."

It took over an hour to go through the rest of the crowd. By that time, some of the patrons had left the vendor area carrying bags filled with literature and various handouts, and taken the elevator up to the convention floor.

Several of the people wore a purple paper hat handed out by one of the vendors. Several others wore a yellow kerchief printed with the vendor's name and logo. One vendor handed out patriotic pennants attached to a thin, flexible pole about two and a half feet long. A straw panama hat with a red, white and blue hatband resembling the U.S. flag was another popular item.

Not seeing the mystery man anywhere, Stephen asked to return to the third floor for one last look.

The crowd there was growing significantly. The two men worked their way around and through the crowd, but still had the same results. Finally, Osborn said, "Let's go back to the security office and see how they're doing."

Returning to the office, it felt good to sit down. Stephen was getting very nervous. "We're not getting anywhere, are we?"

"Not yet, I'm afraid." Janson was also getting rather nervous. "But we don't have much to go on. We're watching the crowd and checking against the drawing we have, thanks to Stephen. But not a thing so far."

Stephen asked, "What time does the President arrive?"

"Sometime just after two o'clock," Janson responded. "He and the Secretary of State are taking Marine One to the Baltimore airport. The limos are already there waiting for them. They will follow a parade route to get here, so a lot of people will have a chance to the see the President as he passes. The route has been published in the paper so people will know where to go to see him go by." He laughed. "They'll be lucky to get a quick glance, but this is politics, and the impression is everything. They want to impress the public and give them some identification with the President. That helps in any election."

"Well," offered Osborn, "With all the crazy stuff going on here today, let's hope that he's still alive to help with the next election."

CHAPTER 41

The morning session of the annual conference on Homeland Security ended at 12:05 with everyone dismissed for lunch. While a few people left the center to eat in one of the nearby cafés or restaurants, most went to the special dining area for dignitaries and guests, or to the upstairs dining area for the general attendees on the fourth level.

Agent Osborn tapped Stephen on the arm, motioned with his head, and said, "Let's go to the security office to see how they're doing. We can have our lunch delivered there."

Stephen nodded. "Sounds good."

Osborn called Janson on his wrist mike, told him what they were doing and asked if he wanted to join them. He was happy to do so. "There'll be plenty of time to talk while we're eating, and I can still be ready before the President arrives. See you there at the office."

Leaving the conference seating area, Osborn and Stephen made their way through the crowd to the special dining area where Osborn greeting several people, smiling, shaking hands and saying hello on the way to the elevator. Relieved to get in and close the door, Osborn pushed the button for the second level.

"That was an interesting trip for you, Randy. Wasn't aware so many people knew who you are, being FBI and all that."

Osborn winked at Stephen. "Some people think Congressmen are terrorists of a sort." He smiled. "Actually, politics is too much a part of my job. I have to appear before various committees occasionally and that's not always much fun. Then I have my bosses to keep informed, and they have people they must deal with, who sometimes call on me also."

"Guess there's no way to get away from the politics, no matter what you do," Stephen replied.

"Yes," said Osborn. "And in my case, it really is politics." He laughed.

Walking into the security office, Osborn called over to one of the FBI agents working there. "Say, Pete, can you call the kitchen and have three extra meals delivered here—one for Stephen here, myself, and Janson? He'll be here in a minute."

"Anything special you want?"

"No, nothing special. Filet mignon, a loaded baked potato, sautéed mushrooms, bacon bits, chives. You know, all the standard stuff, and just one banana split each should do for today."

Pete broke into laughter. "Cloth napkins okay, or do you want silk?"

"Oh, plain ordinary cloth," he nodded his head sideways, smiling, "pressed and folded neatly into thirds covering the plate, but not touching the salad."

"They may be a little late with that, boss. If you're asking for three of them, that is."

"Okay, then. Have them send the regular meal, if they have to."

"Right. Three spaghettis it is." He looked at Stephen, then back to Osborn. "I'll tell them to hold the garlic bread. You don't want to gain any weight."

Osborn winked. "Watch it there, Petey."

When Pete finished speaking to the kitchen, he put the phone down and asked, "Hey, boss. You want some cold coffee while you're waiting?"

"Thanks, Pete. You're so thoughtful." He motioned to Stephen. "I think we're all right. We'll wait for the main entree."

As Stephen and Osborn sat down, Janson entered the room. "Am I too late for a wonderful lunch?"

"No, not at all," Osborn answered.

Stephen said, "We ordered a special one just for you."

"What? Baked FBI?"

Stephen smiled. "No, fried."

"Good. In that case I'll join you gentlemen." He faced the rest of the crew and did a small bow. "If you'll permit me?"

230

One of the Secret Service men answered. "Why sure. Have a seat, Mr. ... uh, what's your name? Smith?"

"Yes, Agent Smith." He shook his head. "Not Jones."

The Secret Service agent stood up and held out his hand, motioning. "Please, won't you join us, Mr. Smith?" He sat back down laughing. They all laughed.

As he sat down, Janson inquired, "Anything new at all?"

"Not a thing," was the reply. "Everything is normal and quiet. Almost too normal when you know something is going to happen."

The other Secret Service agent said, "I wish we had a way of telling what and when. This waiting is hard on my nerves."

"Don't I know it," Janson answered. He turned to Osborn and Stephen. "No sign of our special guest?"

"Nothing."

Changing the subject, Stephen leaned back in his chair and asked, "What time did you say the President should arrive?"

Janson checked his watch and thought for a minute. "He should be on Marine One right now. The city has a special parade route for him to follow. Once he leaves the airport, it should take about fifty minutes to get here. So, he should arrive at about two o'clock. I'd better be downstairs and have our team ready at 1:30. We don't want him to arrive before we're prepared."

Osborn raised his eyebrows. "Not too good."

"For sure," Janson replied.

One of the kitchen staff, wearing his security badge, wheeled the lunch cart into the office. "Here you are, gentlemen." He began to serve each man with their lunch: Salisbury steak, potatoes and gravy, mixed vegetables, and a dinner role. He had thermos containers with coffee and tea, and also had some bottled water.

Small talk persisted among all the men present as they ate their meals. Two of the Secret Service agents kept watch on the security monitors as they ate.

Janson pressed his radio earpiece to his ear. He nodded and announced, "The President has left the airport. He'll be here in just under an hour."

"Then there's time to finish eating," said one of the Secret Service seated by the monitors.

"Yes," Janson looked over and smiled. "for a change."" He took another bite.

Just then another member of the Secret Service wearing a dark gray suit and tie stuck his head into the room. Spying Janson, he walked over and whispered in his ear.

Janson's eyes opened wide as he turned to look at the man. "*What?*" he almost screamed. "You've got to be shitting me."

He jumped up and threw his napkin on the table. Starting toward the door, he told the others, "They've just found some bombs on the conference floor."

"Where?" shouted Osborn, also getting up fast. He motioned for Stephen to follow him.

"Under the speaker's platform," answered Janson. He stopped and turned at the door, pointed to the two Secret Service agents at the monitors. "Call the bomb squad. I want two of their best men there right now! The President's on his way!"

He rushed out, followed closely by Osborn, but then Osborn stopped. He spoke to the Secret Service agents. "Keep this quiet for now. Don't announce anything. We don't want a panic. We'll give the order to evacuate if it's necessary. Wait to hear from one of us."

Osborn turned and moved away quickly, almost running. Stephen hurried to keep up with him. Stephen noticed that Janson didn't wait for the elevator. He went straight for the stairs. Osborn followed him, and Stephen followed Osborn.

Once they reached the third level, they all ran to the conference seating area. It was almost deserted. Only a handful of Secret Service agents dressed in suits were there. All the patrons for the conference were either eating their lunches or gone out of the building. As he got there, Stephen heard one of the men tell Janson, "Mike dropped his cell phone by the side of the platform. When he bent down to pick it up, he noticed a reflection off something under the stand. He stuck his head under and saw the bombs."

"Okay. First of all, nobody touch anything. Stay out from under the platform. Don't go under there. Wait for the bomb crew. Where's Mike?"

"Here, sir." Another agent in a brown suit stepped up from the side.

"What did you see?"

"I had to crawl under to get close enough to see for sure."

"Okay. What did you find?"

"Black plastic pipe. The ends are sealed. That's why the dogs didn't find them." He was breathing hard. "They're attached to the leg stands at the corners where they meet the floor of the platform. There's a whole bunch of them there, sir. At least twenty. There's enough damned explosives there to blow this whole place to smithereens."

"What else did you see?" He held up his hand in a motion to stop. "Just a minute." He turned to the agent who interrupted his lunch with the news. "Where are those bomb guys? Are they here?"

"No, sir."

"Get them. Now!"

"Yes, sir."

He turned back to Mike. "Now, what else did you see?"

"Wires. Each piece has a wire coming out of it. The wires lead to some sort of box strapped to the underside of the floor."

"That's probably the power source, and possibly the igniter. Was there just one, or several?"

"Several of them, sir. Five, I think."

Janson clamped his eyes shut tight and made a face. "Damn!" He shook his head. "That means there are several circuits. We could stop one and the others could still go off." He kicked at the floor. "Damn it! That's just what we didn't need."

He turned back to Mike. "See anything else?"

"Each box had another wire coming out of it. It was short, only about three feet, but each wire is connected to a cell phone."

Janson went white. "They could set these bombs off from anywhere. They don't even have to be here in the building." He shook his head again.

"The bomb guys are here, sir."

"It's about time." He looked behind him to see two men, each carrying a toolbox in each hand, rushing toward him.

"What is it? What did you find?"

"Plastic pipe bombs, about twenty of them."

"Where?"

"Under the platform," he pointed.

"Okay. First question. Did anyone see anything that could be a timer of any kind?"

Janson looked at Mike, who shook his head. "No, no timers. But they are all connected to several central boxes, and each box is connected to a cell phone."

"Oh, shit!" the bomb technician responded. "So there is more than one cell phone?"

"Yes. The wires from the pipe bombs connect to central boxes. Five, I think."

The bomb tech nodded his head and motioned for Mike to continue.

"Then each box is hooked to a cell phone."

"So there are about five cell phones?"

Mike nodded. "That's right."

"Okay. You guys all get back around the corner," he motioned with his arm, "We'll get under there and see if there's a way to disarm them." He turned to walk over to the platform, then turned back. "Have you evacuated everyone yet?"

Osborn answered. "No. We didn't want to start a panic, and we didn't know how bad it might be."

"How much time do we have?"

Janson checked his watch. "Twenty minutes."

He turned, quickly walked to the platform and spoke to his partner. "Let's go under here and have a look."

Stephen could hear them talking after they crawled under the stage. Everyone else remained quiet, waiting, counting the minutes.

The techs began talking very low, back and forth. The man who seemed to be the leader stuck his head out. "This is quite a job. I don't know if we can disarm this or not. We'll give it a try, but since we don't have much time, we're going to have to chance not having any decoys or trip safe wires that'll set the bombs off."

He nodded and started to scoot back under the platform. "Twenty minutes, huh? I'll let you know how it looks." Then he stopped and looked back. "You said you didn't alert anyone yet?"

"That's right," Janson answered.

The tech pressed his lips together, making a face. "There's a lot of explosives here." He shook his head. "Better have a plan on how to get everybody out of here."

CHAPTER 42

"Here we are, sir." The Secret Service agent held the door for the President. As he slid into the limo, the Secretary of State walked around to the other side, where another Secret Service agent held that door open. She got into the limo beside the President.

"All ready for the parade, Mr. President?"

He smiled. "I guess so. This is something we have to do. Just part of the job." He sighed.

"Yes, unfortunately, it is." She sat back and made herself comfortable.

The Presidential motorcade was assembled and ready to leave the Baltimore airport. Howard Ramsey, the agent who held the door for the President, punched a button on his cell phone. When Ed Janson answered, Ramsey informed him the President was on board and they were leaving the airport.

Ramsey waved to each of the other drivers, and they all got into their vehicles. Two motorcycle police led the way, followed by one police car with two officers. Second in line was the black limousine reserved for the mayor of Baltimore and his guest. The third limousine contained the governor of Maryland and his wife, and the fourth limousine held the President and Secretary of State. A black Chevrolet Tahoe with four Secret Service agents followed the President's limo. Another police car with two officers came next in line, and two motorcycle police were last. Two additional motorcycle officers rode along and would be there for traffic control as the motorcade passed through various intersections.

It was a beautiful August afternoon, with the weather providing the perfect day for a parade. The city had planned the route, approved by the mayor, and had it published in the Baltimore Sun. It was also posted with three online newspapers, The Baltimore Times, The Baltimore Post, and The Baltimore News Journal. Baltimore has eight television channels broadcasting locally: WBAL, WMAR, WJZ, WBFF, WMPB, WMDE, WUTB, and WNUV. All eight stations announced the route during their news broadcasts for the last two days, and all had it posted on their websites.

The President of the United States is always on a specific time schedule. Not only are appointments and various activities identified with a start time, but also a planned duration. With such an extremely busy schedule, the President's activities are closely monitored to ensure proper compliance with both the start and duration times.

Leaving the airport and turning the first corner, heading for the initial parade starting point, the people riding inside the vehicles put their shoulders back and sat up straight, filled with patriotic pride. It was a privilege to be part of this wonderful celebration, and they all wanted the State of Maryland and the city of Baltimore to know it. A broad smile decorated each person's face, and a proud feeling of unity and gratefulness for being able to lead their fellow countrymen welled up inside each of them.

As the motorcade neared the parade location, the President leaned forward and spoke to the Secret Service agent sitting in the front passenger seat. "Howard, when we start the parade, I'm putting the rear windows down. I want to be seen waving back at everyone."

"I'm not so sure that's a good idea, Mr. President, security-wise."

The President nodded and said, "I understand. But the people have come out to see their President, and I want them to do that. I don't want them to think that I don't care about them. This is important, and we do have an election coming up in a few months. They don't want their leader to be a snob. I want them to feel good about me. They'll forget a lot of the troubles, if they can remember me taking time to acknowledge them and waving back. This is important. We need the windows down."

"As you wish, Mr. President."

"Thank you." He sat back.

The Secretary of State leaned over and spoke softly. "You were briefed that there *is* a potential threat, weren't you?"

The President looked at her and nodded. "I think it's more potential than real. Besides," he sat up and reached up to pat Ramsey on the shoulder, "the Secret Service is here to protect me. Nothing will happen. Right, Howard?"

"Yes, sir."

He sat back, smiling, and looked back at Madam Secretary.

She returned his smile. "You're right. It's ridiculous to think there's any real danger. No one's going to try to shoot you — or anything else. Not in this day and time. We're past all that stupid stuff."

She sat back and folded her arms across her chest, waiting for the parade to start.

A high-pitched electrical whine could be heard as the rear windows were lowered while the limos squealed around the first corner.

"There they are," said Madam Secretary.

The President smiled and leaned forward, putting his face next to the open window. He was totally amazed at the large number of people gathered along the street. "Look at the crowd. Is your side as busy as this?"

"Yes, we've drawn a pretty fair size gathering. And the parade is just starting. The crowd will get bigger as we go."

The President smiled and put his hand out the window, waving and waving.

The motorcade was not able to slow down, due to the schedule they needed to keep. The President had to get to the convention center and into the conference on time. There would be several people waiting to meet him prior to him being formally introduced. After his special introduction, he would sit on the stage waiting for his turn to speak. He would have to keep smiling during that time, but that was not a problem. It was a pleasure for him to be there, to show he cared, and to smile for all those voters.

The shiny, highly polished black limousines reflected the bright sun into the crowd as they passed. Hurrying just enough to show urgency and keep their schedule, their speed allowed them to see and be seen, and still add a dramatic flair as the tires screeched slightly going around each curve.

It was a day that made everyone proud. People from every walk of life lined the sidewalks three deep. They all smiled and waved. Some pointed. While some people were dressed up, others wore casual clothes. Most of the shorter ones had either made their way to the front of the crowded sidewalk so they could see, or, if young enough, were sitting on their father's shoulders.

School children were present, some wearing their school uniforms or colors. A few young families had spread blankets and sat with their small children, pointing and waving. All smiled. Several grandparents were also there—some with their families or grandchildren, others just a couple leaning on each other, happy to be there.

One man was heard to say, "Look, Gladys. The President is here, in our State, in our town. Look at that — he waved at us. Makes you kind o' proud, doesn't it?"

Then the answer. "Don't be silly, Arthur. He's just a man."

"Yeah, but," he replied, "He's our leader. He's the President of these here United States." One could feel the pride in that statement, which seemed to permeate throughout the crowd.

Some cheered as they waved. Some just stood there in awe. Others just stood there.

Police stationed along the route stood on street corners, enjoying the day, hoping no one in their area dashed into the street or tried to run up to one of the limos. They watched the crowd, moving a few steps this way, then that. They smiled at the small children too young to know why they were there.

Everyone in the crowd seemed to be in such a happy mood, delighted just to share this moment with everyone else. Who knew? They might even be seen on TV, they and the President. It was such a beautiful day that no one questioned if they had voted for the right person. Political ideas and differences had been laid aside for this day and time.

Many people felt like they were at the circus. It was a good day, it was a good time. This was history. The President was there.

The tires screeched around another corner. You could almost hear a band playing patriotic music as the motorcade rolled past. Looking at all the people there, one imagined hearing the words, "And the rockets' red glare, the bombs bursting in air, gave proof — " It was a celebration, and everyone enjoyed it.

"We better get a move on it, George," advised Ramsey. He shook his head one time. "The President has to be there in ten minutes."

"Okay, Howard. Here's the last turn before the end of the parade. I'll pick it up a bit after the turn."

"All right," Ramsey replied.

Finally, as the motorcade moved away from the crowd, the windows were raised and the vehicles increased their speed. It was time to get to the convention center.

CHAPTER 43

"The President will be here in ten minutes!" shouted Janson. "If that's not diffused in five, I'll have to evacuate the building and stop the President."

"Okay. Okay," came the response.

"How's it looking?"

"Give me two minutes without interrupting."

"Okay." Janson held up his hands. "But I'll be waiting."

Turning to Osborn, he wiped sweat from his forehead with the back of his hand. He shook his head and glanced at his watch one more time. He frowned, started to speak, and reconsidered.

Stephen used his left hand to trace the scar running from his eyebrow to hairline. He closed his eyes and tried not to count.

"This is cutting it too close," whispered Janson. He bounced up on his toes then back down on his heels, and rocked back and forth.

Osborn took a deep breath. "I wish I had a cigarette."

"You don't smoke," Janson said.

"It's a good thing," Osborn replied, "Otherwise I'd be bumming one off you."

"I don't smoke," Janson replied.

"It's a good thing," Osborn said.

He glanced over at Stephen, who held up both hands and stated, "I don't smoke either." He lowered his voice. "And I know — it's a good thing."

All three men smiled reluctantly.

Janson looked at his watch again, glanced at Osborn and Stephen, and started walking quickly to the speakers' platform. "What's happening under there?"

"It looks like a pretty straightforward design. Nothing fancy or complicated. At least, not as far as we can tell."

"So what now?" Janson asked as he reached the stage.

"Damn it! I told you to get back out of the way."

Stephen heard a big sigh.

"Hal, get out from under here and take the boss and whoever else back by the stairs. I'm going to cut these wires. We need to disable these cell phones, boss, and I don't see any other way."

The bomb tech stopped for a moment, then spoke again. "Boss, this seems like a simple linear setup, duplicated to detonate five sets of bombs. It looks like all five cell phones will answer to the same number. Which means one phone call, and this goes off. There's enough explosive here to demolish at least half of the entire convention center."

He paused. "As soon as you guys get over by the stairs, call out to me. I'll cut the wires to the cells. There doesn't appear to be any false circuits or other means to cause this to go off, other than the phone call. Get back and let me know when you're away."

The second bomb tech scrambled out from under the stage and motioned with his arm as he started to run. "Come on, boss. Everybody. Let's get back by the stairs while we can."

Running to the stairs, Stephen looked at Osborn, who just shook his head. Safely standing next to the stairway, the tech called out, "We're clear, Russ. Go ahead. Good luck." He looked back at Janson and shrugged.

Stephen stood there, waiting. Waiting.

Stephen thought waiting to hear from the bomb tech under the stage was worse than having a root canal. Time passed so slowly.

Nothing happened.

Stephen looked at his watch, then glanced over at Janson.

Ed Janson was looking at his watch, still sweating. He made a face and looked up.

Osborn glanced at Stephen.

There was nothing any of them could do but wait — and hope — and pray.

"Got it!"

Stephen let his breath out and lowered his head. He muttered "Thank you."

"It's okay. It's safe now. You can come back."

The group of men started the long walk back to the black stage.

Janson asked, "It *is* okay, now?"

"Yes," Russ, the bomb tech answered, crawling out from under the platform. He stood up and addressed Janson. "All the cell phones are now disabled. There's no other way to detonate the explosives." He also wiped a lot of sweat from his forehead. "It's totally safe, so we can remove it later. It'll be okay to let people back here for the rest of the meeting."

He looked at Osborn, then glanced at Stephen and back to Janson. "The phone call could come from anywhere. But most people who would do this would want to be close enough to watch and be sure. If these are radical fanatics, Jihadists or whatever, they could even be in the audience and make the call from there, like a suicide bomber. I've done my job, now it's your turn. Good luck finding them."

He motioned to Hal, his partner, and they moved away and began putting tools back into their toolboxes.

Stephen, Randy Osborn and Ed Janson all turned to face each other. "He's right," Stephen added. "We don't know for sure how many there are, but they could be right here with us."

"How could they do that?" Janson asked.

Osborn tilted his head and offered, "Fake IDs. Maybe someone letting them in one of the back doors." He turned to Janson. "Either way, there would have to be someone on the inside to help."

"This is such fun!" he said with a grimace. He spoke into his sleeve mike. "Okay, guys. Let the people back onto the convention floor. We're clear for now, and we're going ahead with the conference. Let 'em in."

He glanced at Stephen, then back at Osborn. "I need to get down to the loading docks. The President will be arriving in just a couple of minutes."

CHAPTER 44

"I need to get down to the loading docks. The President will be arriving in just a couple of minutes. Want to come with me?"

Osborn looked at Stephen, who answered, "Sure. Why not?"

Walking to the elevator, Janson snapped his fingers as if remembering something. He raised his arm and spoke into his sleeve. "George, you said you checked the computer records for the secure doors, right?" He paused, listening. "When you checked, what time did you start with?" Again he paused. "Okay, and there was nothing unusual?" Another pause. "Great. Let's go back and check again, but look at everything from early this morning. I was told the cleaning crew left at six this morning. Start from that time and see if there's anything unaccounted for. Okay, let me know when you've completed that. Yes, do it right away. Thanks."

Janson turned his head to look at Osborn as they walked, and winked at him.

Osborn nodded. Stephen could tell he was in deep thought. *He must be reviewing every detail in his mind, searching for a way the terrorists could penetrate their security.*

Stopping just before stepping into the elevator, Janson looked up and off to the side. "What time was that?" He nodded at Osborn and Stephen. "The security guard?" Looking away, he nodded very slowly. "Have four men meet me at the loading docks, two at dock three and two at dock seven where the President will be arriving. Tell them to hurry."

After they all stepped into the elevator and he pushed the button for the bottom floor, Janson turned and said, "One of the back doors on the loading dock was opened at 6:50 this morning.

It only remained open for eight seconds. That's long enough for two, possibly three people to enter. Probably two."

"Did the computer show who opened the door?"

"The security guard assigned to that area. That time was before any of my agents were present." He looked at Osborn. "I don't think your people were here then, either. If so, they were just arriving."

As they got off the elevator, Janson held his hand up to his ear, then spoke into his sleeve. "Got it. Thanks." He smiled. "We may have it. The security guard who opened the door was only hired two weeks ago. He had a Mexican visa and green card, but he was originally from Pakistan."

"Shit," sighed Osborn. "And he's let two other people into the center."

Hurrying away from the vendor floor area toward the back of the building, they found the door to the loading docks, marked "Deliveries Here." Two Secret Service agents were waiting for them.

Opening the door and walking out into the dock area, they noticed two more Secret Service agents entering from a door off to their right.

The dock area was huge. Angled like an inverted V, each side supported five individual loading docks. A forklift sat back to the left against the wall, and two hand trucks were available, one for the first five unloading spots, and one for the second five on the far end of the dock. Two short stacks of empty wood pallets stood neatly placed against the back wall.

As they all walked toward the center of the area, Janson said, "The rest of the Presidential team will be here in about two minutes."

A single door on the far end of the dock area swung open, and a man in a security uniform walked into the room. With a look of surprise, he inquired, "What are you all doing here? This is a restricted area." He appeared perplexed. "The President will be arriving in a few minutes. You're going to have to leave now, please."

"That's him!" shouted Stephen, pointing.

The guard's eyes grew big, and he grabbed for the pistol at his side.

"FBI! Stop right there!" shouted Osborn, gun already in hand.

The guard pushed his hand holding the gun out in front of him as he crouched down, then fired wildly.

Everyone ducked. Everyone except Osborn, who broke into a run toward the security guard.

The guard turned and sprang through the swinging door and out of sight.

Stephen broke into a run following Osborn. Two of the Secret Service agents were right behind him.

Running through the swinging door, everyone charged ahead, following the sounds of the guard running from them. A long, empty hallway stretched out before them. It was about nine or ten feet wide and over thirty feet long, with unfinished walls on both sides. A step ladder and several pieces of lumber leaned against the wall on the right. There was no sign of the security guard or Osborn.

Back here in the hallway, all the lights had been turned off, making it darker than normal.

A gunshot shattered the air, then another loud shot echoed through the hallway. Stephen paused only a moment, then kept charging ahead full speed.

Reaching the door at the end of the hall, Stephen heard Osborn's voice on the other side of the wall, shouting. "Give it up. You can't go anywhere!"

There was no answer. The gunfire had stopped. It was quiet. Stephen stood by the door, listening. No sound. He slowly pushed the door open, still listening, and took a few steps forward. Still no sign of Osborn or the guard.

Secret Service agents silently stepped up beside Stephen, one on either side, holding their guns ready for use. One of the agents nodded to Stephen.

Stephen smiled, acknowledging the agents, and took a small step forward. Another loud gunshot broke the silence and the bullet hit something behind Stephen with a smacking sound. He ducked and froze. Waiting, he used only his eyes to look all around.

They had entered what appeared to be a large warehouse area. The wall to the far right was paneled with sheetrock, but not painted. The wall on the left was also unfinished, revealing uncovered metal studs and wires. The ceiling lights were switched off, and it was even darker in this area than in the hallway.

Three islands of empty pallets stood on the left, with a few feet between each. Stephen could see more stacks of building material beyond the pallets. A wide aisle separated the two sides of the warehouse with multiple stacks of all sorts scattered around the large space, some almost eight or nine feet high.

He still could not see either Osborn or the security guard that he had recognized. He hollered out to Osborn. "Randy, that's the guy from the hotel who tried to kill me."

Still no sound.

Their eyes tried to adjust to the darkness, but it refused to fade away, continuing to mask almost everything. Stephen watched for movement. There was none.

Stephen crouched and started forward. He glanced around and saw that the Secret Service agents had moved out next to the wall on each side of him. Holding their guns raised with both hands, they eased forward, scanning the darkness.

Stephen kept his eyes moving from side to side as he crept forward. There was no movement — and no sound, other than his own breathing.

A quick movement ahead to his left caught his attention. Three gunshots shattered the silence, one from his left and two from somewhere in front of him.

Then quiet. No sound. Again, no movement.

"It's over!" Osborn shouted. "Give it up! You don't have to die!"

Stephen couldn't tell where Osborn was, only that he was in front of him somewhere.

It became deadly quiet.

As Stephen inched forward, peering into the dark shadows, he sensed that all hell was about to break loose. The hair on the back of his neck tingled. An icy chill took hold of his shoulders and slowly slid down his back. He shuddered.

Now, he thought. *Right about now*, he quietly sucked in his breath, *something is going to happen. Be ready* —

He stopped. Lurking there, motionless, holding his breath, he stared into the silent darkness, searching for a glimpse of movement.

He exhaled slowly, trying to be as quiet as possible. Knowing he had to be ready to react, he squeezed his right hand into a fist, expecting the solid feel of the pistol in his hand. There was nothing there. He looked down at his empty hand and realized he didn't have a gun. *What am I doing?* He looked from side to side. *Everyone else must have thought I did.* He shook his head. *I don't have a gun.* He swallowed hard as fear flooded over him. *Am I crazy? I must be losing it.* He reached down with both hands to touch the floor and crouched even lower, now hoping the darkness would hide his presence. He waited.

A faint scraping sound came from his front left. Then a loud clang as a piece of metal hit the concrete floor and rolled. Rapid movement ruptured the darkness in that same area as a shadow turned and swung an arm around toward him. A bright flash exploded just before Stephen heard the gun shooting. Two quick shots.

Suddenly World War III broke out and guns fired from his left, from his right, and in front of him. All three agents shot at the shadow before it could flee. Stephen heard, "Uhh," and the sound of a body knocked backward and tumbling onto the floor.

He didn't move. Knowing he didn't have a gun, Stephen wanted to wait and be sure what happened before revealing himself.

Flashlights lit the area as the agents moved to the shadow now on the floor. Stephen saw the outline of one man bend down to examine the shadow. "He's dead."

Osborn called out, "It's okay, Stephen. You can come out now."

"You got him?"

Osborn replied, "We got him."

Stephen made his way to the men. He bent down to examine the man's face. "Yes, that's him. He's the one who tried to kill Sheryl and me." He stood up. "That's him."

One of the Secret Service agents spoke. "Well, that's one down."

"He did open the outside door," the other agent said. "So there must be more."

"Just great," Osborn uttered, looking down and shaking his head. He turned to Stephen. "We think there's probably two more people, and we don't know who they are or what they look like." He gestured with his arms out to his sides. "And they're here to kill the President. Just great!"

CHAPTER 45

Ed Janson and Tim Brown stayed in the loading dock area while the others pursued the security guard identified by Stephen. Janson needed to be there for the President's arrival, or to turn him away if needed.

Janson received details of the shooting on his earpiece. He spoke into his wrist mike. "Good job, fellas. Like you said, that's one down. We probably have two more here someplace. We did get the bombs, but who knows if there's anything else. The President is arriving now. I'll brief him and the rest of the security team, then we'll decide what to do. I'll let everyone know."

He gave the signal that it was okay to pull up to the dock and escort the President inside the building. He also asked Agent Ramsey to explain to the President that they needed to discuss the situation regarding his safety as soon as he stepped inside. Now he paced nervously, waiting for the unlocked door to open.

Originally commissioned in Washington, D.C., as the "Secret Service Division" of the Department of the Treasury, the agency's original mission was to suppress counterfeiting of U.S. currency. Created on July 5, 1865, the Secret Service faced an unbelievable situation with a reported one-third of the U.S. currency in circulation at that time being counterfeit. The legislation creating the agency was on Abraham Lincoln's desk the night he was assassinated.

Following President William McKinley's assassination in 1901, Congress informally requested the Secret Service to provide presidential protection. Now expanded to include many high-ranking officials and diplomats, the Secret Service assumed full-time responsibility for protecting the President in 1902.

Gary Fuller

In meeting with the President, Janson briefly laid out the details of what happened earlier that let up to the existing situation. He did not include opinions without being asked, nor did he offer suggestions. He merely provided the information, so the President could make his own decision on how to proceed.

At the urging of the Secretary of State, the President decided to continue with the plans that had been developed for him while at the conference. He was escorted to a private room, where he shook hands with several high-dollar contributors and greeted three cabinet members and five deputy director level personnel.

He moved to a backstage area with his escorts and waited to be introduced.

Khan sat in the cleaning closet on the fourth floor, waiting. He had learned to practice patience much earlier in life. He understood the parable that revenge was a dish best served cold. However, this time was truly difficult for him. He was eager to finally carry out the plan he had developed some time ago, after his brother's death. He knew Allah had guided him to this point — to the point where he, Kamran Khan, would extract Allah's full revenge not only on Israel, but also on the United States — Little Satan and Big Satan.

The Zionists would reap their final harvest, and the world would see Israel for what it was—a mere pimple or blemish that needed to be removed from the face of the earth. Israel was nothing more than a puppet of arrogant America. The Jews had invaded their land and pushed them to the outskirts of civilization. The world had lost respect for the Arabs, Afghans, Palestinians, Pakistanis, and the rest of the Muslims, thinking they were the ingredients of the lowest life forms. Israel caused nothing but problems for the world, and the world would be happy to see it gone forever.

Israel had already paid for their first installment with the death of their UN ambassador, Colonel Daniel Shavit. Other members of their UN team were disposed of with the restaurant bomb. Now, with their so-called friend, the United States, being perceived as weak, humbled in the eyes of the entire world, Israel

251

would also bow to those countries around it, and shrink away into oblivion. They would no longer be able to hide under the rocks or behind trees. With their support gone, they would wither and die.

And America, positioning its imperialistic military in Muslim countries throughout the Middle East, attempting to impose its own self-centered ideas and moralistic judgment on everyone else, would also see the beginning of its own downfall. America was a country of ignorant, self-satisfying infidels with no appreciation or understanding of the world around them, suffering from the lack of concern they proclaimed to hold for others. He had seen their lifestyle. They didn't even have respect for each other.

America had propped up and paid for Israel long enough. The end of their time was at hand. It would begin today, and he would start it. Israel and America would pay dearly. And Allah would bless him for it.

He checked his watch again. Almost two o'clock. It was time.

He stood and smoothed his jacket and pants, smiling. He wore a medium brown suit with a pastel yellow, open-collar shirt, no tie. His hair had been combed immaculately, and his dark eyes sparkled.

He bent down and checked his pants leg to be sure the pistol he hid strapped to his ankle was still there, ready to use.

He reached over with his right hand and touched the conference identification badge that Tariq gave him. He nodded and pulled back his shoulders, standing tall. He was ready.

Opening the door slowly, he peered out to see if anyone was standing close by. Not seeing anyone, he slipped out the door and quietly closed it.

Walking fast, he wanted to catch up to the last few people who had finished their lunch and were headed back to the conference floor for the second session. As he walked quickly around the tables, he noticed the remainders of food left on unfinished plates—various small portions of meat, mashed potatoes, and dinner rolls.

Two of the men immediately in front of him turned as he walked up. He smiled at them. They returned the smile and nodded. As they neared the open area leading to the elevator, he overheard one person inquire how another liked the meal. The reply was, "The Salisbury steak was good, but I think the chicken looked better."

Another person added, "Yes, I had the chicken and thought it was pretty good."

One of the men right in front of him turned and asked Khan what he thought of the lunch. "I especially liked the cake. Dessert is always good, don't you think?"

"Yes, usually," the man replied. "Sometimes it's too dry, but today it was good."

Stepping off the elevator, the man spoke to Khan again. "I'm Charlie Davis," he held out his hand, "from Atlanta. I don't think I met you earlier, did I?"

"No, I came in a little late." Khan smiled and shook hands as they walked. "Derek Jones. From New Hampshire," he added.

"Nice to meet you." The man nodded and moved away, turning to speak to another man beside him.

Slowly ambling toward the front of the seating area, Khan scanned the area for an empty seat. Spying a few seats in the middle section, he thought that would be perfect. Glancing at his watch, he took his time walking down the aisle, letting others go past him. It was just past two o'clock, and the conference would be reconvening. He noticed several people on the speaker's platform were already seated. He recognized the Secretary of Homeland Security from the pictures he had studied. The Secretary appeared to be comparing notes with another man, who nodded and sat down. The Secretary stood up straight and moved toward the podium with all the microphones. The spotlight came on, highlighting the Secretary as she stepped up to the front.

Khan wanted to be sure the seats he watched were empty. No one else moved in that direction, and almost everyone in the audience was sitting.

He selected the second seat in from the aisle in the seventh row. As he sat down, he casually looked around as if checking for someone. No one right there said a word to him. It was as if he had reserved that seat for himself.

He smiled as he leaned back in the padded folding chair. He had a perfect view of the Secretary as she started speaking. "Please, everyone take your seats. It is time to start our second session of the conference on Homeland Security." She pounded the gavel. "I now call the session to order."

Excited, Khan could not believe his good fortune. He had the best seat in the house for what he wanted. He could not only see the speaker clearly, but he was close enough that he could not miss if he needed to shoot. Only one seat away from the aisle, he might even be able to get away in the chaos that would be happening. And if not — well, that was up to Allah.

I will proudly give my life for Allah, he thought to himself. *I am here. Allah has ordained this effort. It IS his will that these infidels should pay for their sins.* He looked around, smiling, noticing all the men and women looking at the Secretary as she spoke. *ALL these people, every last one of them down here in the front of the audience, they will soon experience the biggest surprise of their lives — and a painful end to all their lives, at that.*

"Ladies and gentlemen." People all over the audience rose to their feet. He could see anticipation on each face. He turned toward the platform. "The President of the United States." The band began playing loudly, and the audience started clapping. Contagious excitement filled the air and everyone smiled broadly.

The President walked out from behind the curtain at the back of the stage, moved to the front of the platform beside the Secretary and waved at the audience. Smiling broadly, he waved to the people on the right, then turned to the left, then back to the center. Throughout the audience, people were cheering. Cameras clicked, strobes flashed and flashed. Reporters could be heard speaking loudly into their microphones. The President kept waving and the band kept playing.

When the music stopped, the President dropped his hand and the noise of celebration faded away. The Secretary motioned for the President to take his seat, and he did so.

The Secretary then introduced the Secretary of State, and she entered from behind the curtain, just as the President had. She took her place beside the Secretary of Homeland Security and waved to the people. Again the noise subsided, and Madam Secretary took her seat beside the President.

Khan checked his watch once more. It was 2:10 pm. He nodded, making a mental note that the Secretary of State would speak first. The President wasn't scheduled to start speaking until 2:30. Plenty of time.

He reviewed their planned schedule in his mind. Saleem would come out of his hiding spot at 2:15. He would mix with other people on the second level, and move to a location by the back staircase. The President would start addressing the assembly at 2:30. It would be the last speech he would ever make.

At 2:35 pm Eastern Daylight Time, Saleem would make his phone call to the number for the cell phones under the stage. If the President started his speech late, then the call would be made after he began to talk. Either way, the bombs would ignite. The blast from the explosion would destroy most of the conference center, annihilating the majority of people in attendance. It would be such a devastating explosion that it would rock the foundations of governments around the globe, and the world would never be the same.

. Khan leaned back in his chair and crossed his legs. He smiled. *I am ready for you, Mr. President. Your war on terror has come to you! ALLAHU AKBAR!*

CHAPTER 46

The Secretary of State addressed the audience first. "I want to thank all of you for your support, and your unwavering dedication and allegiance to making our nation what it is today. Thanks to all the efforts of each one of you, our country is a much safer place in which to live and prosper."

She continued speaking regarding the state of world affairs and the troubling situations around the globe with various terrorist organizations, and assured everyone that, "Thanks to the efforts you put forth, we do not need to fear experiencing those same terrible consequences here in our own country."

Saleem checked his watch. It was past 2:15, and Tariq had not come to check on him. "I guess I'd better go ahead anyway," he uttered to himself. "I wonder what is keeping him so busy he could not come help me."

The men's bathroom was empty, so he removed the ceiling grill from the air vent and lowered himself through the opening. Dropping to the floor, he remained still, listening for anyone that might come into the restroom. When no one did, he moved to the sink and splashed some water on his face, checked himself in the mirror and drew a deep breath.

He brushed the small amount of dust off his checkered sport coat and gray slacks, clipped the plastic identification badge on his jacket breast pocket, and pulled out his gun. After verifying it was loaded, he replaced it in the shoulder holster that Tariq purchased for him. He looked at his watch again. It was time.

Quietly opening the restroom door just enough to check, he saw no one standing anywhere close, and no one seemed to be looking in his direction. He pulled the door wide open and stepped out into the second level area.

256

He started walking casually, heading for the elevator at the far end of the floor. Hearing the speaker from the floor above, he checked his watch again. 2:22.

Saleem wanted to be standing by the far elevator at the time of the explosion to avoid being caught in the mass destruction he was about to cause. That far away from the blasts, he might survive. He was ready to die serving Allah, but he thought he could serve Allah better if he lived a while longer.

Two men in dark gray pinstriped suits stood by the double door off to the right, talking. They would have looked like twins except that one agent, Alan Malone, had a yellow tie while James Thomas, who everyone called Jimmie because he was the youngest agent in their detail, wore a light blue tie. Malone started over to intercept Saleem, who grimaced, thinking, *of course I'm a person to question. No one else is moving around.*

"Excuse me, sir," Malone said as he approached. "FBI." He opened a small leather case and showed Saleem his credentials. "Most everyone is upstairs where the speakers are. May I see your badge?" He held out his hand.

Oh boy. Here goes the first test. Can he tell my badge is a fake, or did Tariq do a good job? Saleem unclipped his badge and held it out for the man. "I — uh — I wasn't feeling well. I've been in the bathroom for a few minutes."

"Okay, sir," Malone said, looking at the badge. He turned it over. "What is your name, sir?"

Saleem paused. *Think, damn it, think.* Suddenly he remembered. "Why, I'm Leon Rogers. From Texas, you all."

Both men smiled.

"Well, Mr. Rogers, may I ask why you were in *this* restroom, so far from everyone else?"

"I told you. I wasn't feeling well. I didn't want a lot of other people around me if I started vomiting. It would be embarrassing."

"Yes, of course." He handed the badge back. "Are you feeling all right now?"

"Yes. I think I'm okay. I'm going to walk a little, to be sure I'm a bit better. I'll take the far elevator over there," he pointed, "to give me a little time." He smiled again at the FBI man.

Malone reached out and gently took hold of Saleem's arm next to his shoulder. "You're sure you're okay? I can walk with you if you like."

"Thanks, but that's not necessary. I just want to be sure I'm okay before I sit down with everyone else."

The agent nodded. "I understand, Mr. — Roberts, was it?"

"Rogers. Leon Rogers. From Texas."

"I understand. Let us know if you need any assistance."

"I will. Thank you."

The FBI agent turned and walked back toward the office door where he had been. Saleem held his breath for a few steps, then slowly let it out. He inhaled deeply and tried to calm himself. He turned his head to look back and make sure the FBI agent wasn't following him.

He saw the two agents standing by the door. Malone, the one who talked to him, was waving his arm and pointing to Saleem. *What is he doing?* Saleem shrugged, waved back at him and kept walking. As he turned back toward the direction he walked, he spied two more men dressed in suits and ties beside the railing overlooking the vendor area. They stood about forty feet away, with both men watching him.

They continued to watch as he neared them. The taller of the two dropped his arm off the railing and took a step to the side. Nervous, Saleem looked around for a closer elevator. There was none, but he saw the sign for the back stairway off to his right. He angled toward it, glancing back to check on the two men. They just stood there, watching him. He exhaled deeply and whispered thanks to Allah.

Checking his watch, Saleem saw it was 2:32. Time passed so slowly. It seemed like it took him forever to reach the stairway, but now he was there, and it was time.

Retrieving a cell phone from his jacket pocket, Saleem flipped open the cover. The graphic for the phone service provider displayed on the screen. He had memorized the phone number he needed to call, but he had also programmed the number into the contact list — in case he became nervous and couldn't remember it. At this point, he decided he didn't want to make a mistake being so nervous and dial an incorrect number, so he selected the call list, then highlighted the number he was to call.

He quickly checked his watch one more time. 2:35. Time to call.

"Allah bless me," he said softly. He pushed the call button. After a few seconds, he heard the number start to ring. He closed his eyes. "Allah, let it be your will."

CHAPTER 47

The phone continued ringing. Saleem opened his eyes and looked at the phone, wondering, *why is it not working? There's no explosion. This makes no sense.*

He closed the flip-top phone to end the call. Inhaling deeply, he opened the phone again, with a slight nervous shake. Again he selected the contact list, highlighted the number and pressed send.

He waited. Again he heard the number ringing. Ringing. Ringing.

No explosion.

Nothing!

He stared at the phone in disbelief. He shook it and listened again. *How could this be?* He closed the phone, opened it again and redialed one more time. Still nothing.

Hearing footsteps behind him, he turned and saw those same two men from the railing walking rapidly toward him. "No!" he shouted. He threw the phone down on the floor, smashing it to pieces.

"Mr. Rogers, can we help you?"

How did they know my name? Something is wrong. He stared at them with a blank expression, not sure what to do. *This has to happen. We planned it.*

They had almost reached him. "No!" he shouted again. With his left hand, he pulled his jacket back, revealing the gun and shoulder holster. He grabbed for the pistol with his right hand.

The FBI agent on the left, Roy Bradshaw, was closest. He leaped through the air and tackled Saleem, knocking him to the ground. The other agent took two rapid steps and kicked the gun

Gary Fuller

out of Saleem's hand. It clattered as it hit the concrete floor and bounced.

Saleem twisted, broke one leg free. He rose up from the waist and slugged Bradshaw, the agent who tackled him, causing his grip to loosen. He swung his free leg as hard as he could, kicking Bradshaw in the side of the head with the heel of his shoe. The agent let out a sound and twisted as his eyes rolled up into his head. He lay there unconscious.

The second FBI agent, Barry Taylor, drew his gun, stepped up beside Saleem and pointed the gun at him. Before Taylor could say anything, Saleem twisted his body very quickly and brought his other foot up to connect with the agent's pistol. Taylor's head turned to follow the gun as it went flying from his hand.

Saleem spun around, rising to his feet, swinging his fist at the same time. Taylor, not expecting Saleem to react so quickly, was not fast enough to block the punch. It threw him off balance and he took a second punch. A fist slammed into his stomach and bent him over slightly. A rabbit punch to the back of the neck knocked the agent to the floor, dazed.

Saleem scooped up his pistol and ran for the stairs. He threw the door open and leaped down the first few steps, bouncing down the rest to the landing. Holding onto the hand rail, he flung himself around the corner and down the first three steps, then every other step until he reached the bottom of the landing. Without looking back, he dashed out the door, onto the floor near the registration area by the vendor displays.

He saw the restroom sign to his left and rushed into the bathroom. He went into the second stall, stood on the toilet so his legs wouldn't show underneath, and held his breath.

Agent Taylor checked on Bradshaw, the first agent, while calling into his sleeve for help. Malone and Jimmie left the office doorway running. Taylor spoke instructions into his sleeve for the men on the first level. When they responded, no one had noticed Saleem come down the stairs.

He dropped his wrist and checked Bradshaw again. He couldn't feel a pulse. He checked a different location. *This can't be,* he thought. He tried another spot on the body, then another, but found no pulse at all.

He raised his wrist and spoke into the mike. "Boss, everyone," he paused, "Roy Bradshaw is dead. He was killed in a scuffle with the suspected terrorist who broke away from us and ran downstairs. He was kicked hard in the head. It must have hit him just right." Another pause as Taylor lowered his head. Tears formed and turned to anger. "I'm sorry, guys, he's gone."

He stood up and pointed, leaving Malone to stay with Bradshaw. "I'm going to get this bastard." He sprinted down the stairs, with Jimmie trailing him. Running onto the first level floor, they stopped and looked around. There was no sign of Saleem.

Taylor spoke into his wrist mike again, calling his boss. Osborn replied he had been listening to everything.

"We've lost the guy, boss. I know he's on this first floor someplace, but I have no idea where. The other guys said no one saw him come down the steps." Thinking quickly, he added, "I guess that means he must be close here. Let's see, where could he hide?" He paused, looking around. "Jimmie, you see any place here where he could hide?" The other agent shook his head.

They both stood there, searching, watching for any movement.

"What about the restroom over there?" Jimmie inquired, pointing to his left.

"Yes." Taylor said and broke into a run.

Reaching the door, they took up a position on each side of the doorway and Taylor shouted, "FBI. Come on out. You can't get away." Quiet. No response.

Taylor stepped back and kicked open the door, then he and Jimmie both rushed in. No one was visible. Two more agents from the first floor arrived at the door and stood there, guns drawn.

Jimmie bent down and checked under the stall walls to see if any legs were showing. None. He stood up, glanced at Taylor and shrugged.

There were six stalls in the restroom. Taylor stepped over by the last one in the row and kicked the door open. No one there. "Give it up now and you can live," he called out. "You don't have to end it here. Come on out." Still no response.

Taylor kicked open the fifth stall. No one. "We're getting closer. Better come out."

He moved to the fourth stall and kicked it open. No one there. Taylor turned to Jimmie who just raised his eyebrows, shook his head slightly and kept his gun raised, ready to fire.

Taylor moved to the third stall and hesitated. "Are you coming out?" He kicked the door.

The door to the second stall jerked open. Saleem jumped out, hit the floor, rolled, and came up on his feet. He had held his pistol close to his body so as not to lose it when he rolled. He came up facing Taylor. Saleem pushed his arms out to point the gun at the agent.

Thunder erupted, permeating the enclosed area as two quick gunshots echoed loudly off the walls in the small room. Saleem's eyes opened wide in surprise as his body, hit from behind, jerked forward, his gun hand flying out to the side. He tried to focus on Taylor and pull his arm around to point the gun again, his eyes red with anger.

Taylor's gun fired, echoing simultaneously with Jimmie's gun as it shot once more.

Saleem's head snapped up, and his body twisted halfway around before collapsing to the floor. Taylor kicked Saleem's gun away from him, and Jimmie bent down to check for a pulse. He looked up at Taylor. "He's gone."

One of the two agents standing at the door raised his arm and spoke into his sleeve. "We got him, boss. He's dead."

It was quiet for a moment, then Osborn asked, "Was he shot?"

"Yes. We had to fire several times, but no one else was hurt." Then with a scowl, he added, "Except for Roy."

"Okay. Good job, people, I guess you couldn't take him down alive. Too bad," Osborn replied. He added, "I'm very sorry about Roy. He was a great part of our team. We all know this kind of thing can happen." It was quiet for a moment, then Osborn spoke again. "Sorry, guys. Shake it off. We have a job to do, and we're not done yet."

Osborn continued, "Frank, stay with Roy until the medics show up, will you?"

"Sure, boss. I'll stay with him."

"We didn't hear any shooting up here, so it didn't interrupt the conference. That's a really good thing right now. We sure don't need that."

The second agent at the door spoke into his wrist mike. Sighing loudly, he nodded his head and said, "That's two down, boss."

"Right, guys. That only leaves one more. Now, where in the hell is he?"

CHAPTER 48

After getting her attention, the Secret Service agent brought both hands up in front of his face. Acting as if he held a string or wire between the thumb and forefinger of each hand, he moved his hands apart, appearing to stretch out whatever he was holding.

Without pausing her speech, the Secretary of State glanced down at her notes, then moved her eyes slightly to observe the agent. He now used one hand, raising four fingers held together while bringing his thumb downward. He then reversed the motion, bringing his finders downward to meet the thumb as it was raised. He repeated the action three times.

Madam Secretary looked directly at the agent and nodded her head, continuing to speak without interruption.

The agent turned around to face the audience and spoke into his sleeve mike. "She got the message."

The President had been called backstage to meet with Janson and Osborn, who spoke. "Madam Secretary will stretch out her speech so we can talk for a few minutes, sir."

"Okay," the President started. "You're telling me there is one more terrorist here someplace? Probably in the audience?"

"Yes, sir. He might be in the audience, we don't know for sure."

"What do you know?"

Janson spoke up. "Mr. President, we *do* know, from all the evidence and the events that happened here, that a security guard recently hired by the convention center was actually a terrorist from Pakistan. He opened a secure door to let two others into the facility early this morning."

"And you say you caught two of them, right?"

"Yes, we did, sir."

"Then why haven't you caught the other one?"

"Unfortunately, sir," Osborn interrupted, "we don't know who this person is or what he looks like." He glanced over at Janson. "We think he is probably in the audience somewhere, and that he might be planning to shoot you."

Frustrated, the President looked at the floor, back at Osborn, then to Janson. "I'm here now, and I need to make this speech. I'm announcing a new bill asking for additional funding to help major cities defend against possible terrorist attacks around the country." He raised his arms out to his sides. "How would it look if people thought I was afraid to announce that at a conference on Homeland Security?"

"Sir," replied Janson. "I know that's a concern, but so is your safety."

"Still," the President nodded, "I'm going to have to do this." He turned to directly face Janson. "Your job is to protect me, isn't it?"

"Yes, sir."

"Then do it. I'm going out there to give this speech."

He looked over at Stephen. "And who are you?"

Janson answered. "This is Dr. Stephen Grant. He works with the UN."

Osborn stepped in. "He's helped with terrorist actions before, and he's been deeply involved in helping us with this one."

"Well, Dr. Grant," the President responded, "I'm glad you're here. Apparently, we need all the help we can get."

He turned back to Janson. "There's enough damn Republicans who would like to shoot me already. I don't need someone trying it for real. Get this son of a bitch before anyone else is hurt. Understand?"

"Yes, sir."

The President strode away from the men standing there and moved close to the spot where he would walk through the curtains when introduced again. He glanced back at the group of men and nodded.

"Let's go," Osborn said, motioning for the others to follow.

Reaching a spot away from the main backstage area, Osborn asked the men to gather around him. "Ed, you guys are in charge of protecting the President. Keep your men around him, all around the stage. Put a couple of men in the primary walkway between the guest dining tables and the audience seating area. Follow anyone who walks out of the audience, even into the restroom if necessary. Let's not lose sight of anyone moving around."

"Got it. You'll take care of the rest?"

"Yes." He looked at the other agents around him. "I want agents in every aisle, not more than twenty feet apart. In fact, I think we have enough men, make it fifteen." He turned from one side to the other and back as he talked. "Stay alert. Constantly scan the crowd for anything unusual. If you suspect something, call me on your mike. Don't go charging into the audience and cause a disruption unless it's necessary. Okay?"

"We do want to be careful, but just because someone stands up," interjected Stephen, "doesn't mean it's trouble. They may need to go to the bathroom or something."

"If someone *does* stand up," Osborn continued, "watch them closely. See how they're going to move. If they come to the aisle, quietly question them. The Secret Service guys will follow them if they leave the seating area, so let them do their job."

He looked around at their faces. "Any questions? None? Okay. Let's do our job, and hope this guy reveals himself in time for us to act and stop him." He clapped his hands as if they were in a game huddle. "Let's do it."

As they began dispersing to various positions, Osborn said, "Stephen, why don't you come help? You can stand in the aisle just down from me, and we can watch each other while we're at it. If either of us sees something, we'll holler to alert the other." He reached around and patted him on the back. "I'm glad you're here to help, Stephen." He smiled. "I owe you one."

CHAPTER 49

The floor of the speakers' platform erected for the conference stood four feet high. This allowed for Secret Service agents to stand in front of the platform without obstructing anyone's view of the speaker addressing the audience.

The planned open space between the platform and the first row of the audience was ten feet wide. This not only provided enough space for the agents, but kept the audience back far enough for the agents to effectively observe those seated in those rows closest to the stage.

Finishing her speech, the Secretary of State was now ready to introduce the President. Several agents, wearing the standard Secret Service uniform consisting of black suit, white shirt, dark tie, black shoes, and close-cropped hair, spaced themselves out across the area in front of the platform. They stood facing the audience, carefully scanning the people seated in front of them and slightly to each side. The agents remained about ten feet apart, positioned to react quickly considering the threat they each knew they were facing.

Not one of them smiled. Neither did they stand still, but rather moved casually from one foot to another, turning from one side to the other. Because each one of them acted the same way, restraining each movement to only a small amount, it was impossible for anyone to notice how nervous the agents were.

Aisles were kept open along each side of the audience next to the walls. Two main center aisles, each eight feet wide, led from the back of the large seating area to the front of the room. Because the conference seating area had been arranged in a pie-shaped fashion, there were extra aisles added with additional sections of seating as you moved further back from the stage.

All in all, eighteen hundred people had been seated and waited patiently for the President to make his address.

Osborn stood in the main center aisle to the left as you faced the stage. He stationed himself close to the front between rows two and three. He positioned Stephen in the same aisle at row ten. Behind Stephen, additional FBI agents stood in the aisle every fifteen feet or so. Stephen glanced around and saw more agents spaced down each side aisle, about the same distance apart.

Osborn paced a couple of steps in one direction, then reversed himself and moved back. Sometimes he moved in a small circle, but no matter how he moved, his eyes were always scanning the audience, observing each person within a radius of about ten feet. He felt that was as much distance as any agent could cover effectively and stop a shooter who might expose himself.

Stephen tried to mimic Osborn's actions, moving back and forth within a short distance in each direction. He would have waved or at least nodded toward the agent about fifteen feet behind him, but the agent was too busy observing the people to notice Stephen.

He heard the Secretary of State say, "Ladies and gentlemen." He turned to face the stage. "The President of the United States."

Again applause erupted throughout the conference presentation area. People started to rise. Stephen quickly looked to his side at the people beginning to stand up all over the place. He glanced back behind him — same thing. To his left — the same. He tried to watch what everyone did, but it was impossible. Some slower people were still getting to their feet. Those standing close to him blocked his view of others.

Don't let anything happen right now. He shook his head. *We couldn't stop it.*

The applause and cheers did not last as long as the first time. *Good,* thought Stephen. *Let's get everyone sitting back down so we can watch them.*

The President nodded to the audience and motioned for them to be seated. Gradually, people began to stop cheering and take their seats. After everyone sat down, the President started speaking.

"Thank you. Thank you. It's a real privilege to be here with you today. It's good to see you. I know some of you have travelled a long ways to be here, and it's appreciated."

Everyone had calmed down and were now listening. Stephen quickly scanned the area around him, then checked other agents moving in circles in the aisles. Smiling, he turned and looked behind him. A man in his early thirties sat in the first seat from the aisle, wearing a white shirt with a gray plaid pattern, dark gray slacks and black shoes, nodding his head, acknowledging what the President was saying. He turned to the pretty ash blonde in a light blue dress seated next to him. The way they smiled at each other and leaned over to bump shoulders indicated to Stephen that they were married — or at least would like to be.

Seated behind that couple were an older man and woman, probably in their late 50s or early 60s, holding hands. Next to them were three teenage boys, nicely dressed in blue jeans and sport shirts—one red, one yellow and one green.

Stephen smiled and turned to face the other direction. The couple seated on the aisle appeared like a normal, uninteresting conservative couple you would not pay attention to. But next to them sat a young threesome, probably in their early twenties. The smiling blonde in the middle, wearing a white top and a short brown skirt, held hands with the young man in a light gray sport shirt, sporting short hair, sitting closest to Stephen, but leaned forward to speak to the man on the opposite side. That man had much longer dark brown hair that appeared unkempt and wore a short sleeved, black shirt and faded jeans.

He thought how young the crowd looked. There were a few older people, but most seemed to be in their early forties or younger. He heard several people shush their neighbors and the place became significantly more quiet. Realizing he had not paid attention to anything the President had said, he turned toward the stage.

"With all that is going on in the world today, these are confusing times." The President looked around the audience. "We certainly want peace for our world, for our city or town, for our neighborhood, and for our own families." He paused and raised his voice. "But although we want peace, we must be prepared for those actions that are necessary to secure peace wherever we are."

Osborn glanced at his watch. 2:45. He nodded to Stephen, who nodded back.

The President continued. "That is why I'm proud to introduce a bill to our Congress which will assist with this goal and help protect us here at home." He waved his arm in front of him. "We all are subject to an unwanted interruption to our way of life. It could happen to you, or to me. Some of these terrorist groups have established a goal of disrupting or even ending our way of life. We cannot allow that to happen."

He paused and smiled as he glanced around the audience. "I am asking Congress to approve additional funding, specifically for cities with a population of more than one hundred thousand, to be used to purchase excess equipment from our military and provide training to the proper city personnel, so they can effectively respond to any terrorist action."

More applause. More people standing again. More uncertainty for Stephen and all those FBI and Secret Service agents trying to watch the crowd for the single, remaining terrorist.

Kamran Khan sat there listening. He could hardly believe the frenzy these people spawned, reaching desperately for new hope that would bring meaning to their pathetic. selfish, meaningless lives. He thought, *If they only knew the truth instead of the crap they are being fed.* He shook his head. *It is no wonder America has lost its way.* Glancing around, seeing the mix of people here, especially so many younger people, he smiled. *They are being led astray, like sheep to the butcher.*

He glanced at his watch. 2:50 exactly. *Well, come on, people. It's time to pay the piper.*

He sat back and smiled, waiting for the bombs to go off.

CHAPTER 50

Something must be wrong. Khan nervously checked his watch again. 2:56. *The President has been speaking for several minutes. Where's Rana? There's no bomb explosion.* He began to sweat. *He should have made the call by now.*

He closed his eyes and lowered his head. A cruel but reluctant smile spread across his face. He now knew Saleem was not going to explode the bombs. There could be a lot of reasons why, but it did not matter. All the planning and work for this event had been in vain. There would be no huge explosion. There would not be the mass casualties he'd hoped for.

Now it's up to me, and only me. I will do what I have to do. Mentally calculating the distance between him and the President, he estimated it at 10 meters, or just over 30 feet. Raising his eyes, he looked up and said to himself, "Allah, help me. I do this for you."

The President paused again, checking the audience to be sure he held their attention. Khan sat up straight to listen to what the President had to say. He wanted the timing to be just right.

"There will be a small tax increase to pay for this. We must all bear this burden together."

There was no applause this time.

"The tax increase is necessary to enable us to protect our cities —"

The audience remained silent, suddenly starting to become restless.

"— and ourselves —"

Someone in the audience shouted a loud "Booo." Another person shouted, "Nooo."

The President glanced toward the area where the shouts originated, and continued speaking. "Against radical fanatics who would *destroy* our way of life." He motioned with his fist, emphasizing the statement.

Another member of the audience yelled, "Nooo." Then a person several rows back on the right side stood up, cupped both hands around his mouth so he could be heard, and cried out, "No new taxes!"

The President acted surprised, dropped his arms to his sides and took a step back from the podium.

A man about midway back on the left side stood. "Bring our military home from the Middle East. They already know how to use the equipment."

Another man on the other side of the audience stood up. "Yeah! Let them protect us here at home."

Khan recognized the next man who stood. He worked at the Seven-Eleven store close to the Embassy Suites. They had visited when Khan went into the store. That man called out, "Bring them home. We don't need new taxes."

The President looked from side to side, flustered, not sure what to do.

Two men sitting next to each other stood. One shouted, "No new taxes." The other then bellowed, "Bring them home." He swung his upper arm back and forth as he said it. The man beside him joined in. "Bring them home."

Several more people rose to their feet and joined in. It became a chant. The man and woman sitting on Khan's right stood. Soon there were groups of five or six standing in various parts of the audience, all chanting. "No new taxes. Bring them home."

Khan stood. He could feel the enthusiasm of the chant building. He joined the others, moving his arm in unison. "No new taxes. Bring them home."

The President held his hands out to the audience and tried to speak. "I'm sorry, but —" The chant continued. The President motioned for quiet, and tried to continue speaking. "These steps are necessary to provide for our own security here at home."

Much of the audience was no longer listening. The chanting increased. Cameras flashed as reporters and delegates began snapping photos. Television cameras swung around, attempting to capture all the action. Again, the President stepped back from the podium.

Smiling, Khan looked around him at the audience and the groups of people standing, chanting. *Perfect,* he thought. *With this confusion, I may even be able to get out of here. I couldn't plan this any better.* He nodded. *Now is the time.*

He bent over to retrieve his pistol from the ankle holster.

CHAPTER 51

The FBI and Secret Service agents went nuts.

Many groups of people stood, scattered all around the huge assembly, waving an arm toward the President. Any one of them, anywhere in the audience, could hold a gun and shoot at the President.

They knew there was one person, somewhere out there, who wanted to try. He wanted to kill the President of the United States. This situation presented the perfect opportunity to do just that.

The President stepped back from the podium and stood there — stood still — shaking his head. He didn't think about being a target for someone to shoot.

Not sure of how to react and caught completely off-guard by the crowd's chanting, the President motioned for the audience to quiet. They refused.

The chant continued. "No new taxes. Bring them home."

Agents jerked their heads around, eyes darting at groups across the audience, watching hands for any sign of a gun as arms thrust forward, over and over.

It had to happen now!

They couldn't watch every single person, there were too many.

One of the FBI agents took a quick step to the side and started to point at one of the groups, then dropped his hand and shook his head.

They all overdosed on adrenaline. Blood pressure went up. Hearts beat faster. They knew it had to happen right now.

"Gun!"

The shout came from Osborn. He saw the black pistol in Khan's hand as his arm went up and back, ready to thrust forward. Osborn tried to point as he broke into a run toward the row of chairs where Khan stood.

Stephen jerked around just in time to see the gun in Khan's hand at the side of his head pause and start to swing forward, toward the President. Khan stood by the second chair in from the aisle, about six or seven feet from Stephen. With no time to think about it, Stephen lunged at Khan, trying to tackle him.

Khan's smile remained as he started bringing the gun forward. His eyes caught the blur of Osborn's movement coming toward him, in front, off to his left. His involuntary reaction caused him to cringe slightly as the gun fired.

The loud explosion from the Kahr .45 automatic startled everyone around him. People jumped from the noise, jerking their heads around to see what caused the noise.

The shot went off target and missed the President, who also jerked in shock. Several Secret Service agents reacted immediately, jumping up to the stage in front of the President while others came from behind to pull him down to the floor and cover him with their own bodies.

Khan's mind had just started to process the fact that his first shot missed the President when Stephen, flying through the air, smashed into him, knocking him to the floor. People standing beside him screamed and quickly jumped back to escape.

Khan squeezed his hand around the gun to prevent losing it as he fell. As his body hit the floor, he kicked, hard. Stephen rolled partially to the side and scrambled to get hold of the pistol in Khan's hand. Using his free arm, Khan slammed his elbow into Stephen's side.

Stephen tried to hang on, still reaching for the gun, when Khan hit him again and again with his elbow. Stephen's hands slipped off Khan's arm, and he was forced to roll away to prevent another elbow smash.

Khan rolled in the opposite direction, twisting and rising to his feet in one motion. An arm wrapped around him while a hand knocked the gun from his hand.

Osborn spun Khan around to face him and swung a right hook that landed on Khan's jaw, knocking him backwards.

With a small space now between them, Khan kicked out and hit Osborn in the stomach, knocking the wind out of him. Osborn involuntarily bent over just in time for Khan's second kick, which connected with Osborn's chin. He flew backwards, landing flat on the floor.

Stephen, now on his feet, charged Khan, grabbing him with both arms. Khan squeezed his own arms together, causing Stephen's grip to loosen. He bent over, throwing his hip into Stephen. It forced Stephen to drop his arms and step back slightly. Khan slammed his left fist against Stephen's jaw.

Stephen staggered backward a couple steps. Before he could recover, Khan was there with his right fist aimed at Stephen's face. Stephen ducked, turning away so the blow glanced off his shoulder. Stephen countered with a punch to Khan's stomach, followed by a quick left uppercut. This time Khan staggered back.

Stephen charged in, ready to hit Khan when a surprise punch caught him on the chin and sent him sprawling. A second punch knocked him to the floor.

Khan saw the gun on the floor and scooped it up. He had already fired the semi-automatic pistol once, so it was already cocked and ready to shoot again. It would only require a small amount of pressure on the trigger to fire.

He aimed the gun at Stephen as he stood up. Stephen knew there was nothing he could do. There wasn't time to react.

Khan squeezed the trigger.

CHAPTER 52

The explosion of gunfire was deafening. Two shots rang out, almost simultaneously.

Stephen thought he was shot, but didn't feel any pain. *Is this how it feels — like nothing?* He looked down at his chest. *How could he miss?*

He glanced up in time to see the shock on Khan's face. Khan dropped the gun, clutched his chest and staggered. Stephen saw surprise in Khan's eyes as he looked down at Stephen, then fell to the floor.

Standing in the aisle, behind where Khan had been, Osborn's face was intense. He slowly lowered the pistol to his side. Jimmie came running down the aisle to him. He looked at the gun in his hand and put it back in the holster under his jacket. "I didn't know if you would get it in time, boss. I had to shoot."

"I know, Jimmie. You had a good shot. We both hit him, just in time." He turned back to look at Stephen. "Are you all right, Stephen?" He stepped over to where he lay on the floor. "Here, let me help you up."

Jimmie asked, "Sure you're all right, Dr. Grant?"

Stephen smiled sheepishly as he got to his feet. "Yes, thanks to you both." He shook his head. "That was way too close. Thank you again."

"Just doin' our job, huh boss?"

Osborn slowly shook his head. "Yes. Our job. Sometimes we get away with it. This was one of those good days."

They all turned when they heard some noise on the stage. Ed Janson stood at the microphone. "Ladies and gentlemen. Just a word, please. Sometimes events preclude even the best of plans. This is one of those times. For your information, you can rest

278

easy, the President was not hurt. The quick action of several people, including the FBI and Secret Service, prevented that from happening."

He looked around at the audience. "More information will be released later, but I can tell you we were fortunate here today. Bad things planned for all of us were prevented from happening. The President will not be able to continue his speech. He is being taken back to the White House for his own safety, not that there is any reason for concern now. You need not worry. We will break for the rest of the afternoon, then rejoin for the banquet as scheduled for tonight. I might add, you may want to think about what happened, or didn't happen, here today, when you consider what our President was saying. Be careful for the rest of the afternoon. Thank you."

Osborn turned to Stephen. "Well, I guess that's it for the afternoon. Sure you're okay, Stephen?"

"Yes. I'm fine." He grinned. "You'd think I'd be getting used to this by now."

Both Randy Osborn and Jimmie smiled. "I'll be up in the security office," Jimmie told Osborn, and moved away.

The crowd slowly moved toward the back of the conference area. Osborn motioned by tilting his head, "Let's move over to the side and let the others leave. I know you'd like to get out of here, too, but you're not in a hurry at the moment. Come on." He started moving toward the right side of the chairs.

Arriving at the far aisle, Osborn spoke. "Have a seat, Stephen."

After sitting down, Osborn thanked Stephen for his help. "If you hadn't been here, and acted as quickly as you did, this entire thing could have turned out much different. I — we — owe you a big thanks for what you did."

"I'm just glad I was here to help. Thank you for that."

Osborn reached out and put his hand on Stephen's knee. "I'm truly sorry about Sheryl, Stephen. I know how much she meant to you."

Stephen put his head down and nodded. When he looked up, tears wet his eyes.

Osborn said, "It will take time to get over it. I know, remember. I've been there too." They stood up. Osborn continued, "If you just need to talk sometime, you've got my number."

They started walking toward the center's exit. "When the After-Action Report is finished, I'd like you to read it before I submit the final copy, all right?"

"Sure."

"I'll let you know when it's ready. Do you want to go back now, or spend the night and go home tomorrow?"

"I think I'll catch a cab to the airport and hope I can find a flight home."

"Okay. Call if you need me."

"I'd say the same to you, but you *would* call me. I'm afraid I need some time before I can help with another problem."

Osborn slapped him on the back. "At least you didn't say no."

They walked out the exit.

CHAPTER 53

The sky, crowded with various shades of gray clouds, threatened rain. Observing the dark shapes shifting with the wind tempered one's attitude, pushing toward melancholic depression. However, this was mitigated since the visibility below the clouds to the north side of Manhattan remained reasonably clear.

From a table by the windows at Terrace in the Sky, the penthouse restaurant high atop Columbia University's Butler Hall, he scanned the horizon while sipping a glass of Cabernet. He moved his glass in a swirling motion, staring at the wine as if seeking his future in any reflection he might detect.

Loneliness had again invaded his life. The pain of loss caused a feeling of emptiness to rise from deep within himself. Forced to work hard at not surrendering himself to those painful feelings, he struggled to find some source of meaning in his life.

Yes, he was a college professor, a teacher who touched many young lives, helping them discover many facets of life — their lives, and the lives of others — and how they become intertwined in each other's journey.

Yes, he was part of the United Nations, and he hoped he somehow assisted in efforts not only toward world peace, but toward making the lives of others bearable and even enjoyable.

Contemplating the dark gray carpeting on the floor, he remembered becoming involved in the actions of the CIA, trying to preserve peace and save many lives. That was two years ago. Recently he assisted the FBI in finding and eliminating a terrorist threat here in the United States, possibly even saving the life of the President and many others. He wondered what type of event might come next.

He marveled at how all these things could happen to just one man — him.

Closing the wooden presentation case, he ran his finger over his name engraved on the brass plate centered on the polished oak box. Dr. Stephen A. Grant.

A broad smile crossed his face. He recalled chasing the security guard through the convention center warehouse in Baltimore. Actually a terrorist, the guy had shot at both him and the FBI agents. Stephen charged ahead with them through the dark building before realizing he didn't have a gun himself. *What an idiot.* He shook his head. Fortunately, it turned out all right.

That event, along with some others, were the reasons for this gift sitting on the table in front of him. The oak presentation case contained a Glock Model 23, .40 caliber semi-automatic pistol and two magazines. It was accompanied by a note from Agent Randy Osborn. "Thanks for all your help. This is the standard issue presented to new agents when they graduate from the FBI academy. Next time we ask for your help, please don't go chasing the bad guys without a gun."

A letter was also included in the box, stating that Dr. Stephen Grant was recognized as a special assistant called upon to assist the FBI at various times as needed. He should be considered a regular law enforcement officer for the Federal Bureau of Investigation with regard to issuing a concealed weapons permit for the State of New York. The letter had been signed by Supervisory Special Agent Randall Osborn, and also by the Director of the FBI.

So maybe there was a purpose to his life after all. He did more than touch other lives, he helped stop a number of bad things from happening and enabled others to continue their lives. That helped relieve some of the sad feelings.

He raised his glass and enjoyed the full taste of the dark Cabernet as he sipped the wine.

He also had the pleasure of sharing many wonderful wines with more than one love during his lifetime.

Wait a minute. My life's not over yet. What am I doing? Yes, I've deeply enjoyed love. I may not experience that kind of love ever again, but when you think about it, I've been blessed with three great loves.

Smiling, he remembered his wife Becky and the wonderful times they shared. It was what love was meant to be. Full of laughter, she became the sunshine in his life, and he thought his life had ended when she was taken from him in a horrible traffic accident. Tears of happiness flooded his eyes and mixed with tears of sorrow created by the memories.

With the sunshine gone, he went into a deep depression for over a year. He recalled how terrible it had been for him during that time. His friend Peter helped bring him back to life and gave him new hope.

Not long after starting to date again, he met Dr. Samantha Sorkin. He was attracted to her immediately. There was something special about Sam, about almost everything she did. He smiled, imagining her beautiful face and the effect her charms had on him. He fell deeply in love with her and imagined sharing a full life with her forever. Tears from the emptiness he felt inside returned to his red eyes.

They had gone through good times and some bad times, even facing death together. He thought they'd gotten through all that fairly well, but when it was over, Sam decided she had to deal with demons of her own. After looking into the face of death, she said she needed to find her true self—who she really was, and what she truly wanted for the rest of her life.

Even though she might love Stephen, any future she could imagine with him would hold too much danger and indecision for her, as long as he continued his "daring escapades."

She had to work through issues from her childhood, her young adult life, and her adventures with Stephen. She felt compelled to go on a soul-searching journey alone, without him, to discover the truth about herself. She told him this, then walked out of his life forever.

Forever, that is, except for his haunting memories and visions of her in the mirror. However, Stephen had made the decision to leave her memory behind and live his life with a new love.

That new love was Sheryl Houser. More tears appeared. All three loves had been real, but this one would be his last. He put his memories aside and acknowledged his love for her. He knew he was the luckiest man on earth when she agreed to marry him.

He wiped the tears from his face and tried to smile as he recalled their plans for the future together. It would have been wonderful. He pictured her standing in front of him, her smile and the way she tilted her head, looking demurely at him. But it was not to be. Killed by the terrorists in Baltimore, she died citing her love for him.

Excruciating pain stabbed his heart, cutting him into pieces. *Why did she have to die?*

Uncontrolled tears again streamed down his cheeks. Lowering his head, he knew he couldn't continue to cry. This wasn't the place to let his emotions to run wild.

He shook his head. *Snap out of it. How can any man be so lucky? Three wonderful, true loves in one lifetime. Riches can never replace that type of love, real love.*

Using his napkin, he dried the tears from his face, set it down, and picked up his wine glass. He stared at it a moment, then slowly put it to his lips. Taking a small amount into his mouth, he moved his tongue through it, tasting it, savoring it. *Life can be wonderful. Even when you don't know what's ahead, it can still be good. I don't know what I'm going to do, what will happen. Oh, teaching, and the UN of course. My life will go on.* He enjoyed another sip of wine. *I guess I'll just enjoy it anyway. I'm strong. It won't be the same, but I can make it. And it will be okay.*

He glanced out the window. It was now raining. *The weather was like this the last time I was here.* Lightning flashed on the distant horizon. *Wow, that was over two years ago.* He shook his head. *I haven't been back since ...*

Pressing his lips together, he tried to clear his mind. Again he gazed at the fading skyline as dark, heavy clouds released buckets of rain. *No. Don't let this dismal weather get to you. I can't limit my thinking to only those painful memories of the horrible moments in my life. I had many happy times, too.*

He sipped his wine. Looking at the glass, he thought, *should I have another glass — or just go home?* Setting the nearly empty glass on the table, he decided he wasn't going to be unhappy. He didn't have to. *No, life may not be the same, but it doesn't have to be sad.* He would have another glass of wine. Then he would go back to his apartment, listen to music and drift off to sleep.

He saw the waiter move to a couple two tables down. The waiter nodded, wrote down their order and started to turn away. Stephen held up his glass for the waiter to see. The man nodded the acknowledgement and moved away.

Stephen picked up his napkin and wiped the tears from his eyes. He decided to smile, waiting for his new glass of wine.

There was a noise behind him. Someone was walking by. He didn't pay any attention, until he realized the person had stopped walking and now stood directly behind him. He waited a moment, but the person continued to stand there and not move away. Nervously, he turned around to see why the person had stopped right there.

"What — " He stopped. The shock of surprise slammed him like a sledgehammer and took his breath away. A flaming volcano of emotions erupted within him. Although shaking inside, he sat still with his mouth open, staring.

There, facing him, wearing a beautiful smile, stood Samantha Sorkin.

"Hello, Stephen."

CPSIA information can be obtained at www.ICGtesting.com
Printed in the USA
BVOW01s0355260215

389172BV00001B/5/P

9 781621 376644